All three men walked to the nearest window as [illegible]d a rumbling outside. Looking down into the gardens they saw a battery of four-pounders being driven into position. The six guns, each weighing in excess of six hundred pounds, were limbered and lined up facing the palace.

'Do you think they are going to fire at us?' Lausard said, smiling. He watched the crews of each gun swarming around the pieces like ants around their hill, each of them with a specific job to perform.

'What the hell is going on around here?' Rocheteau wanted to know.

Lausard had no answer. 'All anyone wants is peace,' he said quietly. 'And yet this city looks as if it is about to explode.'

By the same author:

Bonaparte's Sons
Bonaparte's Invaders
Bonaperte's Warriors

Bonaparte's Conquerors

Richard Howard

WARNER BOOKS

A *Warner* Book

First published in Great Britain in 1999 by Little, Brown and Company
This edition published by Warner Books in 2000

This is a work of fiction. Characters, organisations, situations and philosophies are either the product of the author's imagination or, if real, have been used fictitiously without any intent to describe or portray their actual conduct.

A CIP catalogue record for this book
is available from the British Library.

ISBN 0 7515 1813 1

Typeset in Stempel Garamond by
Palimpsest Book Production Limited,
Polmont, Stirlingshire
Printed and bound in Great Britain by
Mackays of Chatham plc, Chatham, Kent

Warner Books
A Division of
Little, Brown and Company (UK)
Brettenham House
Lancaster Place
London WC2E 7EN

Bonaparte's Conquerors

One

Alain Lausard looked up at the mass of dark cloud that filled the sky and heard another growl of rolling thunder. It sounded like distant cannon fire – a noise he had come to know well during the last three years.

The dragoon sergeant patted the neck of the bay he rode, steadying the animal, reassuring it. As it shook its head, rain water flew from its mane, spattering Lausard; the sergeant smiled. He tilted his head further up towards the sky and felt the October rain brush his cheeks and chin. It ran in rivulets over the dark green cape he wore. His brass helmet and its horse-hair mane were sheathed in protective oil skin to preserve them from the elements.

The road along which he and his men travelled had been transformed into a quagmire by days of inclement weather and, in many places, horses sank as deep as their fetlocks in the mud.

Lausard looked behind him at the remainder of the column. Most of the men, their heads down, looked as uncomfortable as their horses as they moved through the countryside. These men he had come to know well. These men he called comrades, even friends. The men of the second squadron. One of the three that comprised his regiment of dragoons. *His* regiment. He smiled again at the thought. He belonged among these men. He had their respect. He was one of them. And yet only he knew the truth of the situation.

They knew him as Lausard the thief. A man who, like them, had lived a life of deprivation in the streets of Paris, fighting for food until his imprisonment. Like him they had suffered in reeking, damp cells until the newly formed Republic's need for troops had ensured that he and those like him had been spared the guillotine, forced into uniform and trained as soldiers. And in their new guise they had conquered. Under the guidance of Napoleon Bonaparte they had swept through Italy, driving all before them. Then on, to the other side of the world, to Egypt. To blistering heat and choking sand. And more victories.

They had left that God-forsaken country forty-five days ago. The sea voyage had been as rough and uncomfortable on their return journey as it had when they had first embarked on what their commander had chosen to call an 'Oriental interlude'.

It was an interlude that had cost the lives of many men, some of them close to Lausard. But that was in the past. All that mattered now was that they were back in France. Away from the dysentery and flies, the hunger and thirst, the heat and the plague.

Another rumble of thunder shook the sky and the sergeant glanced up again. The sound was like the greeting of a distant and long-lost friend and Lausard smiled at its salutation.

'I didn't think I'd ever be so happy to see rain,' he remarked.

Beside him, head bowed, the rain pouring from the peak

of his helmet, Rocheteau grunted something under his breath and looked up at the bruised sky.

'It is like a gift from God after Egypt,' Moreau offered. 'We should thank Him for our safe return home.'

'I thank the captain of the frigate who brought us across the sea,' Lausard said. '*You* thank your God if you wish.'

Up ahead, the road curved to the right, forging a way through some trees. Lausard could see Captain Milliere and Lieutenant Royere riding at the head of the column, just ahead of a wagon and several other horses, which moved in an untidy group and were ridden by men in civilian dress.

'Why did they choose *us* to act as wet nurses to those "pekinese"?' Delacor complained.

'Be grateful,' Lausard told him. 'If not for those men we would still be in Egypt. They were our ticket back to Paris.'

'And then what?' Rocheteau enquired.

Lausard could only shrug. '*They* report to the Directory. What becomes of us I have no idea.'

'The Directory,' snorted Delacor. 'It's a wonder we had a country to return to with those overfed lawyers in control.'

'Is it true that when Bonaparte returned to France he brought only members of the Scientific Commission with him?' Rocheteau asked. 'Men like those.' He nodded in the direction of the civilian riders.

'And three hundred of his guides,' Roussard added. 'He would have let the rest of us rot in Egypt.'

'Well, he's been back over two weeks now. I did hear that more troops were to be evacuated when the time was right,' Lausard said. 'If there are any left alive by then.'

'To hell with those left behind,' Delacor snapped. '*We* are back. That is all that matters.'

'I will offer a prayer for those we left behind,' said Moreau.

'Pray all you like, your holiness,' Rocheteau chided, 'it won't help them.'

'I would imagine that the women of Paris will think their own prayers have been answered,' Giresse interjected.

'Why is that?' Lausard asked.

'Because *I* have returned safely. Those fortunate enough to know me will rejoice that a true lover is once again amongst them.'

The men laughed.

Delacor cursed loudly as his horse stumbled in a deep pothole.

The animal whinnied in terror and almost overbalanced but the trooper tugged hard on the reins and managed to keep the frightened animal on its feet. Mud and filthy water sprayed up around the horse as Delacor struggled to keep control. Some of the other mounts neighed in protestation and Joubert gripped the reins tightly as his mount lifted both its forelegs clear of the mud and threatened to rear up.

'These damned horses,' Delacor said angrily. 'Where the hell did the Directory dig them up?'

'You can't blame the horses,' Tigana protested. The big Gascon met Delacor's withering gaze with indifference. 'They are undernourished. They probably weren't intended for military use. The horses we usually ride are bred in Brittany. Bigger and sturdier mounts. These are more like pack animals. I should know, I bred them myself for long enough before I became a soldier.'

'Before you were arrested, you mean,' Delacor corrected him.

'I used to be an expert where horses were concerned,' Giresse interjected.

'Yes,' Lausard said, grinning. 'An expert in *stealing* them.'

The men nearby laughed again, the sound eclipsed by a loud rumble of thunder.

'But I agree with Tigana,' Lausard continued seriously. 'We are riding unsuitable horses because they have been supplied by civilian contractors. The sooner Bonaparte stops dealing with those leeches the better.' He patted the neck of his horse. The animal flicked its head skittishly and Lausard eased the pressure on its bridle.

Few horses had survived the journey back from Egypt, and the seas were littered with their bloated carcasses. However, some of the animals had been used as food and the men had been only too happy to take advantage of the supply of meat. In fact, Lausard thought there had been more food available *during* the voyage than there had been since they had returned to France. Granted, it had mainly comprised salt meat and dry biscuits but the provisions had been adequate. On a number of occasions they had even managed to catch and cook fish.

Since returning to home soil they had received a canteen of fresh water, some bread and a few vegetables, most of which had been consumed during the first day. It was a far cry from the official rations each man was supposed to receive. Lausard wondered how long it would be before they were all given the regulation twenty-four ounces of bread, eight ounces of meat, one ounce of rice, a quart of wine, one-sixteenth of a litre of brandy, and one-twentieth of a litre of vinegar.

In Egypt they had even been granted a ration of coffee amongst their meagre victuals.

Thoughts of food made Lausard's stomach rumble. He concentrated instead on guiding his horse through a small stream that had burst its banks and flooded the narrow road.

They had landed in the province of Herault two days ago. The journey to Paris, Lausard guessed, would take them another four days. If the rain stopped and the roads became more accessible, they could be there sooner.

Up ahead, the wagon lurched wildly to one side. For an instant Lausard feared it would overturn but the driver snapped the reins and drove on the team of four. The exhausted animals managed to haul the vehicle forward, and its steel-braced wheels left deep ruts in the sodden earth.

'Is there anything valuable in that wagon?' Rocheteau asked, a familiar glint in his eye.

'Not to *you*,' Lausard said, smiling.

'I was speaking to a member of the Scientific Commission the other day,' Bonet volunteered. 'He said they had some particularly fine geological specimens that they had found in Egypt.'

Rocheteau looked blank.

'Rocks,' Lausard told him. 'The wagon is carrying rocks.'

'What is the purpose of bringing rocks halfway across the world? We have rocks in France.'

Lausard chuckled.

'Citizen Caminarro says they are unique in composition,' Bonet explained. 'He has been a geologist for ten years and—'

'All right, schoolmaster,' Rochteau interrupted. 'I don't care about rocks unless they're valuable. They are useless to me unless I can trade them for food or wine.'

'Or women,' Giresse added.

'No, just food,' Joubert insisted, rubbing his large belly. 'I'd give my soul for a good meal. Perhaps we will finally eat well when we reach Paris. What do you think, Alain?'

Lausard shrugged. 'Do you think the Paris we know has become wealthy since we left it?' he mused. 'Have the gutters and backstreets where we lived been transformed? When did any of *us* ever find food in abundance in Paris?'

'Things might have changed, Alain,' Rocheteau offered.

Lausard didn't answer. He simply looked up at the cloud-choked sky.

The rain continued to lash down.

Two

Lausard looked up and saw the sails of the windmill turning gently. The rain had eased slightly, only to be replaced by an ever stronger wind, which had swept in from the west. The late-afternoon sky was turning the colour of gunsmoke and the sergeant wasn't the only one who suspected that night would bring with it the cold.

As the column passed by the windmill, the men heard it creaking. It had been battered by the passage of time and Lausard wondered how long it had been standing. Ten years? Twenty? About a mile beyond, visible on the slope of some hills, lay the town of Bixente. The column would stop there for the night, rest and replenish its supplies as much as possible.

Lausard glanced towards the small house beside the windmill and saw a man emerge. He stood watching the dragoons for a moment then waved. Some of the troopers returned the gesture as they rode past, Rocheteau among them. He nudged Karim, who rode alongside him, head low, the collar of his cloak pulled tightly around his neck.

'You see, the people here are more friendly then they were in *your* country.'

'Egypt was not *my* country, as I keep telling you. I didn't belong there any more than you did.'

'And what do you think of France, Karim?' Bonet wanted to know.

'It's wet,' the Circassian said flatly.

Lausard grinned and looked across at the trooper, whose tanned, healthy complexion was in marked contrast to the sanguine visages of the other dragoons.

'Are you beginning to wish you had stayed in Egypt, my friend?' asked the sergeant.

Karim shook his head. 'At least here I'm free,' he said, wiping rain from his face.

'None of us is free,' Sonnier complained. 'Our lives are in Bonaparte's hands. We live or die at his whim. We are his slaves now.'

'We are soldiers,' Lausard corrected him. 'You should be grateful. What would you prefer? To be sitting in a cell waiting for them to come to execute you? To be starving to death in a Paris gutter? We all have more freedom here than we will ever know and I for one welcome it.'

'Better to be the slaves of Bonaparte than of the Directory,' Rocheteau added.

'You know nothing of slavery,' Karim said. 'I was a slave from childhood. I was taught what to think, how to act. I knew only to obey. To obey a master I neither wanted nor asked for. True slaves have no mind of their own because they are not permitted one. Be grateful for your circumstances. Do not question them.'

Lausard listened to the words of the Circassian. However, his attention was caught by movement from the head of the column. He squinted through the veil of rain and saw

Lieutenant Royere guiding his horse across the sticky ground, the folds of his green, silver-trimmed cape flapping around him like the wings of a gigantic bat.

The officer reined in his mount close to Lausard.

'Sergeant, take five men with you and ride into Bixente. We need provisions and possibly billets for the night. Captain Milliere suggests staying in the town until dawn, to see if the weather relents. It is slowing our progress.'

Lausard nodded. 'A number of horses have thrown shoes too, Lieutenant. The farriers will need to attend to them.'

'A night beneath a roof would seem infinitely preferable to riding on through this infernal weather,' Royere observed before tugging on his horse's reins and heading back towards the head of the column.

Lausard pointed at the five men closest to him and the dragoons swung their mounts out of formation, following the sergeant along the rutted, rain-drenched road, mud flying up behind them.

They passed the wagon and the civilian riders, then rode on, towards the officers who led the squadron and beyond.

The outlying houses of Bixente were hidden from view by a wood and some thickly planted hedges. Lausard was not surprised to see that many of the residents had not ventured outside their dwellings; others, meanwhile, were going about their business with scant regard of the weather. Those who spotted the dragoons looked on with either disinterest or curiosity, dependent, it seemed, on their age. Lausard noted a group of children standing at the windows of a wooden building, peering out at the horsemen. Elsewhere, a large man with a cloth tucked into his belt stood in a doorway watching the soldiers disinterestedly. A blacksmith barely gave them a second glance as he worked at an anvil, hammering a piece of metal into shape.

It was a scene that was, Lausard thought, being repeated in thousands of small towns throughout the length and breadth of France. But it was a scene somehow alien to him. He regarded these men of the land, these artisans and labourers, with a dispassionate eye. Not just because, prior to the frenzy of The Terror, they were of a different class to him, but because they were civilians. He was a soldier. What did they know of the horrors he and his companions had endured? How could they ever begin to know? Lausard felt a sense of alienation, the force of which surprised him. These civilians were not like him. They had not known the lifestyle he had enjoyed before the coming of the Republic. They could never have hoped to understand his wealth and his status. They would have despised him because of it. And now they could never hope to know of his feelings as a soldier. Commoner or aristocrat. Civilian or soldier. Whichever way he looked at it, he and these people were as different as it was possible to be.

He knew that most of his comrades came from exactly this kind of stock. Men like Bonet, Rostov, Tabor, Gaston and Tigana had all lived and worked on farms. And yet he felt a kinship with those men because they were soldiers; they shared his hardships on a daily basis. Lausard glanced around at his companions and wondered if they felt the same.

Rocheteau was gazing about him at the townspeople, noting, like Lausard, that most of the male population was made up of either children or men in their forties and older.

'Where are all the young men?' Carbonne pondered aloud.

'If there are no young men then there will be many very grateful young *women*,' Giresse was quick to observe.

The six horsemen turned into what appeared to be the

centre of the town. A cobbled square that may well have been a market place. The sound of horses' hooves on the solid ground echoed through the sodden air.

Two women, one holding a small child, paused to look at the horsemen, then continued on their way, seemingly oblivious to the heavy rain.

Giresse smiled longingly after them.

Lausard looked around the square, his horse pawing the cobbles impatiently.

'What do you want here?'

The voice came from behind Lausard and he turned to see a powerfully built man hobbling from one of the nearby buildings. His left leg had been severed from the knee down and a wooden one scraped across the cobbles as he approached the dragoons. The man was in his fifties, his face and hands gnarled by age.

'My name is Guinon,' the man announced, moving amongst the soldiers. He reached up and patted the muzzle of Rocheteau's horse. 'I am a tanner here in this town.'

'Who is in charge around here?' Lausard asked. 'Who must I speak to in order to secure provisions and billets? A squadron of dragoons and some civilians are even now on their way to your town. We need shelter for the night and food for ourselves and our horses.'

'You won't find many willing to help you in this town or any other around here. They have all seen enough of soldiers.'

'And you?' Lausard asked. 'Why are you prepared to?'

'Because I was a soldier myself.' Pointing at his wooden leg, the older man explained, 'That is how I got this. I was with General Montcalm in Canada. The same cannon blast that killed him took my leg at the Heights of Abraham. There are others here who will accommodate you too. We are not all so hostile to our fellow Frenchmen. Tell me what it is you need and I will try to help.'

Lausard explained briefly about the column and its mission to Paris. Guinon listened intently, nodding occasionally.

'Bring your men in,' he said finally. 'There are enough here who will help you. We can find shelter for twenty or thirty of you, perhaps more. The innkeeper, Dorleac, has stables he will allow you to use and so do I. My daughter Rosa will cook for you. She cares for me since her mother died.'

Lausard saluted.

Guinon returned the gesture with remarkable precision, watching as the six dragoons wheeled their mounts and rode out of the town.

The fire that roared in the grate of Guinon's house was a welcome sight and Lausard gazed into the leaping flames, taking a sip of his wine and feeling comfortably full. The meal he'd eaten had been most welcome and he, like the other dragoons who sat around the table, had finished every scrap. Even Captain Milliere had used the freshly baked bread to wipe every last drop of gravy from his plate.

He, Lieutenant Royere, Citizen Caminarro and two other members of the Scientific Commission were to stay with Guinon that night. Lausard had declined the offer, feeling it was unfair that he and Rocheteau should enjoy the comfort of shelter while their companions were camped outside in the rain. Rocheteau had thought about protesting but one look at Lausard had persuaded him otherwise. For now, he contented himself with enjoying the warming fire and the excellent wine.

Another fifteen men were billeted with the innkeeper. Some of them were sleeping in his stables but, in such foul weather, any cover was welcomed by the dragoons. Outside, those not so fortunate sat shivering around smoky camp fires, wrapped in their cloaks, trying to sleep on the sodden ground.

The talk over the dinner table had been of war. Guinon had amused the men with his tales of his own military service in Canada and the dragoons had been only too happy to speak of their own privations in Egypt. Guinon had listened attentively, astounded by some of the stories.

Rosa entered carrying a plate of biscuits and set them down on the table before excusing herself. She was a pretty girl in her early twenties, her cheeks carrying that familiar ruddy hue prevalent in those who live in the countryside.

Lausard smiled at her as she left, aware that Rocheteau was also gazing at the young woman; the corporal's expression, however, was more a leer than a smile. Lausard kicked him sharply under the table and Rocheteau looked towards the biscuits instead.

'I noticed that there were very few young men in the town,' Lausard commented. 'What happened to them?'

'Conscription,' Guinon said flatly. 'A law was passed last year. The Jourdan Law. Men are called to serve the Republic according to age, profession and marital status. It has not been popular. Many have rebelled against it, particularly in the west, in Brittany and Normandy. The regular army has been fighting a guerilla war against these rebels. It has spread too. We have our own problems with *chouans*.'

The dragoons looked vague.

Guinon smiled. '*Chouans*,' he repeated. 'It is what these rebels call themselves. They refuse to fight for the Directory, or even to acknowledge it. Their name originates from the call of the screech owl; they use it as a signal among themselves. Regular troops patrol this area and many others within

France. Rumour has it that over twenty thousand men are tied up trying to combat these rebels. Men that are needed elsewhere.'

'What kind of problems do these *chouans* cause you?' Lausard pressed.

'They steal food and grain. Horses sometimes. We are powerless against them. They will kill if they have to. They care only for themselves. Our own hardships are of no concern to them.'

'What do the regular troops do to protect you?'

Guinon shrugged. 'They can do little,' he said wearily. 'The *chouans* are like ghosts. They appear, strike and then vanish back into the forests and the hills. Have no fear, they will have seen you arrive. They miss nothing. The last two years have yielded excellent harvests, there is plenty of grain for them to steal.'

The men sipped at their wine, the momentary silence filled with the crackle of burning wood.

'What of the other theatres of war?' Milliere's voice broke the silence. 'How does the army fare against the enemies of France?'

'I know only what I learn from those troops who ride through here,' said Guinon. 'But it is not good. The Austrians are pushing into Italy, forcing back our troops. Everything that Bonaparte gained in 96 and 97 has been lost, with the exception of Genoa and some of the Ligurian coast.'

'Land *we* conquered,' Lausard mused, sipping at his wine.

'It is the same in Prussia,' Guinon continued. 'General Jourdan has been driven back into the Black Forest, towards the Rhine. The army has nicknamed him "The Anvil", because he is always being hammered.'

Milliere ran a hand through his hair and exhaled deeply. 'Is what we fought for now so worthless?'

'We fight for the Republic, Captain,' Royere said. 'A Republic that we helped to build.'

'A Republic built on the bodies of the rich and the excesses of the Directory,' Lausard interjected.

'Those bastards have run France into the ground,' Guinon said venemously. 'They could all do with the same kind of treatment they visited upon the Bourbons and the aristocracy. I myself would gladly carry each one of them to the guillotine. They have done more damage to France than Austria, Russia, Prussia and all our other enemies combined. Perhaps now General Bonaparte has returned some kind of order will be restored.'

'Bonaparte is a soldier, not a politician,' Royere said. 'He has no power over the Directory.'

'Then he could do worse than turn his army on them,' Guinon snapped. 'Bonaparte seems to be our only hope. I for one am glad that he is back in France. I would always trust a soldier above a lawyer.'

'I would trust a thief above a lawyer,' Lausard said, grinning. 'And, believe me, I know enough thieves to be an expert.'

The other men around the table laughed.

Guinon set about refilling any empty wine glasses.

'When do you leave?' he asked.

'At first light,' Milliere told him.

'Then may God speed your journey,' the older man said, raising his glass. 'Let us drink a toast.'

'To France?' Royere enquired.

'To the army,' Guinon said.

They drank.

Three

From the large windows of the room in the Tuileries, Charles Maurice Talleyrand looked out across the perfectly manicured gardens and beyond to the imposing edifice of the Palais Royale.

The Minister of Foreign Affairs gazed in wonderment at the former symbol of royalist power. The white walls were now grimed, some of the windows broken. The building was as obsolete as those who had once inhabited it.

Behind him members of the Directory either busied themselves or sat idly at the large table that occupied the centre of the room. The five men responsible for the government of France seemed to be dwarfed by the massive room, the high vaulted ceiling causing each sound to echo. The winter sunlight streaming through the windows occasionally glinted on the magnificent crystal chandelier that hung like an inverted frozen fountain from the gold inlaid ceiling.

'What do you find so fascinating, Talleyrand?' asked Louis Jerome Gohier. 'You have been staring out of that window for the last ten minutes.'

'I was thinking how ironic it is that the regime you and

your companions sought to destroy still dominates your every waking hour,' the foreign minister mused. 'You govern the country from a former Bourbon palace, within sight of another and close to their private residence. I am surprised you did not order the destruction of these shrines to feudalism.'

'Each of the buildings serves a purpose,' Paul Barras justified. 'It is fitting that our work should continue in the very places where the corrupt Bourbon monarchs destroyed this country.'

'Indeed, these places are certainly the breeding grounds of corruption, Citizen Barras. I would not disagree with you on that. Buildings so saturated with corruption perhaps carry that residue on to *all* those who inhabit them in time.'

There was a note of derision in the foreign minister's tone that Barras was not slow to recognise and he glared at the younger man.

'It seems that your piety did not leave you when you renounced your position of Bishop of Autun,' Barras said acidly. 'Do you imply that there is still corruption at the heart of this government?'

'I imply nothing. I simply gave voice to my thoughts.'

'Do you feel yourself above the rest of us because of your religious background?' Gohier asked. 'If there has been any corruption in evidence perhaps you should look more closely at yourself. Or your mistress. I feel that some of the money you and Madame Grand enjoy would be difficult to account for if close examination were required.'

Talleyrand turned, running a hand over his satin breeches, brushing away an unseen piece of fluff. 'I am not overburdened by scruples,' he said, smiling. 'But then again, who in this room is?'

'I think we have more important matters to attend to than money,' snapped Pierre Roger Ducos. 'When is General Bonaparte expected?'

Sieyes glanced at his pocket watch. 'He is already late,' he noted.

'You cannot impose timetables upon conquerors,' Talleyrand observed.

'Conquerors?' snapped Barras. 'The subjugation of Egypt is not even complete and yet Bonaparte has returned to France leaving a campaign he initiated in the hands of others less able.'

'Kleber is an excellent general,' Gohier observed. 'Fully the equal of our Corsican. And he is a good Republican.'

'But Kleber is in Egypt,' Talleyrand reminded the others. 'Bonaparte is here.'

Outside the room, in the long marbled corridor that led to the chamber, the men heard the sound of booted feet marching in perfect unison. They took up position behind the large table and waited for the knock at the door. It came a moment later.

Napoleon Bonaparte entered the room dressed in the uniform of a chasseur. He was flanked on either side by blue-clad grenadiers who towered above him, their bearskins giving them the appearance of giants. Bonaparte swept his bicorn from his head, the small feather attached to the tricolour cockade billowing in the breeze. He saluted the two grenadiers, who marched from the room, leaving their general alone in the company of the politicians.

Bonaparte accepted the seat offered to him and adjusted the sash he wore around his waist. His hair was long, his features gaunt but, as ever, his eyes sparkled. He shifted constantly in his chair, uncomfortable within the strictures of such formality. Like a lion pacing a cage, he appeared ready to spring. The energy contained within his small frame was phenomenal.

'It is my pleasure to welcome you back to France,' said Gohier.

Bonaparte met his gaze and that of the other men without blinking. 'The news that reached us in Egypt was so alarming that I didn't hesitate to leave my army, and set out at once to come to share your perils.'

'An admirable sentiment,' Barras chided. 'I trust that your men were as understanding of your desertion?'

Bonaparte shot him a venemous glance. 'I did not *desert* my men,' he said quietly. 'They are more than capable of fulfilling their duties without me and, besides, I felt that my presence was of greater importance here. France is menaced by three nations. All I have previously won has been lost. I felt that my rightful place was here in the service of the Republic.'

'We have gloriously overcome any perils we may have faced, General Bonaparte,' Gohier insisted. 'You return in good time to help us celebrate the triumphs of your comrades in arms.'

'Triumphs that have seen the Austrians retake most of Italy. Triumphs that have also seen them push through Prussia towards the very borders of France herself. You see *those* as triumphs? Perhaps we hold a different interpretation of the word.'

'Contrary to what you may think, General,' said Barras, 'this country is perfectly able to function without you.'

'If you had anything to do with it, Citizen Barras, I would still be in prison.' Bonaparte glared at the older man. 'Is your memory so short? It is only five years since you ordered the elimination of Robespierre. During the "White Terror" you decreed that all his followers were to be arrested. I spent three weeks in the Chateau d'Antibes because of you and your compatriots.'

'You cannot blame me for that,' Barras protested. 'Besides, it was well known that you were a protégé of Augustin Robespierre. It was right to view you as an enemy of the state at that time.'

'Because I dared to commit my views to paper?' Bonaparte snapped. 'I wrote a pamphlet outlining the ideas upon which this Republic would best be founded. I sounded a call for democracy and for that I was imprisoned.'

'What did Robespierre know of democracy? He was a dictator. As obscenely autonomous in his rule as the Bourbons before him.'

'Gentlemen,' said Sieyes, raising a hand. 'We gathered here today to hear General Bonaparte's reports and greet him. To welcome him back to France. Not to hurl recriminations back and forth like children throwing stones. What happened in the past between the two of you is unimportant now. We should be united in our quest for a greater France, not divided by petty politics that belong to another time.'

Bonaparte continued to glare at Barras who lowered his gaze, unable to retain eye contact with the furious Corsican.

'I am a servant of the Republic,' Bonaparte said finally, 'and I swear that this will never be drawn except in the defence of the Republic and its government.' He gently touched the hilt of his sword.

'An admirable sentiment, General,' Gohier observed. 'The Executive Directory, like all of France, greets your unanticipated return with pleasure, mingled with a little surprise. Only your enemies, whom we naturally regard as our own, could put an unfavourable interpretation on the patriotic motives that induced you, temporarily at least, to abandon your colours.'

'I think General Bonaparte has made it quite clear that his reasons for leaving his army in Egypt were valid, based on genuine concern for the Republic,' Talleyrand interjected, sipping at a glass of water.

'But there will be some who will question our Commander in Chief's loyalty to his own men,' Barras persisted.

'Then let those who would do so confront me personally with such accusations. I have nothing to hide and nothing to be ashamed of. I made all of you rich with the spoils from my campaigns in Italy and Egypt. I ensured that the economy of France remained stable due to the money and treasures acquired during those same campaigns. If you accuse me of anything then accuse me of patriotism. It is the only accusation I will accept.' Once again Bonaparte's gaze settled on Barras.

A heavy silence descended on the room, finally broken by Bonaparte, as he rose to his feet and placed the bicorn on his head.

'If you have any more questions regarding my conduct, Citizen Directors, I will be happy to answer them. If not then I have business to attend to.'

The other men in the room also stood up.

Gohier walked around the table and embraced the general, a curt, perfunctory gesture that was returned without a hint of sincerity.

Sieyes looked on silently, stroking his chin.

Ducos glanced across at the older man and something unspoken passed between them.

'If I might have a word with you, General,' Talleyrand said, hurrying to catch up with Bonaparte. 'I will not intrude upon your time any longer than I have to.'

Bonaparte nodded and the two men left the room.

* * *

'Where are the principles of the Republic now?' snapped Bonaparte, pointing an accusatory finger at the Tuileries. 'Those fools who claim to govern France misplace them as easily as a child misplaces a toy.'

The Corsican clasped his hands behind his back and turned away from the huge edifice, striding purposefully along one of the gravel paths of the palace gardens, his face set in hard lines. Despite the bright sunshine, there was a sharpness to the morning, and when the general exhaled, his breath frosted in the chilly air.

Talleyrand kept pace with him, finally guiding him towards a carved bench beside the path. The foreign minister sat down but Bonaparte seemed content to stand before him, his gaze occasionally alighting upon the palace. Each time it did so, his expression would darken a little more.

'What did you expect to find when you returned?' Talleyrand enquired. 'A country at peace with itself, where everyone lived idyllically? Where there was no unrest, no deprivation and the equality everyone called for during the revolution was a reality?'

Bonaparte held the politician's gaze for a moment then shook his head.

'It should not have been such a fanciful notion, Talleyrand,' he said, finally sitting down. 'I did not expect to find a country tearing itself apart. One tyranny has merely been replaced with another.'

'That is the way in politics. It is like an ocean. There are constant upheavals. Waves and squalls. This particular ship of state would seem to need steadying somewhat. There are too many hands on the tiller and they are all pulling in opposite directions.'

'Very poetic,' Bonaparte said scathingly. 'But that is of no help to France or to me. These lawyers have ruined this country. They sit there like kings, they flaunt their wealth. Wealth that belongs to the people.'

'There is nothing wrong with wealth, my friend. You and your family do not live the lives of paupers. The revolution was only ever concerned with stripping away the privileges of birth, not inequalities of fortune. If the Directory has achieved only one thing of any note, it has shown that *anyone*, no matter what their background, may rise to a position of wealth or power if they have the ability. You are a perfect example of that.'

'I don't need your flattery, Talleyrand. I need to know what has been happening in France while I have been away.'

'Where would you like me to begin? Would it interest you to know that some members of the Executive Directory were intent on seeing you arrested for abandoning your army in Egypt?'

'Barras.'

'Gohier,' Talleyrand corrected him. 'But I am sure that Citizen Barras would not have objected if that course of action had been pursued. The inefficiency and unpopularity of this government has passed all rational limits. They attempted to replace *assignats* with *mandats* but discovered that paper money was no better than hard currency. In fact, all they succeeded in doing was giving us two depreciated currencies instead of one.'

'And has there been any opposition to their incompetence?'

'Little else. But the opposition is not strong enough. Jacobins. Royalists. None has the power to displace this government. The Executive locates its enemies and removes them. In the departments of France during elections, votes that went against the ruling body were later reversed by acts of law. One political coup has followed another. But each has been initiated by the government itself. The *coups d'état* of 22 Floréal and 30 Prairial were purges, designed to remove all opposition to the Directory. Barras spoke of Robespierre's dictatorship earlier. Well, my friend, that is what we have now. The only difference is, we have a dictatorship of five men instead of one.'

Bonaparte stroked his chin thoughtfully.

'It is their mismanagement of the war that is their greatest crime,' Talleryrand continued. 'After you had defeated the Austrians in Italy in 97, only England stood against us, and even then I feel Pitt would have agreed to peace. But it is not in the interests of the Directory to have peace. Any external threat prevents the French people from concentrating on the problems within their own country. The Directory did not *want* peace. They formed the League of the Rhine with Bavaria. This antagonised both Prussia *and* Austria. They annexed Holland and formed the Helvetic Republic. But elsewhere both Scherer and Moreau have been defeated by the Russians. Macdonald was forced to abandon Rome and both Britain and Russia have moved against us in Holland. The army is short of boots, muskets, horses and ammunition. Yet still they fight on. The only men the people believe in any more are soldiers. This country is being run by lawyers and no one has any respect for *them*.'

'What is to be done then? You are a diplomat. A politician. Is the solution a diplomatic one? I think not.'

'The time has come for change. It is the nature of that change and how it is to be achieved that are the problems.'

'Then the sooner these problems are solved the better. France faces civil war again. That must not be allowed to happen. I will not *permit* it to happen. Whatever measures needed for the well-being of this country must be put in motion quickly and decisively.'

'There are many others who agree with you, General. You have friends in places you would not begin to imagine.'

'Do you look to me to save this country?'

'It would not be the first time, my friend.'

Bonaparte gently touched the hilt of his sword.

'I said I would draw this in defence of the Republic,' he mused. 'If that is the case, I will be true to my word. You have your saviour.'

Four

The rain that had been falling steadily for the last few days had eased to a drizzle. Lausard looked up at the washed-out sky, the wind driving curtains of moisture across his line of vision. The valley rose steeply on either side of the column, the slopes thickly wooded.

They had left the town of Bixente a little over thirty minutes earlier. The men had woken in darkness and set off as the first meagre light of dawn had coloured the sky. They had been permitted to cook themselves some breakfast using the few rations they possessed. The officers had been more fortunate and both Captain Milliere and Lieutenant Royere had enjoyed mountainous repasts served to them by Guinon's daughter. The tanner had waved all the men on their way, saluting as the dragoons passed.

Lausard had eaten from a huge metal container that the men of his unit had used to cook what little provisions they had. Rocheteau had caught a couple of wild rabbits, which Gaston and Bonet were only too happy to skin and add to the simmering soup. None of them knew when they would eat again, or indeed what their next meal would consist of. Lausard wondered if they would dine again before they reached Paris, now reckoned to be three days away.

The civilians in the column looked particularly uncomfortable. Cold, wet and hungry, these men were not used to the rigours of army life and this journey must seem like purgatory to them. However, Lausard mused, all of them had spent time in Egypt. Surely this trip was to be welcomed when compared with the horrors they must have endured there?

The sergeant pulled his cloak more tightly around his neck and, once again, glanced up at the hillside.

The road seemed to be getting narrower. It was as if the hills were actually closing in on the muddied thoroughfare, trying to crush it out of existence. Up ahead there was barely enough room for the horsemen to ride two abreast. The wagon lurched on, its driver forcing the exhausted horses to even greater efforts. But the more the helpless beasts tugged and fought their way through the sucking mud, the more difficult their task became. Lausard could see one of the wheels sinking deeper into the ooze. The wagon tipped slightly to one side and there were gasps of concern from the civilian riders around it.

'Why get so worried about a load of rocks?' muttered Rocheteau. 'Now, if they had diamonds or gold in there, *I'd* help them move it.'

'You might have to help them anyway,' Lausard informed him. 'It's going to block the road if it stays there and none of us will be going anywhere.'

'Let *them* move it. It belongs to them,' Delacor hissed. 'Let those preening "pekinese" get their precious hands dirty for a change.'

'Lausard!'

The shout made the sergeant turn in his saddle. He recognised the voice and the figure riding towards him from further down the column.

Sergeant Delpierre rubbed a pockmarked cheek with one hand and then pointed a finger at the stricken wagon. 'Get some of your bastards to help move that wagon,' he snapped. 'Now!'

'Are you trying to give me an order?' Lausard asked. 'You forget, we both share the same rank. I take orders from Lieutenant Royere or Captain Milliere. Not you. And that goes for my men too. If you want the wagon moved, move it yourself, you horse's arse.'

There was a chorus of chuckles from the men nearby, silenced by a withering glance from Delpierre.

He and Lausard locked stares for a moment then Delpierre wheeled his horse and rode back down the column. He returned a moment later with six men from his own unit, who dismounted and took up position to the rear and sides of the stranded wagon.

'Not helping them?' Lausard asked the sergeant, who sat astride his black horse watching as the dragoons struggled to free the wagon. One of them slipped and fell face down into the clinging mud. Cursing, he hauled himself upright and continued pushing.

'*Your* men should be doing that,' Delpierre observed. 'It is the work of criminals and scum, not *real* soldiers. But then you think yourself above the rest of us, don't you, Lausard?'

'I think myself above *you*, but then again, I would imagine a sewer rat would feel superior in your company, Delpierre.'

'I think we should meet again when we reach Paris. Perhaps you could get some of your thieves, rapists or murderers to act as seconds for you.'

'Are you challenging me to a duel?' Lausard asked evenly.

'I look forward to killing you.'

'You can try,' Lausard said, looking directly into the other sergeant's eyes.

They both looked up towards the hillside as they heard the sound of breaking wood. A groan which grew into a high pitched shriek.

'Look!' shouted Giresse, pointing to a point on the easterly slope.

They all saw it.

Three of the large oaks there were toppling over. With a deafening crash they struck the ground and rolled towards the valley floor, gathering pace as they reached the bottom. Horses whinnied in panic. Riders looked around, desperately seeking a means of escape in the narrow pass. Some troopers even leaped from their saddles and ran for the opposite slope in their eagerness to escape the rolling timber.

Lausard saw the first of the tree trunks smash down across the road like a huge club wielded by some massive invisible hand. Half a dozen men and horses were bowled over by the impact and the sergeant saw two men crushed beneath the rolling logs. The second took out four more men, and horses both in front and behind the disturbance seemed to go wild. Joubert clung desperately to his reins as his mount reared violently, threatening to hurl him from the saddle. Charvet shot out a hand and grabbed the bridle of his companion's horse, trying to steady the frightened beast.

There was another loud noise from the opposite slope.

Lausard saw more trees crashing down, rolling inexorably towards the trapped column and the stranded wagon. And now, for the first time, he also saw figures moving amongst the trees.

There were several loud cracks which he recognised as musket fire.

One of the balls struck the ground a few feet from Lausard, throwing up a small geyser of mud and water.

It was followed by several more.

'*Chouans*!' snapped Lausard, seeing more shadowy figures moving amongst the trees. 'It's an ambush.'

Ahead, one of the dismounted dragoons went down clutching his shoulder, blood staining his green cape.

Sonnier pulled his carbine from his saddle, swung it up to his shoulder and aimed in the direction of one of the attackers. The Charleville thudded back against his collarbone as it spat out its load. He smiled as he saw one of the rebels pitch forward but immediately he took another cartridge from his cartouche, bit off the ball, poured powder into the muzzle, spat the ball after it and then rammed the remaining powder and wadding into the barrel, ready to squeeze off another round. All around him other dragoons were doing the same, some firing blindly into the thick woods that surrounded them.

A bullet struck Carbonne's horse and tore off one of its ears. The terrified animal reared and hurled Carbonne from the saddle. He landed with a groan in the mud and rolled over, trying to regain his senses and also to escape the pounding hooves of his injured horse. The animal finally bolted into the trees.

Lausard pulled one of his pistols from its holster and dragged hard on his reins, urging his mount towards the woods on the westerly slope.

'With me,' he shouted and half a dozen of his men followed him.

The rest, firing from the saddle, returned the musket fire that was now peppering the column from front to back. Some riders dismounted, using their horses as cover but, with the fire coming from both sides at once, many decided they were just as safe astride their mounts.

Thick, sulphurous smoke was already beginning to fill the valley as the dragoons intensified their fire.

Lausard sent his horse hurtling up the slope and into the woods, reining it in immediately when he saw just how dense the trees were.

'Fight on foot,' he shouted, leaping from his saddle.

Rocheteau followed his example.

Karim drew his wickedly curved sabre and did likewise, his two pistols tucked into his belt.

Bonet, however, managed to remain in the saddle, his horse twisting and turning in the woods, weaving in and out as if it was on some kind of training exercise. He was taking the animal further up the slope, getting behind the enemy.

Lausard pointed ahead to where several of the *chouans* were crouching behind a felled log, firing into the column of dragoons trapped in the valley.

Ducked low, the sergeant and his men moved closer.

Delacor slipped the axe from his belt and gripped it tightly. He'd claimed it from a dead sapper after the Battle of the Pyramids, and the edge was razor sharp.

Tabor fitted his fifteen-inch bayonet to the end of his carbine and held it across his broad chest as he moved through the underbrush, scurrying with remarkable agility and finesse for a man of his size.

Lausard could see their opponents clearly now.

Sheltering behind several of the oaks were eight or nine of the rebels, all dressed in rags, unkempt and unwashed in most cases. Some were shoeless. They all carried Charleville muskets and were firing them with a proficiency that surprised Lausard.

He had no idea how many more *chouans* were secreted in the woods on either side of the valley but the only ones that concerned him now were these men directly before him.

They had been so preoccupied with firing at the column of dragoons that none had seen the sergeant and his handful of men enter the trees and make their way up the slope.

Lausard watched Bonet as he guided his horse expertly through the trees until he was behind the rebels. The other dragoons followed.

From the valley the dragoons in the column were still returning fire and several times lead balls sang through the air above the heads of Lausard and his men.

'Our own troops will kill us at this rate,' whispered Rocheteau, dropping down behind a gorse bush. He slid the knife from his belt and ran the pad of one thumb along the sharp edge.

Lausard looked around at the other men, checking that each was ready.

The *chouans* were less than twenty yards away, still oblivious to the presence of the dragoons.

'Now!' bellowed Lausard, and the men launched themselves into the attack.

Hurtling down the slope into their foe, they had the element of surprise on their side. One or two of the rebels reacted and tried to get off shots at the charging men, but it was useless.

Bonet rode his horse straight into one of the men, knocking him off his feet. As the man rose, the former schoolmaster drew his sword and thrust it into the back of the rebel's neck.

Lausard raised his pistol and shot another in the forehead, then he too pulled his sword from its scabbard, driving the pommel into the face of another rebel.

One of the *chouans* swung his musket like a club but Karim ducked beneath the blow and struck out with his sabre. The wicked curved blade sheared through his opponent's leg just above the knee, slicing effortlessly through bone and muscle.

The severed limb fell to one side and the rebel shrieked and toppled over, blood jetting from the stump. Karim finished him with a blow that almost split his skull in two.

Rocheteau drove his shoulder into the midriff of his foe, using his body weight to force the man down. As they crashed to earth, the corporal ran his knife into the man's throat just below the larynx.

Those *chouans* who remained alive were concerned only with escape now and they fled.

Delacor raced after one of them and caught him with a mighty blow of the axe. It shattered the man's collarbone and stuck in his shoulder. Grunting, Delacor wrenched it free and hit him again, this time burying the blade in his enemy's skull.

Bonet dug his heels into his horse and prepared to give chase but Lausard caught his companion's bridle and pulled to prevent the horse bolting.

'Let them go,' he said, glancing around him at the dead rebels. One was still moving, clutching at a wound in his chest, which was weeping blood freely.

Up and down the valley, the men could still hear the sound of gunfire but it was beginning to die off. Lausard guessed that the *chouans* on both sides of the valley were fleeing. He knelt beside the wounded rebel and looked into his face.

The man was in his early twenties, his features pale, but there was anger in his eyes as he met the sergeant's gaze.

'You steal from your own people,' said Lausard, leaning close to the man. 'You shoot at your own soldiers. Why?'

The wounded rebel coughed, blood spilling over his lips. 'They are not my people,' he rasped. 'And you are nothing to me. You fight for the Directory. I want no part of anything they do.'

'We are soldiers of France,' Lausard told him, watching

as the man's eyes rolled upward in their sockets. He released his grip on the rebel's torn and bloody shirt, allowing him to sink back on to the sodden earth.

The sergeant stood up and turned away from the body.

Rocheteau prodded the man with the toe of his boot. 'I thought the revolution was supposed to unite this country,' he mused.

Lausard shook his head and looked around at the other dead *chouans*.

'What have we returned to?' he murmured. 'A land where men still kill their brothers. And for what? How many were carried to the guillotine? How many died in the streets? All the killing and suffering. All the pain. All without purpose. *Nothing* has changed here.'

He stalked off, heading back towards the valley floor.

The other dragoons followed.

Five

Talleyrand looked admiringly around the dining room of Emmanuel Joseph Sieyes, marvelling at some of the priceless artwork that adorned the walls. The foreign minister sipped at his wine then brushed some crumbs from his jacket.

'A fine meal,' he said, nodding in the direction of his host. 'It seems only right that plots should be hatched on a full stomach.'

Sieyes regarded him silently.

It was the third man in the room who finally spoke.

'You make light of such serious business, Talleyrand,' Ducos said irritably. 'We could all be imprisoned for what we are doing here tonight.'

'We are *planning* what everyone else in Paris, indeed the whole of France, desires. The Directory is a blemish on the face of this country. Removing it will present a more pleasing countenance to the people.'

'Nevertheless, what we are attempting is treason,' Ducos insisted.

'What we are attempting is to wrest true democracy away from those who have imposed dictatorship,' Talleyrand reminded him. 'There is nothing so terrible about that.'

'There are many dangers involved,' Sieyes said. 'Not only must we induce a *coup d'état* we must also determine what kind of regime is to follow the fall of the Directory.'

'Is it feasible that the fall can be achieved without recourse to military intervention?' Ducos wanted to know. 'If you remember rightly, the coup of 17 Fructidor required the aid of General Augereau. Had he not occupied the Councils of the Elders and the Five Hundred then that may well have signalled failure.'

'I feel we need military help of some description,' Sieyes said. 'As to who will be our sword, that is a different and more complicated matter. There are as many ambitious soldiers in Paris at the moment as there are politicians. But the views of all these men are not known.'

'Potentially, the most dangerous group is led by Augereau and Jourdan,' Talleyrand observed, 'both Jacobins and both members of the Council of the Five Hundred.'

'What of Bernadotte?' asked Ducos. 'He has no love for the Directory. They removed him from the Ministry of War. I think we could count on *his* support.'

'When Sieyes was instrumental in forcing his resignation?' Talleyrand said, peering at his host over the rim of his wine glass. 'I hope he has the capacity for forgiveness.'

Sieyes remained silent.

'And Moreau and Lefebvre?' Talleyrand continued. 'It would be most convenient to have Lefebvre on our side. He is, after all, Military Governor of Paris. Does anyone know either his or Moreau's attitude towards the Directory?'

'I doubt if either would bestir themselves to protect it,' Ducos offered.

'As you know, had he not been killed in Italy, I would have

preferred General Joubert to take charge should a military situation arise,' Sieyes said.

'There is a more obvious choice,' Talleyrand interjected. 'A hero, beloved of the people. A conqueror who commands the respect of his own subordinates and who, I am sure, would be delighted to aid in the removal of men he himself detests. I speak of General Bonaparte.'

Ducos nodded almost imperceptibly.

'I don't trust him,' Sieyes intoned. 'He has political aspirations of his own. He might not react very favourably to being used as an instrument of insurrection.'

'I don't think that General Bonaparte has ever been *used* by anyone in his entire life,' Talleryrand chuckled. 'He is as eager as you for change. For the good of France. And your doubts about him, you will be overjoyed to learn, are more than mutual. He detests you, my friend. I heard his wife say so.'

'I care nothing for the opinions of that harlot,' snorted Sieyes. 'All of Paris knows of her infidelities. Bonaparte is a fool to let her continue humiliating him in public.'

'He is in love and love does strange things to men,' Talleyrand observed.

'The bedroom manoeuvres of Madamoiselle de Beauharnais are of no concern to us,' Ducos reminded his companions. 'There is the more pressing matter of the government of France in case it had escaped your attention. It is her husband we need. Will he join us?'

'He sees the need for change,' the foreign minister said.

'Under whose terms?' Sieyes demanded.

'Both you *and* our Corsican have your own ambitions,' Talleyrand observed. 'I feel that those ambitions could be best served by working together.' He grinned. 'After all, there is room for only *one* plot against the government, isn't there?

Bonaparte's family will be useful to us as well. His younger brother, Lucien, recently became President of the Council of the Five Hundred, and Joseph, his elder brother, is a deputy and also eager to see the same changes as we in this government.'

'There is the matter of money to be considered too,' Ducos interjected. 'It seems that overthrowing a government requires considerable financial resources too.'

The three men laughed.

'Bonaparte amassed considerable personal wealth during his campaigns in Italy,' said Sieyes. 'Let us hope he will be willing to use some of it in pursuit of this cause.'

'I was hoping you would be prepared to part with some of your own considerable fortune too, Sieyes,' Talleyrand mused. 'There are plenty of others more than willing to help finance a return to democracy. Army contractors, bankers and speculators are all willing to provide financial support. Cambaceres, our current Minister of Justice, is already liaising with financiers such as Recamier and Perregaux. We have administrators, commissioners and deputies in both chambers with us too.'

'So what precisely is Bonaparte's role in this?' Ducos asked.

'He can count on the support of most of the generals we have mentioned,' said Talleyrand. 'But Bonaparte's true worth will be his control over the army. Should force be needed, there is no more able man in the whole of France than Bonaparte.' Talleyrand refilled his glass. 'There is a delicious irony to this entire venture when you consider that it was Bonaparte who saved the Directory back in 95 from the very people he now purports to represent. He had no compunction about ordering his cannon to fire on the populace then, but now he says he wants democracy so that those same people may flourish. It appears that the saviour of the Directory is about to become its destroyer.'

'And after that destruction is complete? What then?' Sieyes wanted to know. 'You know Bonaparte better than any of us, Talleyrand. What will he want? What reward will this Corsican consider appropriate?'

'There you have me, my friend. Even though I know him, I do not possess the ability to read his mind. But I am very sure you will be one of the first to discover what he desires.'

'So, what is the next step for us?' Ducos asked.

'A meeting of conspirators,' said Talleyrand with a wry smile.

Six

Lausard looked around at the houses and shops that flanked the narrow street. The sound of the horses' hooves echoed loudly on the cobbles and more than one window was thrown open as curious inhabitants cast inquisitive eyes over the column of dragoons.

There was a uniformity to the buildings that Lausard remembered only too well. Grey, lifeless houses inhabited by grey, lifeless people, he mused, broken only occasionally by a more brightly painted shop front. The rain that had fallen for most of their journey from the south had stopped earlier the previous day but the gutters were still full. Even the roads, both inside and outside the city were awash in places. Rivers had swollen menacingly, some threatening to burst their banks. Lausard wondered if the Seine itself had risen. Perhaps if it did, it would wash away all the filth and scum from the streets of Paris once and for all.

Paris. The word, the city itself, held little in the way of welcome memories. The trees that lined the streets were, in the midst of this bleak November, devoid of leaves and stood like skeletal sentinals, guarding the thoroughfares of the French capital – the place he had called home prior to pulling on a uniform. The city where he and so many of his unit had been imprisoned for a variety of crimes, some petty, some not so. And before that he had walked these streets as a thief. The gutters that now flowed with dirty water had been his home. He and Rocheteau, and so many others, had barely survived in those overcrowded, filthy streets where stealing had been their only means of existence.

He, Alain Lausard, who had fled the life of opulence to hide with men he would normally have avoided at all cost. Men who would have ordinarily cut his throat for the contents of his moneybelt. For in that belt he had carried more money than most residents of Paris would ever see in a lifetime.

He had fled the wrath of the mob, as many of the rich had tried to do. Lausard felt that he had been luckier; he had escaped with his life. His family had not been so fortunate and now, as the column headed across the vast open expanse of the Place de la Revolution, memories at last came flooding back. Recollections he had been trying to purge. He could still remember it as if it had been yesterday. The sight of the guillotine set up in the middle of the square, surrounded on all four sides by the baying hordes of citizens. Then the tumbril arriving with its latest consignment of victims, destined to lay their heads beneath the blood spattered blade of the revolution's killing machine. But on that particular day, the four figures who had been hurried to their deaths had been his father, his mother and his two sisters. He had stood, transfixed, watching as their lives were taken. He, who should have been with them on that bloodied scaffold. He, who had fled to escape his fate. Alain Lausard, the thief. Alain Lausard, the coward.

Six long years had passed and still the feeling of self-disgust was just as strong, and it returned now with even greater ferocity as he passed the very spot where his family had been slaughtered.

'Is something wrong, Alain?'

Rocheteau's voice startled Lausard from his waking nightmare and he looked across at the corporal.

'I was just thinking,' he said quietly.

'So was I,' Rocheteau confessed. 'Who'd have thought we'd ever see Paris again as free men? It's been two years now, hasn't it?'

'Nearly three,' Lausard corrected him. 'Nearly three years since they came and took us from the Conciergerie. Released us from those stinking cells and gave us these uniforms.' He looked down at the green surtout he wore.

'Who'd have thought we'd be back here as soldiers?' Rocheteau continued.

'I didn't think we'd *ever* get back alive,' Sonnier offered.

'It's good to be home,' Giresse said, looking around at the buildings and the civilians who wandered past going about their business. Some glanced in the direction of the dragoons but most paid them little attention.

Lausard was not surprised. Troops were hardly an uncommon sight in the streets of any major city in France now. However, what did surprise him was the sheer volume of soldiers moving about the capital. Ever since they had entered the outskirts of the city, he had seen men from every conceivable regiment or branch of the army. Infantry, artillerymen, cavalrymen. Some wandering about in small groups, others moving in a more martial fashion. They had exchanged salutes with over a dozen officers from various regiments, including two colonels, one a chasseur, the other from Bonaparte's guides.

'I hope there's some food where we're going,' Joubert complained, rubbing his large belly.

'Shut up, fat man,' Delacor snapped. 'You could go without food for a month and still survive.'

'I feel as if I *have*,' Joubert groaned.

'Where *are* we going, Captain?' Lausard addressed Milliere, who rode just ahead of him.

'My orders were to report with my men to the Luxembourg Palace. What is to happen when we arrive I have as much idea as you, Sergeant.'

'It looks like a city under siege,' commented Royere. 'So many troops.'

'Perhaps the news of the war was worse than anyone told us,' Rocheteau mused. 'Perhaps the Austrians and the Prussians are at the gates of Paris now.'

Some of the men laughed.

'What's so funny about that?' Roussard wanted to know. 'I thought returning to Paris would mean we'd all stay alive a little longer.'

'The sooner we get back to fighting the better,' Charvet said. 'At least when we're at war, those bastards in the Directory won't try to lock us up again. I hope the Prussians and the Austrians *are* at the gates of Paris. What do you say, Alain?'

'I fear the true enemy is somewhat closer,' Lausard murmured.

The boys were no older than twelve or thirteen. Dressed in short trousers, wooden shoes and jackets of various colours, most of which were far too large. Lausard watched them as they went about their business. Moving with all the speed of trained monkeys, they carried their small barrels with relative ease, moving from dragoon to dragoon and pouring a measure of brandy into each metal cup that was held out.

The sergeant looked across towards Gaston, the trumpeter,

who was barely two years older than the boys who now served him. The lad sat with his legs crossed, his brass helmet between his legs, the top button of his scarlet surtout unbuttoned. He accepted the brandy when it was offered and sipped it with as much vigour as his older companions. Lausard marvelled at how nearly three years of war had aged the youngster. Worry lines were etched deeply in his skin. His blond hair was past his collar and was badly in need of washing. And like most of the dragoons he had several days' growth of whiskers.

Lausard scratched at his cheek and ran appraising eyes over the Luxembourg Palace. Some beautiful linden trees stood in front of the main building but the square itself was strewn with rubble – the ruins of other buildings. Lausard could only wonder how and when they had been destroyed. The garden too was a ruin. Some chestnut trees waved leafless branches in the November breeze but the rest of the garden was barren.

Still carrying his brandy, Lausard walked slowly into the building before him, Rocheteau and Karim close behind. Their heavy boots echoed on the stone steps, the sound becoming even louder as they entered a large vaulted chamber.

'The sacristy,' Lausard observed. 'No wonder Moreau was so happy we were quartered here. It appears our home is to be this chapel for the time being. He can be closer to his God.' He sipped at his brandy.

'Alain,' Rocheteau said, tugging at his sleeve, 'what did you mean earlier when you said the enemy are closer?'

'We have all seen how many troops are in Paris. There is a reason for that. What that reason is I do not know but I suspect we may see action sooner than any of us imagined.'

'Perhaps the citizens of Paris are preparing to fight, just as the *chouans* did in the countryside.'

'It's possible. And if they do, the Directory will call upon us to stop them. They will order us to kill our own people once more.' He looked unblinkingly at the corporal. 'And we will do it. Because we are ordered and because we are soldiers.'

Rocheteau drained what was left in his cup.

'Have this,' Karim said, passing his companion his cup. 'I never did care greatly for it.'

Rocheteau took it gratefully.

'I hope Allah, all praise to Him, does not look down upon me with too much anger for sleeping in the home of *your* God,' Karim grinned.

'I have no God,' Lausard told him.

'You must believe in something, my friend,' observed the Circassian.

'I believe in this,' Lausard said, patting the hilt of his sword.

All three men walked to the nearest window as they heard a rumbling outside. Looking down into the gardens they saw a battery of four-pounders being driven into position. The six guns, each weighing in excess of six hundred pounds, were unlimbered and lined up facing the palace.

'Do you think they are going to fire at us?' Lausard said, smiling. He watched the crews of each gun swarming around the pieces like ants around their hill, each of them with a specific job to perform.

'What the hell is going on around here?' Rocheteau wanted to know.

Lausard had no answer. 'All anyone wants is peace,' he said quietly. 'And yet this city looks as if it is about to explode.'

Seven

The house of Josephine de Beauharnais in the Rue Chantereine was impressive but lacked any outward hint of ostentation; its exterior masked the opulence that filled it. Josephine's husband, though only too happy to enjoy the grandeur and riches acquired from three years of campaigning, felt it would be betraying the principles of the Republic to wallow openly in his new wealth. Napoleon Bonaparte still believed in what the Republic stood for.

He now sat gazing into the flame of the candle, his dark eyes reflecting the dull yellow light. Around the table others watched him. His elder brother Joseph sipped at his wine. The younger of the Bonapartes, Lucien, picked at a piece of pastry on his plate. Talleyrand was brushing crumbs from his sleeve. Sieyes and Ducos looked on impatiently, waiting for someone in the room to break the silence. It was towards the Corsican in particular they looked.

'If force should be needed then I will not hesitate to use it,' Bonaparte said finally. 'Against whoever opposes this coup. And there is a simple reason why I would have no hesitation in ordering such action. Whoever opposes us cares nothing for

France. My only concern is for the well-being of this country. Under the Directory, I can see more problems succeeding those they have already created. That is one of the reasons they must be removed.'

'And what of the men you called comrades?' Sieyes pressed. 'Men like Jourdan, Kleber, Brune and Bernadotte? What if it is men such as they that oppose you? Will you fire on them? Will you command your own troops to confront theirs? They are all committed Jacobins. They have their own interests in a change of political power.'

'Kleber is in Egypt, Brune on the north-east frontier. Jourdan is no threat. Bernadotte is the problem. But we cannot delay any longer. If power is to be wrested from the Directory then we must act with or without the collusion of Bernadotte. Whatever his stance it must not deflect us from our objective.'

'He appears immune to *all* approaches,' Joseph Bonaparte observed. 'A political solution has proved ineffectual when dealing with him and he seems not to fear the possibility of open confrontation either. Even feminine wiles have failed to convert him to our way of thinking.'

'Meaning what?' Sieyes demanded. 'What has any of this to do with women?'

'More than you would suppose,' Joseph answered. 'As you know, Bernadotte is married to Desiree Clary. I married her sister, Julie. That makes Bernadotte my brother-in-law.'

'That much I had managed to deduce for myself,' Sieyes said, dryly. 'Make your point.'

'My wife and Bernadotte's wife tried to persuade him to join us, as did my brother's wife,' he nodded in the direction of Napoleon. 'To no avail. He was amiable and amenable, only too happy to dine with us at his home, but still no one is sure of his position. No one knows whether he will support or oppose us.'

'We cannot sit around forever waiting for the decision of one man,' Bonaparte said impatiently. 'If he chooses to stand against us, then so be it.'

'He would be a powerful enemy,' Talleyrand interjected.

'So be it,' Bonaparte said again, with an air of finality. 'As I have already stated, I would have no hesitation in fighting him if the need arose, though I would prefer not to. One of the purposes of this coup is to restore unity, not rekindle the fires of civil war.'

'What of the people themselves?' Ducos asked. 'How do you expect *them* to react to the removal of their government?'

'Despite what the Directory has done to this country, there may well be some who mourn its passing,' Talleyrand observed. 'That mourning may become a little, shall we say, hysterical? There is a possibility of popular uprising against our new regime.'

'Then it will have to be dealt with in the same way as any other kind of opposition,' Bonaparte insisted. 'Swiftly and resolutely.'

'By force?' Sieyes muttered.

'If necessary.'

'In one breath you speak of not wanting civil war again and yet you insist that anyone who opposes this venture is to be removed by force,' Sieyes observed.

'What other solution is there?' Bonaparte said, glaring at the older man. 'Do you think I enjoy the prospect of ordering my own countrymen to be fired upon? This coup must succeed, no matter what the cost.' He glanced at his younger brother. 'What kind of opposition can we expect from the councils?'

Lucien shrugged. 'The Council of the Elders should prove no problem. It is in the Council of the Five Hundred where the problems could arise. There are many Jacobin deputies concentrated there. My own chairmanship of the council may go some way to relieving the situation. But I cannot say with any certainty how amenable that chamber will be to the removal of a government that gave it power.'

'I suggest removing the legislative councils to Saint Cloud,' Talleyrand said. 'It is ten miles to the west. Away from the centre of the city. Away from the prying eyes of the populace.' He smiled. 'I suggest the situation may be more easily managed there.'

'I agree,' Bonaparte said. 'Reconvene the assemblies outside the capital.'

There were murmurs around the table.

'When the meeting is called,' Lucien said, 'several selected deputies will denounce a Jacobin insurrection. They will say that subversives have been arriving in Paris from all over Europe. It will be suggested that transferring the councils out of the city is for their own safety. Article 102 of the Constitution empowers the Elders to transfer the legislature as they see fit. They need no permission from the Council of the Five Hundred or the Directory itself. At that same meeting, it will be proposed and ratified that you, my brother Napoleon, should take charge of all available troops.'

'This is a copy of the address that will be read to the deputies present,' Talleyrand added, pulling a piece of paper from his tunic. '"The Council of the Elders invokes its constitutional authority to transfer the location of its proceedings in order to defeat the factions that wish to overthrow the national representation. Public safety and general prosperity, these are the objectives of this constitutional measure. Long live the People, by whom and in whom the Republic resides."' He folded the paper and handed it to Bonaparte, who glanced at it indifferently before returning it.

'But the army is to remain in the background at all times,' Sieyes protested. 'This was always to be a political not a military coup. The army is to be called upon only if the worst eventuality occurs.'

'Politics is your province, Sieyes,' Bonaparte snapped. 'Let *me* worry about the military implications of our actions.'

'So, when do we begin?' Talleyrand wanted to know. 'Which date is to be consigned to history as that on which France regained her democracy?'

Bonaparte raised his wine glass in salute. 'Eighteen Brumaire,' he said.

They all drank.

Lausard watched as the thick soup was ladelled into his metal bowl. Pieces of mutton, beans and lentils floated around in the brown liquid but it smelled good and he, like the rest of his squadron, had consumed far worse in his time. The dragoons had formed four lines, one in front of each of the large iron kettles that had been set up over a small fire within the sacristy. Thick black smoke from the fires had formed a cloud at the pinnacle of the vaulted ceiling and the aroma of burning wood mingled with the smell of the soup.

The sergeant collected his ration of bread and wandered back to his straw mattress, one of over a hundred laid out in the disused chapel. Men sat on them eating and talking, some trying to sleep, others smoking. A card game was going on nearby. Lausard thought how subdued all the men seemed. An air of expectancy hung over them, a feeling of uncertainty, which had been prevalent ever since they had reached Paris.

Lausard raised a hand and waved at Corporal Charnier

of the third squadron. The other man waved back and continued drinking his soup. He was a bull of a man, powerfully built with a neck so thick it appeared to be merely an extension of his muscular shoulders. He had a small silver snuff box beside him from which he kept taking pinches of the brown powder and snorting it loudly.

'This is sacrilege,' Moreau said indignantly, as Lausard rejoined a group of his men. 'This is the house of God, not some kitchen.'

'If it's God's house then he should take better care of it,' said Lausard, looking around at the inside of the sacristy.

The other men laughed.

'Does God own every church in France?' Tabor asked.

'I don't think God's allowed to own any land, idiot,' Delacor chided. 'Even priests aren't allowed to. The Directory owns it all, doesn't it?'

A chorus of laughter greeted his remark.

'Priests have no need of material possessions,' Moreau insisted. 'Everything they have, they owe to God. They have their piety and they are blessed in the knowledge that they are close to Him.'

'If the church isn't concerned with material things, then how is it that the Pope is one of the richest men in the world?' Lausard wanted to know.

'He used to be,' Rocheteau chuckled. 'I hear Bonaparte took over three million francs from him.'

'And our men pillaged Rome when they took it,' Roussard echoed. 'I doubt if the old boy has enough left to buy a loaf of bread.'

There was more laughter.

'You are all blasphemers,' Moreau snapped. 'Do not expect mercy from God when we next go into battle.'

'I expect mercy from no one,' Delacor said acidly. 'I give none, I expect none.'

'Why didn't you become a priest, Moreau?' Lausard asked.

'My family could not afford to send me to school to learn what was required, otherwise I would have taken Holy Orders.'

'The priest from my village was a rogue,' chuckled Tigana. 'He had more knowledge of women than he did of God.'

'A man after my own heart,' Giresse intoned.

The others laughed.

Moreau glared at the horse thief.

'It's true,' Lausard interjected. 'There are very few holy priests in France. The others are reprobates and charlatans. Every second bastard born is fathered by a priest.' He supped at his soup. 'But if Moreau ran the priesthood that would not be, would it, my friend? For then the priests would be very holy, and therefore very few.'

The men's laughter echoed around the sacristy.

Karim looked on in amusement. He was sitting cross-legged on one end of his straw mattress smoking a pipe, almost invisible behind the thick curtain of smoke billowing from the bowl.

'What is that you're smoking, Karim?' Rostov questioned him. 'It smells like camel droppings.'

'It is Turkish tobacco. It is a fine blend. I took it from a Mameluke outside El Rhaminaya not long before we left.'

Lausard heard footsteps coming towards them and looked up to see Lieutenant Royere stepping crisply among the mass of dragoons.

'Will you join us, Lieutenant?' he said, gesturing for the officer to sit.

'I have already eaten, thank you, Sergeant, but I will sit with you if you can tolerate my company.' He grinned, making himself as comfortable as he could on the stone floor.

'Any news on why we are here or what we are to do?' Lausard enquired.

Royere shook his head.

'No one seems to know anything,' he replied. 'Or if they do they are not prepared to say.'

Lausard watched as the officer reached into one of the pockets of his tunic and withdrew a tiny bottle of clear fluid.

'Diluted nitric acid,' Royere said, answering the unasked question. 'May I have your sword?' He was looking at Lausard.

The sergeant hesitated a moment then slid the three-foot blade from its scabbard and handed it, hilt first, to the officer. Royere turned it in his hand then laid it before him, gently unscrewing the bottle of acid. As the men watched he tipped three small drops on to the blade of the weapon and leaned close. Three tiny black spots appeared. Royere wiped the blade clean with a piece of cloth and returned it to Lausard.

'Captain Milliere and I have been ordered to ensure that checks are carried out on all swords issued within the past six months. Apparently several deliveries from civilian manufacturers have blades of polished iron, not steel. This test reveals the true nature of the metal. The acid will turn white when dropped on iron. Black on steel.'

'So the iron weapons are useless,' Lausard said flatly.

'For all but a few days,' Royere told him. 'They buckle and bend. They rust very quickly.' He handed the small bottle to the sergeant. 'Good luck.'

'Civilian contractors give us poor horses, civilian manufacturers send us bad swords,' muttered Rocheteau. 'What next? Do we discover that our ammunition does not fit the barrels of our weapons?'

'The men who the army deals with care only for money,' said Royere. 'They are not interested in the welfare of those they sell to.'

'Why should they be?' Lausard asked. 'They know nothing of how we live or of what we endure. That is why they are civilians and we are soldiers. But wasn't the revolution supposed to encourage free enterprise, Lieutenant? It gave men like these contractors the freedom to trade, to make fortunes.'

'I didn't come here tonight to argue the validity of the revolution, my friend.' The officer grinned. 'Or the men it spawned. We will save that argument for another time.' He got to his feet. 'There is something else. You are all to remain in this place until morning, and to stand ready. Post sentries as if we were in the field.'

Lausard looked deep into the officer's eyes. 'What *is* going on, Lieutenant?'

'I wish I knew,' Royere said. 'I really do. We prepare to meet an enemy but who that enemy is no one seems to know.'

'An enemy within Paris itself,' Lausard said, his voice a whisper. 'This is another revolution.'

Eight

Sleep never came easily to Alain Lausard. No matter how comfortable his surroundings or how exhausted he felt, the oblivion that shrouded most of the men with such ease eluded him. For with that sleep came dreams and memories he preferred not to relive; those same dreams he had endured earlier in the day, as he had ridden across the Place de la Revolution. The recollections were always painful and, no matter how far into the mists of time the actual events receded, the anguish of their passing still remained. The murder of his family was still like an open wound in his consciousness and he feared that gaping cut would never heal. To Lausard, the loss of honour and pride was as damaging as the loss of any limb. Perhaps even more so. A man could live for years minus an arm or leg. But for how long could a man exist when his sense of self-hatred burned so brightly? When the only thing that would assuage the thirst for penance was death? And so it was again in the dead of night he awoke, an all too famiiar panoply of dreams having spread across his subconscious, like blood soaking through bandages. Those same dreams.

Lausard sat up, the last vestiges of the nightmare fleeing with the arrival of consciousness. Around him other men were awake here and there. He watched one man on a mattress a few yards away writing on a piece of crumpled paper. A note to a loved one perhaps? His candle-holder was a potato, propped beside his straw mattress. Elsewhere the room rumbled with the sound of snoring as many of his companions enjoyed much longed-for sleep.

Lausard had found lately that faces other than those of his dead family had been intruding his dreams. Men he had fought with. Those who not been as lucky as he. Men who died on the battlefields of Italy and Egypt. For now, they were as much a part of his life as his family had ever been. They were the only people he could feel close to and he knew the feeling was mutual; men flung together in the service of their country, united by their experiences and sometimes bonded by a fear of what horrors they would face next. Lausard looked around at these sleeping men. These men he called comrades. Men from the opposite end of the social strata but whom he now called friends.

He got quietly to his feet, moving cautiously, not wishing to disturb the men around him.

A few yards away, the man writing the letter glanced at him then returned to his note. More words of love? Lausard wondered.

He was about to step over the sleeping form of Gaston when he was aware of someone standing close behind him. The sergeant turned to see Karim standing there.

The Circassian nodded and Lausard saw a look in his eyes that seemed to convey understanding. As if Karim had been reading his troubled mind.

'You find sleep as elusive as I,' Karim said. 'For what reason, my friend?'

'Let's walk,' Lausard said quietly. 'I want to check on the sentries anyway.'

The two dragoons made their way towards the exit at the far end of the high-ceilinged room, their boots tapping out a gentle tattoo on the stone floor. Karim's sabre clanked against his leg as they progressed towards the stairs and down towards the main doors and the garden beyond.

'Do you miss home, Karim? Do you wish you had stayed in Egypt instead of coming with us?'

'How could I miss a life of slavery? I had no life to speak of until I fled from the yoke of the Mamelukes who sought to control me. I found freedom when I joined you, and for that I thank Allah, all praise to Him.'

'Can you remember your family?'

'I was a child when the Mamelukes enslaved me. I have no recollection of them. Therefore I feel I have no family.'

'Nor I.' Lausard paused and wondered if he should share the truth of his past with this man. The Circassian had no comprehension of what revolutionary France had been like; he had no hatred for men of any class. And yet, Lausard chose to keep his secret to himself.

They emerged into the garden where, on either side of the great doors, Bonet and Sonnier drew themselves to attention.

Lausard waved a hand in the air for them to stand easy.

'I would ask you if all is quiet but I suspect that it is,' mused the sergeant.

'What's going on, Alain?' Bonet questioned. 'There are grenadiers guarding the entrance to the gardens. That battery of horse artillery has been cleaning its guns for most of the night and we just saw a detatchment of "big boots" ride past.'

'"Big boots"?' said Karim, looking puzzled. 'What manner of men are these?'

Lausard grinned. 'It's the nickname given to the heavy cavalry.'

'They descend upon the enemy like a thunderbolt,' said Sonnier. 'And they are covered in iron.'

'They wear a cuirass on their chests and backs,' Lausard informed Karim. 'They ride horses specially bred to take the added weight. As soldiers they are no better than ourselves.'

Bonet grinned.

'Men have been moving back and forth all night, Alain,' Sonnier continued. 'If we haven't seen them, we've heard them. There must be more French troops gathered in Paris at the moment than there are in Italy, Prussia and Switzerland combined.'

Lausard nodded. He glanced around the gardens of the Luxembourg, illuminated by campfires. The scene did, indeed, look more like a campsite the night before battle than the centre of the French capital. Those men of the horse artillery who were not sleeping were cooking. A corporal was stirring the contents of a large iron pot with the wooden end of a portfire while the others waited eagerly for their share. Several gunners were feeding the horses hay and oats. As Lausard watched, he heard the sound of horses' hooves on the cobbled street beyond the privet hedge surrounding the gardens. Squinting through the gloom he could make out the familiar mirliton caps worn by hussars, and he looked on as a detachment of these flambuoyant horsemen rode by, their harnesses jingling, their sabres rattling. Gradually the noise receded into the darkness. Lausard wondered how long this concentration of troops had been going on and for how long it would continue. Even now, were more men massed *outside* the city, waiting for the signal to enter? And if so, whose signal? And for what purpose? The questions tumbled around inside his head.

'Tell Charvet and Carbonne to relieve you,' he ordered Bonet and Sonnier, watching as both men made their way back inside the chapel.

'What troubles you, my friend?' Karim asked, looking at Lausard's expression. 'Why is the presence of so many of your countrymen of concern to you?'

'It is the *purpose* of that presence I find disturbing, Karim. France has already suffered more than her share of internal strife. Frenchman killing Frenchman. And yet, when I see so many troops gathering together in one place my instincts tell me just one thing: that they, that all of us, await orders that may well signal the beginning of more bloodshed. This republic was built on death. It seems to be the only thing that can sustain it now.'

Napoleon Bonaparte stood in darkness, peering out of the bedroom window down into the street. He had no idea how long he'd been standing here, only that when he had glanced at his pocket watch when he'd first entered the room, he'd noticed that the hands had showed it to be two o'clock.

He had stood looking down at the sleeping form of Josephine. Her dusky skin appeared so smooth in the candlelit glow that he had been unable to stop himself touching her cheek and forehead tenderly, almost guiltily, before moving away to take up his current station at the window. Behind him, he could hear her slow, even breathing. He remained where he was, gazing out into the night but seeing beyond the darkened street to the following day. Of course he had no window to see into the future but, in his mind's eye, that future was a glorious one, both for him and for France. The Directory would be removed; the windbags who ran the country discarded forever to make way for the kind of government his country deserved. He would deliver it from its plight and the country would thank him. He had never stopped to wonder before what kind of reward would be suitable for his forthcoming actions. Perhaps now was the time to consider what manner of prize was fitting for freeing an entire country and its people.

'I sometimes wonder if I married a man or the entire Republic.'

The words made him turn.

Josephine was sitting up in bed, her long dark hair cascading over her shoulders, her white nightdress a wonderful contrast against her beautiful Creole skin. She fixed him in her gaze and ran a soft hand over the sheet beside her.

'Must I lose a husband to state matters? Am I to be a widow of diplomacy?'

Bonaparte smiled and wandered across to the bed, where he seated himself beside her, reaching out to touch her cheek.

'I do not mean to neglect you, but you know how important these coming days are for France and for us.'

'But it is not just days, is it? It is weeks. Months. Years. One thing follows another. Politics. War. I sometimes wonder if *they* are your true love, not I.'

'There is nothing in this world I love more than you. I would give my heart, my soul, my life for you. But France needs me.'

'*I* need you. I need a husband by my side, not a man who deserts me to wage war.'

'You knew when you married me what kind of man you had chosen. I am a soldier; my place is at the head of an army.'

'Would you prefer to be at war than with me?'

'If I could have peace tomorrow I would. If the armies of our enemies left the borders of France there would be no happier man than I. But until they do my place is on the battlefield. And there I must remain until France is free again. Then when the fighting is over I shall return to you. A husband like any other.'

'But you are *not* like other men, are you? You pursue greatness as a hunter pursues a fox.'

'I do not pursue greatness,' he snapped. '*It* pursues me. If that is my destiny then so be it.'

Bonaparte got to his feet and walked slowly back towards the window, his back to his wife. She swung her slender legs from beneath the sheets and joined him.

'And tomorrow?' she asked. 'Will those streets run red with blood?'

He didn't answer.

'And what if some of that blood is yours?' Josephine persisited. 'Am I to lose my husband here, on the streets of Paris? You returned to me from Italy and Egypt. Must I see you die in the city where we make our home?'

He turned to face her, running his hand through her silken hair. 'Whatever happens tomorrow happens for the good of France. I will see to that. You have my word.'

'As a soldier?'

'As a husband.'

Nine

Dawn rose cold and grey over Paris. Lausard watched a watery sun struggling to climb into the washed-out sky, and as he walked across the grass of the Luxembourg gardens, his boots left imprints in the heavy dew. Outside in the streets surrounding the palace he could hear the tramp of feet and the clattering of horses' hooves. Troops were already on the move.

All around him the palace and its surrounding gardens were a hive of activity, as weary men struggled to their feet at the urgings of officers and NCOs. He made his way inside the chapel and up to the sacristy, where the men of his own unit were dragging themselves from their straw mattresses as Sergeants Delpierre and Legier woke the sleeping dragoons with shouts and kicks. Lieutenant Royere and Captain Milliere moved amongst the men. Meanwhile two men from the quartermaster's detail were hauling a heavy wooden box through the sacristy, distributing packs of ammunition to each man. Fifteen cartridges in each. Every man got three. Lausard took his own and began feeding them into his cartouche.

Other men were busy polishing their saddles or rearranging the contents of their portmanteaus. A kettle of water had been set up over a small fire in one corner of the room and four or five men were busy shaving. Lausard could smell vegetables cooking close by as the men of the third squadron attempted to consume some breakfast before they were given orders to move.

Rocheteau was cleaning his brass helmet with a piece of oily cloth. Karim had unsheathed his sabre and was polishing the wickedly sharp, curved blade.

Bonet and Tabor were also cleaning their swords. Sonnier checked the firing mechanism of his carbine, occasionally holding the weapon against his shoulder and squinting along the barrel, and Delacor wiped the blade of his axe with some straw from his makeshift mattress.

'There is to be an inspection by General Bonaparte himself,' said Captain Milliere as Lausard drew nearer. 'Until then, the entire regiment is to wait here.'

'Have you any idea what is to happen, Lieutenant?' Lausard asked Royere.

The officer shook his head.

'Someone should have checked these mattresses for fleas,' Giresse complained, scratching at the back of his neck. 'The damned things are crawling with them.'

'Just like the old days when we were in prison,' Rostov reminded him.

'I used to eat the fleas I found on me,' Joubert said. 'A man like me needs all the nourishment he can get.'

Gaston wrinkled his nose at the thought.

'What time is it?' Lausard asked.

Rocheteau pulled his pocket watch from his tunic and flipped open the lid. 'Six fifteen.'

Lausard nodded. He glanced around him again and wondered what the coming day held.

* * *

As Napoleon Bonaparte entered the dining room of the house in the Rue Chantereine he glanced around at the uniformed men gathered there, some sipping wine, others talking amongst themselves. Despite the early hour there was much movement both inside and outside the house, and Bonaparte noted the sound of many horses in the street. Crossing to the window he looked out to see a unit of blue-uniformed chasseurs passing.

'General Sebastiani is leading them towards the Tuileries,' General Louis Alexandre Berthier explained.

'Sebastiani is a good man,' Bonaparte observed. 'He can be relied upon in a crisis. I hope I can expect the same of all you gentlemen today.'

'I trust there will *be* no crisis,' General Lannes said. The officer was leaning against a wall, supported by crutches, the legacy of wounds he had received at Aboukir. 'At least none that any of us has to run from.'

A chorus of laughter greeted his remark.

Bonaparte looked around at the men; he knew he could rely on them all. Every one of them had proved his worth in combat. Like Lannes, Murat still bore wounds from the Egyptian campaign; Berthier was more delighted than most to be free of that pestilential country; and the brilliant young artillery general, General Marmont, five years younger than Bonaparte, was also a good ally. He stood next to Serurier, the oldest of those present. Beside him, Macdonald, the son of an exiled Scottish Jacobite, warmed his hands around a cup of coffee.

'I trust that you gentlemen have eaten,' Bonaparte said. 'I fear we will have more important business to deal with today than food.'

The men smiled.

'You all know what is expected of you,' Bonaparte continued. 'What we accomplish today will save France. I cannot emphasise too highly how important it is that all orders are carried out to the letter. Look upon the day's events with the same solemnity you would look upon a battlefield.' He looked at each man in turn. 'You are aware of your orders?'

'I will take the cavalry to the Palais Bourbon,' Murat said.

'I am to command at the Tuileries,' Lannes offered.

'I will take the trip to Versailles and watch the Jacobins,' Macdonald intoned.

'I will take three hundred men and surround the Luxembourg,' said Moreau.

'To the Point de Jour and then to Saint Cloud,' Serurier finished.

Bonaparte nodded. 'We must not fail,' he said earnestly. 'The fate of France is in our hands.'

The door of the dining room opened and the uniformed men turned to get a better look at the newcomer.

General Francois Joseph Lefebvre took off his bicorn and wiped a hand across his forehead. He looked agitatedly from one face to the other, finally turning his gaze on Bonaparte.

'Have you come to join us, my friend?' Bonaparte took a step towards the older man. 'If ever I needed your skill and your friendship it is now.' He put an arm around Lefebvre's shoulder.

'I am here on duty,' Lefebvre replied. 'As Governor of Paris it is my province to discover why so many troops are marching through the city at such an early hour and under whose orders.'

'You know the answers to these questions, my friend. You know of our plans, but would you oppose us? Would you come to the aid of the miserable crew of windbags, profiteers and lawyers who have brought our magnificent country to its knees? These men know nothing of the rigours we have experienced. If one of them could, only for a few moments, feel the same kind of courage in his heart that pulses through your veins, then he would be a very worthy man. But none of them knows this feeling; none has any comprehension of what makes men like you and me.'

Lefebvre looked at Bonaparte, tears welling in his eyes.

'I marvel at your courage,' Bonaparte continued, well aware that his rhetoric was having the desired effect. 'All of us do. We can only stand back in awe at your achievements, your nobility and your bravery. I beg you, do not sacrifice those things you hold most dear in the service of liars and frauds. Join us. Men like yourself. Men who know the meaning of honour. On this day, of all days, I need a man close to me who I can trust above all others. That man must be you. For there is none more worthy. There is no man I would sooner have at my right hand on this day of destiny.'

Tears began to course down Lefebvre's cheeks and he embraced Bonaparte, who returned the gesture, his gaze meeting that of Murat.

'You have my loyalty,' Lefebvre sobbed. 'Now and always.'

'Good man,' Bonaparte said, gripping him even more tightly. 'Now we can be sure of victory with *you* on our side.'

The door opened again and this time it was Bessiéres who entered.

'General Bernadotte is outside,' he said flatly. 'He says he must speak with you now.'

'It is what we feared,' Murat observed. 'He means to oppose us. He means to fight.'

Bonaparte headed for the doorway, his boots beating out a

tattoo on the parquet floor as he crossed the hall and opened the front door.

General Jean-Baptiste Bernadotte stood in the middle of the Rue Chantereine dressed in civilian clothes, a cane gripped in one hand.

Bonaparte looked to his right and left, relieved when he saw no troops. Several of the other generals joined him but the Corsican waved them back inside. He approached Bernadotte, who raised his cane as if it were a sword, the end pointing threateningly at Bonaparte.

'I know what you plan to do,' the Gascon said, loudly. 'I know of your desire for advancement. I am not a fool to be coaxed or threatened into joining you.'

'When I heard you were here I rejoiced,' Bonaparte told him, the lie ready on his tongue. 'I need men such as you. Men who have graced the uniform I now wear. Go, and return here in that attire you rendered so glorious. You are needed today.'

Bernadotte rolled up the sleeve of his shirt and held up his arm. 'Look there,' he demanded, pointing to a tattoo. 'Read the words: "Death to Traitors". The sentiment is burned into my flesh as surely as it is imprinted upon my soul.'

'Then join us now,' Bonaparte urged. 'What else are those fools in government but traitors? I know that your love for the Republic runs as deep as mine. I realise that you have seen this country we hold so dear ruined, as have I. Were we not willing to die for it and the ideals for which it stands? Is that not still the case?'

Bernadotte regarded the Corsican warily. 'How do I know that it is not you who are the traitors? It is you who gather secretly to discuss the future of the government, as if you have some mandate from the people to change it.'

'The only mandate I need from the people of France is their

willingness to allow the government that has caused them so much suffering to be replaced.'

'Replaced by what? You have plotted and schemed for months now. You have threatened and bribed those who oppose you.'

'I have bribed no one,' Bonaparte snapped. 'I have no need of false promises. Those who support me do so because they too care for the well-being of this country and its people. A sentiment I thought you shared, Bernadotte. Perhaps I was wrong.'

'You serve up platitudes with as much ease as a baker serves up bread. I hear no sincerity in your voice. I see no purity in your actions. And I see but one motive. Your own betterment.'

'So, what is your answer?' Bonaparte insisted. 'Are you with us or against us?'

'And if I say I am against you, what will you do? Call half a dozen of your fellow conspirators to shoot me down where I stand?' He jabbed his cane at the ground.

The two men regarded each other in silence for a moment then Bernadotte spoke again.

'I will not interfere. Do as you will. You will find me neither an enemy nor an ally today.'

Bernadotte turned and walked up the street, watched by Bonaparte, who finally strode briskly back into the house, where Berthier and Lannes were waiting.

'There will be no opposition,' Bonaparte said, looking at each man in turn. 'And now, gentlemen, we have work to do.'

Ten

Captain Milliere gave the order to draw swords as soon as the dragoons had mounted. The deafening metallic hiss of hundreds of weapons being pulled free of their scabbards filled the air, before they were rested gently against the shoulders of the green-jacketed horsemen. They made their way slowly along the Rue Saint Jacques, the sound of their horses' hooves clattering in the early morning air. To their left, the glittering façade of the Sorbonne reflected the weak sunlight, while up ahead the towering edifice of Notre Dame thrust its twin towers towards the clouds. The men rode in silence, most of them, like Lausard, oblivious to their destination and the purpose of this exercise.

Ahead marched a demibrigade of light infantry. From their bearskin bonnets, sporting drooping red plumes and red cords, Lausard recognised them as carabiniers. The shoulders of their blue jackets were trimmed with red epaulettes, and the small brass grenades on their cartouches sparkled as they marched, the sound of their booted feet a perfect complement to the noise of so many horses' hooves. Fifteen-inch bayonets were fixed to their Charleville muskets, the sun glinting wickedly on the sharp tips.

Behind the dragoons came a squadron of mounted chasseurs led by General Sebastiani. Like his men he was dressed in the familiar short green jacket and Hungarian-style breeches of the regiment. Like all the other cavalry, he had his sabre drawn.

The column of troops moved effortlessly over the bridge, the dark waters of the Seine flowing swiftly below. For a moment Lausard wondered if the structure might collapse beneath the weight of so many men and horses, particularly when a battery of horse artillery and their four-pounders came rolling over close behind.

Once across, at the junction of the Rue Saint Honore and the Rue Saint Denis, the entire column turned left. Lausard saw the imposing outline of the Tuileries Palace. What had once been the home of the French royal family was now the seat of French government. Lausard could not help but think that one form of inefficiency had simply been replaced by another, but it was an opinion he chose not to vocalise. Glancing quickly he saw that the faces of his companions were almost without exception set in grim lines. Wariness shrouded the dragoons; none had the slightest idea what was going on and this ignorance caused them both resentment and fear.

There were more troops outside the Tuileries Gardens. Blue-coated infantry, muskets in the 'Present' position, stood in phalanxes four deep on either side of the wide thoroughfare. Mounted officers walked their horses back and forth to ensure that the lines remained straight. Standards fluttered in the light breeze. Lausard saw General Lannes standing with two senior aides-de-camp, the officer finally moving stiffly on his crutches, pointing at the oncoming cavalry.

Captain Milliere led the dragoons into the gardens and Lausard and his companions found themselves facing the front of the palace. It was a magnificent sight and the sergeant saw more troops outside, mostly line infantry in their familiar uniforms of black bicorns with blue jackets faced with white lapels and cuffs. Lausard had never seen so many troops in full dress uniform. After the rigours and privations of the Italian and Egyptian campaigns, he was more used to seeing the infantry without shoes and dressed in rags. It was a startling contrast, made even more striking by the determined expressions on the soldiers' faces. Without exception, the troops faced the Tuileries.

The dragoons moved into position just behind the first wave of infantry and Lausard wondered if the building was to be stormed. His heart began to thud a little harder against his ribs. He caught Rocheteau's gaze and the corporal raised his eyebrows to signal his own puzzlement. Lausard could only shake his head, the horse-hair mane of his helmet sweeping back and forth, stirred by the breeze as much as by his movement. He patted the neck of his horse and waited.

He, like the other troops gathered outside the palace, saw Bonaparte emerge. The Corsican strode confidently towards the top of a flight of stone steps leading down into the garden and ran approving eyes over the mass of men before him. Behind him Murat and Marmont stood like sentinels, the gold lace on their uniforms glinting in the sunlight.

'I have, this very morning, sworn to the deputies in there,' he motioned behind him, 'that I and my soldiers will carry out the instructions we have been given. They called upon me to command their army and I accepted that responsibility. But with provisions. I told them that we want a Republic founded upon liberty, equality, property and upon the sacred principles of national sovereignty. I promised them that we would achieve our goal. I gave them my word.'

There were some rumblings from the many troops gathered. Lausard heard a shout of '*Vive Bonaparte*!' to his right.

His horse began to paw at the ground, as if it too was unsure of what to do next.

'In what sort of state did I leave France?' Bonaparte continued. 'And in what sort of state do I find it again? I left you peace and I find war! I left you conquests and the enemy is crossing our frontiers. I left our arsenals full and I find not a single weapon! I left you millions from Italy and I find extortionate taxes and poverty abounding everywhere.'

The cheers became more numerous now. Men lifted their weapons into the air as they roared their agreement. Lausard looked around and saw that men of his own squadron were joining in. Tabor and Giresse were brandishing their swords before them and greeting each fresh exhortation with a bellow of approval.

'The Republic has been badly governed for the past two years. You hoped that my return would put an end to all these evils, and it will. You celebrated my homecoming with a display of unity that imposes obligations upon me, which I will hasten to fulfil. It is up to you to carry out your duties and support your general with the energy, resolve and confidence that I have always admired in you. That is the way to save the Republic.'

The watching men erupted in a frenzy of shouts and cheers. Every soldier Lausard could see was roaring Bonaparte's name while the general waved his hat to accept their adulation.

Lausard remained upright on his horse, his eyes moving alternately between Bonaparte and the cheering mass of troops all around him.

'Do you not share our general's sentiments, Sergeant?' asked Lieutenant Royere, smiling.

'Indeed I do, Lieutenant. I was merely wondering at what cost the Republic would be saved. Will it be measured in financial terms or in human lives? After all, it was founded on murder. Killing seems to be the currency of this administration.'

'Surely those who oppose the principles of the Republic deserve to die.'

'Your idealism is showing again, Lieutenant.'

'As is your cynicism, my friend. Did you not once say that the army would eventually be the most powerful force in France? It would appear you were right.'

'Bonaparte commands the army. It would seem that he is intent on commanding France too. I am just relieved to be a part of his instrument of power. Woe betide those who oppose it.'

'Do you think any will?'

'Who can say? But those that do, what will become of them? Will you shoot them down, Lieutenant? Will you ride through mobs of your own countrymen, cutting a path through them as a sythe cuts corn?'

'If necessary. What about you?'

'I am a soldier. I will do as I am ordered. There is no place for conscience or question in *this* army.'

The roars of '*Vive Bonaparte*!' grew ever louder. A deafening affirmation that seemed to reach to the very heavens themselves.

Paul Barras turned as he heard the door of his chamber open, surprised and a little irritated that he had heard no knock. He was about to berate his maid when he saw Talleyrand standing there. On either side of him and in the corridor outside stood grenadiers. An officer, his sword already unsheathed, waited by the door for orders and retreated only when Talleyrand nodded to him.

'The diplomat becomes a soldier,' Barras said scathingly.

'Has your association with Bonaparte transformed you into a man of violence?'

'I came here in friendship, not seeking to inflict harm,' said Talleyrand. 'The escort is purely cosmetic.' He smiled.

'And on the orders of Bonaparte no doubt.'

'It is over, Barras. The Directory is no more. It is time for change.'

'What of the others?'

'Sieyes and Ducos tendered their resignations this morning. Moulin and Gohier were less forthcoming. They are now under guard in the Luxembourg.'

'And what is to be *my* fate? You know as well as I that Bonaparte has been waiting for just such an opportunity to take his revenge against me. Are you here to arrest me?'

'I am a diplomat, as you said, not a policeman. I am sure that if our Corsican had wanted you in irons he would have sent Fouché with me to perform that task. After all, the Minister of Police would be far more able, wouldn't you agree?'

'So what is it that you want of me?'

Talleyrand reached inside his waistcoat and pulled out a piece of paper, which he handed to Barras. The other man glanced at it and smiled bitterly.

'A letter of resignation,' Talleyrand told him. 'Sign it. That is all I ask. By doing so, you help to save the Republic again.'

'Do not flatter me with your empty words, Talleyrand. I know you too well for the duplicitous deceiver you are. It is small wonder you and Bonaparte are allied. There is much similarity in your treachery.'

'There have been few men, Barras, during the course of this Directory's existence, who have lied and cheated with such expertise as yourself. Do not think to lecture *me* on the morals of this venture.'

'Your piety is showing once more, *abbé*. And it does not sit comfortably on shoulders bent with the weight of such betrayal.'

'I offer you the honour of a comfortable retirement. The knowledge that you have *gained* from this transfer of power, not lost as some have. You may retire to your estate and live unhindered. All I ask in return is your signature on that piece of paper.'

'And if I refuse? Why should there be no place for a man such as I in this new regime?'

Talleyrand smiled. 'Sign, Barras. You, like the Directory, are dissolved. You are obsolete. The refuse of the past. Do not make me dispose of you as some would wish. Perhaps you should be thankful that it is I who came here. If Bonaparte himself had sought you out then your final journey may well have been straight to the Conciergerie.'

The men locked stares, then Barras snatched the quill on his desk and scratched his signature at the bottom of the note. He hurled it across the desk towards Talleyrand, who caught it before it floated to the floor.

'A noble gesture,' Talleyrand murmured, as he blew on the still-wet ink. 'One which, in years to come, I feel you will understand was both necessary and very sensible. I suggest you leave Paris before nightfall. As a sign of your sincerity.'

Barras glared at the other man, the knot of muscles at the side of his jaw pulsing angrily. 'And what next for Bonaparte?' he said, finally.

'He meets with the Council of the Five Hundred tomorrow. If they have any sense they will see the wisdom of the measures he proposes and they will act upon them.'

Talleyrand turned to leave.

'He will not be satisfied until he alone controls France,'

Barras said. 'And he will not care who he has to remove to achieve that goal, Talleyrand. Perhaps you should treat this Corsican viper with a little more caution or you too will feel his bite.'

'The best way to handle a snake is to know its temprement,' Talleyrand said, smiling. 'Failing that, one should always wear thick gloves. Mine are particularly resistant to venom.' He bowed and left, closing the doors behind him.

Lausard pulled on his horse's reins and brought the animal to a halt. He patted the neck of the bay and swung himself out of the saddle.

Rocheteau and the others watched as the sergeant strode across the wide expanse of the Champs Élysées and reached for a placard, which had been nailed to a tree. He returned to his horse and remounted. The unit moved on, towards the top of the thoroughfare, the horses walking slowly. The sun was setting, bleeding its colour into the clouds and staining the heavens crimson. A chill wind, which had been building steadily throughout the afternoon was now whipping along the streets and several more placards, like the one now held by Lausard, were tossed around in the swirling breeze.

'"Let the weak take heart",' Lausard read aloud as they rode, '"they are supported by the strong. Everyone is free to go about their business and follow their daily routines in perfect confidence . . . all the necessary measures of security have been taken." It's signed by Fouché, Minister of Police.' Lausard tossed the placard into the street. 'They must have plastered these on every wall and tree in Paris.'

'Everyone is free,' Rocheteau echoed. 'It *sounds* convincing.'

Some of the men chuckled.

'But not Moulin and Gohier,' Giresse said, a smile on his lips. 'Those windbags are still locked up in the Luxembourg.'

'Now they know what we felt like when *we* were prisoners,' Delacor snapped. 'Good riddance to the Directory and all its members. They can rot in hell as far as I'm concerned.'

'Bonaparte was right when he said the country had been badly governed for the past two years,' Bonet opined.

'What difference does it make?' Rocheteau asked. 'We weren't here anyway. We were getting shot at to keep those bastards living in luxury. Perhaps *you* should have taken care of them, Carbonne.'

'In the old days I would have been delighted to help them,' the former executioner chuckled. 'Out of the cart, up the steps of the scaffold and straight on to the guillotine.'

The other men laughed.

Lausard led the unit of dragoons in a wide arc at the top of the Champs Élysées, so that they were heading back down towards the Place de la Revolution and their quarters beyond.

'So who will run the country now?' Tabor wanted to know.

'Does it matter?' Delacor snapped.

'It matters very much,' Lausard told him. 'With the Directory gone there is nothing to replace it, unless Bonaparte himself intends to take over.'

'But he is a soldier,' Rocheteau mused.

'He has the power to rule if he so wishes,' Lausard continued. 'Because he has control of the army. Whoever controls the army controls France. Bonaparte knows that. Why do you think he is always telling us how much he cares for us? How valuable each of us is to him and how he strives to see that we are well looked after? It is in his interest to have our loyalty. Men fight for a number of reasons. Duty. Belief in a cause. Love of their commander. Regard for their country.'

'And what about us, Alain?' Rocheteau pressed. 'Could any of us say why *we* fight?'

'You tell me. For love? For beliefs?'

'We fight because it's better than sitting in a stinking jail cell,' Delacor said.

'I believe in France,' Bonet offered. 'I am proud to fight for my country.'

'So am I,' Roussard echoed. 'I just don't want to *die* for my country.'

There was more laughter.

'I would fight for the love of a good woman,' Giresse said, smiling. 'Or perhaps *several* good women.'

'I would fight for God,' Moreau added. 'I would willingly give my life for Him.'

'At the moment,' Joubert complained, 'I would give my life for a decent meal.'

'I would fight for peace,' Tigana offered. 'If I thought that the world would be a better place for my sacrifice then that would be worth fighting for.'

'Very noble,' Rostov said. 'I would fight for my own life. No one else. I want peace too but I want to be alive to see it. I want to return to Russia, to my birthplace, and I want to live the quiet life and die peacefully in my bed when I am one hundred years old.'

'What about you, Karim?' Lausard said, glancing at the Circassian. 'Why do you fight? This isn't even your country. These aren't your people. You could walk away at any time and yet you remain.'

'Ever since I was a boy I have known only conflict. Perhaps it is in my blood. Perhaps Allah, all praise be to Him, intended me to live my life this way. At the end of a sabre.' He patted the hilt of his blade.

'And you, Alain?' Charvet asked. 'What do you fight for?'

'We all fight because there is nothing else for us. If we left the army what would we have? Is there a man among us who would be better off out of uniform? I think not. Those times have gone. All we are and all we have we owe to the army. Our possessions, our pride. If not for the army we would all be dead now.'

'It will be the army that *gets* us killed,' Sonnier protested.

'It will be Bonaparte and his thirst for power. The man who set us free will bury us all in time. Perhaps even tomorrow. Only Bonaparte knows who will face us when we reach Saint Cloud.'

'It is only ten miles from Paris,' Bonet observed. 'Could there be an enemy force so close without us knowing?'

'I bet it's the Austrians,' Rocheteau said.

'The Prussians,' Giresse countered.

'I wager one day's rations that it is the Russians,' Tigana interjected.

'I'll match that wager,' Rostov grinned.

'If you win, be careful that the fat man doesn't eat your winnings,' Delacor said, nodding towards Joubert.

Again the men laughed.

'Who do you think it will be, Alain?' Bonet asked. 'Who will we fight tomorrow?'

'Whoever Bonaparte *tells* us to fight.'

Eleven

The Château of Saint Cloud was a magnificent building, an imposing, monolithic edifice that dominated the landscape. The afternoon sunlight reflected off the windows, making it appear as if diamonds were embedded in the walls.

As Lausard looked around he could see a demibrigade of grenadiers ahead of his own unit, their muskets held at the ready, their red plumes blowing in the light breeze. As on the previous day, infantry had marched with them during their journey. The march from the centre of Paris had taken a little over an hour, and again, as was the case the previous day, the men knew little or nothing about why they were here.

Earlier they had seen Bonaparte himself ride past, mounted on a great black horse and accompanied by Murat and Bessiéres. Now Lausard could see the Corsican pacing back and forth outside one of the entrances to the château, gesticulating angrily, sometimes towards the building and occasionally towards the troops, who awaited his orders.

'What the hell are we waiting for?' Rocheteau wanted to know.

'Orders,' Lausard reminded him, his gaze fixed on Bonaparte, who had removed his bicorn and was sweeping it back and forth in a series of expansive gestures.

'They should let us go in and kill all of those bastards now,' Delacor interjected. 'Get this over with.'

Captain Milliere looked round, as if to rebuke the man who had spoken. Instead he ran appraising eyes over his men before turning back to face the château.

'How much longer?' Rocheteau murmured. 'We've been sitting here for more than two hours already.' His horse tossed its head once or twice, seemingly as impatient as its rider.

Lausard said nothing, simply keeping his eyes on Bonaparte. Every so often, the general would take a couple of steps towards the entrance then stop. Only Bessiéres' gently persuasive hand on his shoulder prevented his advance at one point.

As far as Lausard was aware, deputies from both the Council of the Five Hundred and the Council of the Elders were already in session inside the château and had been since late morning. He wondered what they could be discussing and how much longer Bonaparte's patience would hold. He looked desperate to get inside and, as time ticked slowly on, even the protestations of his fellow generals seemed to do little to assuage his growing impatience.

Lausard watched Murat walk away from the general, mount his horse and walk the animal slowly back and forth in front of the waiting troops. What purpose this gesture was meant to convey, the sergeant could only guess, but he contemplated the cavalry general's actions for only a moment before sharply returning his attention to Bonaparte.

'What is the purpose of this?' Bonet asked.

'You are an educated man, schoolmaster,' Lausard said quietly. 'What do *you* think?'

Even as Lausard spoke, he saw Bonaparte pull away from

Bessiéres and advance towards the nearest entrance. This time he did not stop.

The Gallery of Apollo inside the Château of Saint Cloud had been chosen as the meeting place of the Council of the Elders. A huge, high ceilinged chamber, decorated with magnificent frescos and ornamented by gold and marble, it had not been acoustically designed for raised voices and as Bonaparte entered the room, he was met by a wall of sound emanating from the deputies. However, as they spotted the general striding purposefully into their midst, his gold-trimmed tail coat flapping behind him, their conversation died down rapidly. All eyes turned to the Corsican.

Bonaparte took up position in the middle of the room, hands planted on his hips, and looked around, satisfied that he had the attention of the assembled throng.

'Citizen Representatives,' he began, his voice reverberating around the room. 'The situation in which you find yourselves is far from normal. You are sitting on top of a volcano.'

There was a babble of voices.

'Time is short. It is essential that you act quickly,' he continued. 'The Republic no longer has a government. Together let us save the cause of liberty and equality.' He looked around at the sea of puzzled, bemused and angry faces, then glanced briefly at Marmont and Bessiéres, who stood close behind him.

'I am speaking frankly as a soldier, because I know no other way,' Bonaparte persisted, forced to raise his voice above the steadily growing tumult. 'The situation in which you find yourselves must be resolved and it must be resolved quickly. For the sake of France. If there is no government then there are no leaders. This country *must* have a leader. A leader who will prevail no matter what pressures are brought to bear on him and his administration. Times have changed. You should all recognise and acknowledge that.'

'What about the Constitution?' a voice close by shouted.

Bonaparte spun round, his expression darkening. 'The Constitution?' he snapped, angrily. '*You* destroyed it. You violated it on 18 Fructidor. You violated it on 22 Floréal. You violated it on 30 Prairial. No one respects it any longer.'

'Then what would you have us replace it with?' called one of the deputies, pointing an accusatory finger in Bonaparte's direction. 'The preachings of a soldier?'

'Better the preachings of a soldier than the rantings of a lawyer. Remember even now that my brave grenadiers surround this palace.'

'You threaten us with force,' another voice called. 'You threaten us with our own army.'

'Is not the army itself composed of men of France? Sons of the Republic who, like me, have marched accompanied by the God of War and the God of Fortune. These men are tired of the inefficiency that has ruined their country. And yet you ask them to give their lives in your name and with what reward? A country crippled by taxation and menaced on her very borders by enemies those troops once crushed.'

'You treat this council as if it were a toy for your private use, General Bonaparte,' one of the deputies shouted.

'A platform for views that only you seem to hold,' another added.

Bonaparte held up both hands to silence the throng. 'Citizen Representatives, I have just told you some truths that everyone has at some time whispered to himself and which must now finally be spoken out loud. The means of saving the people are in your hands. If you hesitate, if liberty perishes, you will have to answer for it before the universe, before posterity, before France and your families.'

A great eruption of noise greeted Bonaparte's words and the gallery echoed with the sound of raised voices. Bonaparte remained in the centre of the room, allowing the sound to wash over him. Some of the deputies were pointing at him, others arguing amongst themselves. He waited a moment longer then turned and marched out, pushing the doors open with a great crash. Bessiéres followed, aware that the Corsican was heading for the Orangery.

The shouts that greeted him there almost stopped him in his tracks.

'Down with the dictator!' several of the council shouted and the clarion call was hastily taken up by others.

Bonaparte hesitated then strode towards the centre of the room, casting a glance in the direction of his younger brother. But Lucien was powerless to prevent the furious tirade, despite his position as President of the Five Hundred.

Bonaparte raised a hand to silence the deputies but to no avail.

Bessiéres drew nearer to him, his hand falling to the hilt of his sword.

Bonaparte opened his mouth to speak but it was a futile gesture.

'We have no wish to hear the words of a dictator,' someone close by shouted angrily.

Bonaparte was aware of several figures moving quickly towards him across the floor of the Orangery. They were led by a heavily built man named Destrem, who shot out a hand as if to grab the smaller man. Bonaparte was sure that more than one of the men carried daggers. Bessiéres stepped between them as Bonaparte took a faltering step back. The other figures surrounded them; some pushed angrily at the Corsican. Bessiéres felt rough hands clawing at his uniform and he shook himself loose. He was aware of more movement behind him and spun round to see half a dozen grenadiers march into the Orangery, their bearskins nodding threateningly as they headed towards their general. The infantrymen pushed aside the furious deputies and formed an escort around Bonaparte, who looked around with glazed eyes, only too happy to accept the supportive arms of his men.

'Get him out of here,' snapped Bessiéres.

'Yes, take your tyrant and leave,' Destrem snarled. 'There is no place for him or his kind here.'

'Citizens!' shouted Lucien Bonaparte, desperate to make himself heard above the cacophony of sound. 'We must have order.'

His words either were not heard or, he surmised, were ignored. 'Remember who you are,' he continued. 'Remember your positions. You act like rabble not like representatives of your country. My brother sought the freedom to speak. To address you. Is that not the purpose of our chamber? To uphold freedom of speech and action?'

'Your brother desires only to conquer,' Destrem snapped. 'If there is no military opponent then he chooses political ones. I will not submit to his thirst for power and neither will this chamber.'

A great roar of approval greeted the remark, and as Bonaparte was being helped from the Orangery, he turned to see more angry fingers pointed at him. A sea of furious faces were turned in his direction. Several of the deputies followed him from the hall and down the stairs towards the courtyard, still gesticulating madly.

Lucien left his seat and followed his brother and the other troops outside, where Napoleon finally shook loose of his escort.

Lausard saw the little group stumble outside and he sat up straighter in his saddle to get a better look.

'Bonaparte has been attacked,' Rocheteau said, a note of concern in his voice. 'Look at him. He is bleeding.'

Lausard saw a thin ribbon of blood running down the general's face.

'You see how these windbags react to a challenge,' Bonaparte bellowed at the watching troops. 'They hide their cowardice in numbers. I promised them my sword and they declined. They sought to attack me. Perhaps to them I am a symbol of what they would destroy. A free man who dares to speak his mind and who has the effrontery to question them. A man who wants nothing more than the best for the country he loves. Are we not all united in that belief?'

There were a few half-hearted shouts from the watching troops and, for fleeting seconds, Lausard saw uncertainty cross the general's face.

'The cause of liberty will not be sacrificed,' Lucien shouted, turning to face the assembled troops. 'My brother has sworn to uphold it. He will not go back on that oath.' The younger Bonaparte suddenly drew his sword and pressed it to Napoleon's chest. 'If he does, I myself will kill him.'

Lausard allowed his hand to drop to the hilt of his sword.

Bonaparte suddenly pulled away from his brother and stood facing his men.

'Murat!' he bellowed. 'Clear the Assembly.'

The cavalry general saluted and turned in his saddle.

'Draw swords!' he roared and Lausard and his unit did as they were ordered.

Simultaneously, the demibrigade of grenadiers began marching up the steps towards the entrance of the Orangery.

Murat put spurs to his horse and forced it up the stone stairs beside them.

From where they sat, Lausard and most of the other dragoons could see the deputies inside the Orangery. Dressed in their red togas and plumed hats, they looked as if they belonged to a different age, and as the first of the grenadiers entered the chamber, many of them tore off their robes and fled.

'Go on, run you pompous windbags,' Rocheteau grinned.

'Is this our conflict, Alain?' Bonet wanted to know. 'Are we to battle politicians now?'

'Attack them. Ride them down,' Lausard said quietly. 'Whatever we are ordered to do. Why does your conscience prick you about having to perform such a duty? They are only men. We have each lost count of how many men we have killed during the past three years. If they are enemies then they threaten us.'

'Do you really believe that?' Bonet said.

'It doesn't matter what I believe. All that matters is that we do our duty and I, for one, would happily cut down any of those scheming "pekinese" in there.'

'As far as I can see,' Giresse offered, 'the only thing wrong is that this day did not come sooner.'

Lausard looked up to see Murat at the top of the steps, his horse rearing wildly.

'Citizens, you are dissolved,' he bellowed at the fleeing deputies, waving his sabre in one hand. Then, to the grenadiers who were still pouring into the Orangery, 'Throw these bastards out of there.'

The stream of troops continued to swarm into the chamber, bayonets glinting in the beginnings of sunset.

'Does this mean that Bonaparte will become our king now?' Tabor asked.

'There'll be no more kings in France, idiot,' Delacor retorted.

Karim looked on, a smile on his thin lips.

'Does something amuse you, my friend?' Lausard asked.

'You came to Egypt supposedly to restore order to a *dis*ordered land, and yet your own country is in uproar.'

'It is the way of the world,' Rostov observed.

'It is the way of the Republic,' Lausard said acidly. 'If, indeed, we still have one. I suspect what we have witnessed here today is the death of that Republic. Only Bonaparte knows what will replace it. All *we* can do is wait.'

Napoleon Bonaparte sat at the table in the Château of Saint Cloud, the room lit only by a single candle, which was burning slowly down to a waxen stubb. Whisps of black smoke rose from the orange flame and the Corsican sat seemingly mesmerised by the ethereal plumes as they rose and then dissipated in the still air. He sipped at his wine but didn't touch the plate of food that had been placed before him.

It was late. Well into the early morning and yet there were still constant comings and goings both inside and outside the château. He had heard the marching feet of infantry, the steady rumble of cannon and the sound of horses' hooves. Despite the exertions of the day, sleep held no appeal. Instead, he rose to his feet and crossed to the window, peering out into the courtyard, where several ranks of chasseurs stood guard.

'It is done, my brother.'

Bonaparte turned as he heard the voice.

Lucien walked in, crossed to the table and poured himself a glass of wine.

'Did everything proceed as we planned?' Napoleon asked.

'The Council of the Elders remained in session,' he explained. 'I explained to them that it was because of Jacobin excesses that the other chamber had required military dissolution but they remained hostile. Nevertheless, they adopted a resolution to create a temporary executive body in place of the Directory. They also agreed to adjourn the legislature for one month.'

'And was I named specifically in these arrangements? I hope they realise that they owe their well-being to me and my army.'

'To many you are still their enemy, but that is of little importance any longer. At nine o'clock tonight I called a meeting of thirty deputies from the Five Hundred, all sympathetic to our cause. They approved the military action taken against the chamber earlier today. They then established a Provisional Consulate comprising Sieyes, Ducos and you, my brother. You are responsible for restoring order in the country and pursuing peace negotiations with the external enemies of France.' He raised the wine glass in salute.

'Do they readily accept the power I have now?'

'You, Sieyes and Ducos. Yes.'

'Those lawyers,' Napoleon hissed. 'They were never anything more than pawns in this entire charade. Sieyes was a Trojan horse within the Directory. One of its own who plotted its downfall. They have played their part. *I* no longer need them and France most certainly does not.'

'In time you may exert the power you so desire but presently we have to consider the reactions of those who remain in our political arena. Two parliamentary commissions, chosen in equal numbers from each chamber, will revise the Constitution. Remember, my brother, this is not merely some political hiccup. We are altering an entire system of government with the eventual object of making *you* its supreme and unchallenged leader.'

'Surely the people will welcome this change too? I have rid them of the shackles placed upon them by the Directory. I trust they will thank me for it.'

'Most, I suspect, will. We have the support of the more

influential newspapers too. Roederer's *Journal de Paris* has long been sympathetic to governmental change and Talleyrand has close links with *Le Publiciste*. They will help spread the message and reassure those who may have doubts. But there could be opposition from those who fear a repeat of what happened during Thermidor in 94. Few will want to see another regime like that organised by Robespierre.'

'Then it is our job, as administrators and law makers, to ensure that does not happen. We must do whatever it takes to convince the people of France that what happened today was for their own good *and* the good of their country, both now and for years to come. The power engendered in a consulate is infinitely preferable to that previously held by the Directory.'

'And if there *is* resistance?'

Napoleon turned and glanced out of the window once again.

'Then, my dear Lucien, it will be dealt with quickly and summarily. I was called a dictator this afternoon. Well, if I must assume that mantle in order to ensure that France remains strong, then so be it. And if there are enemies out there, I will deal with them the same way I would deal with an opponent on a battlefield. And, believe me, if the time comes I will not hesitate. I will isolate them and then crush them.'

Twelve

Lausard walked through the piles of fallen, rotting leaves, occasionally kicking them. He glanced up at the bare branches of the trees, which rattled in the December wind. The entire landscape of the park was a dirty brown, the grass covered for the most part by the wintry blanket of leaves and what remained uncovered had been churned into mud by the constant comings and goings of cavalry mounts.

The park was close to the École Militaire, which formed a dominant part of the Paris skyline. It also represented the most convenient area in which those regiments of horsemen stationed nearby could ride, both for practice and for pleasure. The Tuileries Garden had also become a magnet for officers anxious to exercise their mounts but the majority of troops used this larger park. Entire regiments, including Lausard's, practised manoeuvres here. Here they learned and relearned the art that had become second nature to them during three years of rigorous campaigning. Each squadron would deploy from column to line and then back into column again, all the time ensuring that each dragoon never lost contact with the knee of the man next to him. Three times a day they would groom their horses, Lausard and the other NCOs watchful of new soldiers, ensuring that the task was carried out with as much precision and expertise as weapon training. Lausard always ensured that these new men sponged the eyes *before* they sponged the dock of their mounts, a fault that could be as potentially damaging as fastening a girth strap around a puffed-out belly or putting a damp sword back into the scabbard. He instructed these newcomers in the correct way to charge a saddle and insert a bit. He taught them to recognise which piece of harness or equipment should be polished and which should be greased. For those who wore their spurs too high, he would explain that once mounted and in the ranks this could cause lacerations to the flanks of horses on either side of them. The same thing happened when having lost their stirrups in the canter they pointed their toes in an effort to retrieve them. If a trooper asked how a particular movement was carried out, Lausard would patiently explain then watch as the man executed his instructions. Many NCOs, he knew, merely performed the action themselves and expected the recruit to copy it.

During weapons training, all the men stood in the barracks square, swinging their blades and blocking imaginary sword thrusts, toughening their wrists. Sometimes pairing off and fighting mock combats to hone their craft to perfection. For, in Lausard's eyes, killing was indeed a craft to a soldier.

Now he wandered slowly through the park, watching as a group of recruits were put through their paces by a man he recognised only too well.

Sergeant Delpierre was bellowing orders and instructions at some youthful-looking dragoons, occasionally hurrying across to a fallen man to roar his disapproval as the recruit struggled to his feet.

A number of hurdles had been set up and Lausard, who

had now been joined by his companions, watched as the first of the recruits guided his horse over them. As was usual with recruits, they were allowed saddles but no reins and stirrups. They looked terrified as they trotted and jumped with their arms folded across their chests, in order to strengthen their legs and buttocks, and most fell from the saddle at some time. On every occasion, Delpierre would bellow at them, even kicking one young trooper as he scrambled to his feet and ran after his fleeing horse.

'That bastard doesn't change, does he?' said Rocheteau. 'France has a new leader but Sergeant Delpierre clings to his own ways.'

'He was a horse's arse under the Directory,' Lausard mused. 'He will continue to be one under the Consulate.'

The men with him laughed.

'I rode my first horse at the age of five,' said Karim, watching the antics before him. The Circassian looked on indifferently as another of the recruits toppled from the saddle.

'I *stole* my first horse when I was twelve,' Giresse chuckled.

They continued to walk across the park, closer to the terrified recruits.

Lausard spun round as he heard a loud whinnying close by.

A large grey was standing riderless, tossing its head defiantly. One of the recruits took a step towards it but the animal reared and lashed out with its forelegs, almost striking the man with its thrashing hooves.

'He's a lively one,' said Tigana.

'He looks like he's crazy,' Roussard agreed.

Delpierre turned angrily on the grey and reached for his riding crop. He slashed at the animal several times, striking it across the flanks and rump. This only served to inflame the horse more and it neighed even more loudly and bucked.

Lausard moved towards it, catching Delpierre's arm, preventing him from striking the grey again.

'What the hell are you doing?' Delpierre snarled, shaking loose. 'This beast understands nothing else. It is unrideable. It is fit only for a cooking pot.'

'It has sense enough to know that *you* cannot control it, you fool,' Lausard said, stepping closer to the horse.

'Go on, let it trample you into the ground, Lausard. I will enjoy watching that.'

Lausard said nothing. He stood gazing at the grey. Its nostrils flared and it was heavily lathered but it remained still as he approached it, one hand extended towards its muzzle. The animal backed off but Lausard continued his advance. The horse reared but he barely flinched. The watching men looked on with a combination of bewilderment and concern. Lausard was less than ten feet from the animal now. It remained still, as if daring him to come closer.

Five feet.

He reached out towards it once again, palm upturned, whispering beneath his breath.

Two feet.

The animal shook its head wildly.

Lausard touched its muzzle gently.

The grey didn't move.

He stood alongside it, patting its neck, stroking its flank, his mouth close to its ears.

Lausard gripped the pommel of the saddle and hauled himself up on to the horse's back. It reared wildly but he grabbed its mane and clung on, digging his knees in. The grey dropped back down and bucked once but it was a half-hearted gesture. Lausard patted its neck then gently tapped its flanks with his heels. The animal moved off at a walk, then, at Lausard's urging, at a trot. He guided it back and forth before Delpierre and the watching men.

Karim was grinning broadly, nodding his approval at this exhibition.

Lausard wheeled the grey and forced it into a canter, swinging it around until it was facing the hurdles. He crossed his arms over his chest and urged the horse on. It jumped the obstacles effortlessly, coming to a halt close to Delpierre. Lausard looked down at the other sergeant then slid out of the saddle.

'Your unrideable horse,' he said flatly, rejoining his men.

Delpierre glared at him.

'The words of Xenophon should be painted on every stable door,' Lausard announced, meeting the other NCO's angry stare.

'Who is this Xenophon?' Delpierre sneered. 'What has he to do with me? Which squadron is he in?'

'He was a Greek general, you idiot. He said that horses should be taught not by cruelty but by kindness. You would do well to heed his lesson. Perhaps for you, Delpierre, that message should be inscribed on your forehead. In Greek.'

A great chorus of laughter filled the air.

Lausard turned his back on the other sergeant and wandered away, aware of but unconcerned by Delpierre's furious stare.

'I will kill you one day, Lausard,' Delpierre shouted.

'You will try,' the younger man called back. 'I look forward to it.' He raised his hand in mock salute.

'If ever there was a man who deserved to meet a roundshot head on, it's Delpierre,' Rocheteau observed.

'Ours or the enemy's?' Lausard grinned.

'We shouldn't wish death upon our own comrades,' Moreau interjected.

'To hell with that bastard,' Delacor snapped. 'I wish him nothing else but death. Don't you remember how he treated us when we first joined this stinking army? We were queueing up to put a blade in him.'

'We still are,' Rocheteau laughed. 'Us and half of the regiment.'

Lausard led them across the park, occasionally turning to look at the new recruits still struggling to master control of their mounts. The wind was growing stronger, bringing with it a biting cold.

'If it gets much colder, you'll think you're back home in Russia, Rostov,' the sergeant mused.

'You boys don't know the meaning of cold,' said the Russian. 'When I lived with my family in the Urals I saw snow six feet deep. One of my brother's lost two toes to frostbite during a hard winter. He came in from working the fields, took off his boot and his toes came off with them.'

'No wonder you left that stinking country to come to France,' Delacor observed.

'I left because of the tyranny of the Tsar. My family died because of his economic measures. My family had worked that land for over one hundred years. It had been passed down from generation to generation. It would have been mine eventually.'

'You left one tyranny for another,' Lausard pointed out. 'Isn't that why you were imprisoned here?'

'I was imprisoned because they thought I was a spy, come to find out secrets for the Russian army. One day I will go back and I will have a farm and a family of my own. Until then, I am a servant of Bonaparte.'

'As are we all,' Lausard muttered.

'He was once a man like us,' Bonet observed. 'A poor man from a large family. His rise to power symbolises everything that is best about the Republic.'

'Power can be a corrupting force,' Lausard countered. 'It remains to be seen how Bonaparte deals with such limitless control. It may well destroy *him.*'

'He is no better than those he replaced,' Delacor rasped. 'He enjoys riches and privileges as if he were a king. Perhaps he will be the next one to be carried to the guillotine.'

'Not by me,' Lausard said. 'Remember, he gave us our freedom. He gave us the chance to die with honour. For that alone I thank him. And so should you.'

'Freedom,' Rocheteau repeated. 'What are we supposed to do with that freedom now? Sit around here with our thumbs up our backsides until God knows when? We are soldiers and yet we have no enemy to fight.'

'The time will come for combat, have no fear.'

'Against who?' Roussard pressed.

'France has no shortage of enemies,' Lausard told his companion. 'But I would guess it will be Austria first.'

'Again?' Rocheteau said wearily. 'Didn't we teach them enough of a lesson two years ago?'

The men laughed.

Lausard turned and heard the thundering of hooves drawing closer. He looked up to see Gaston and Carbonne riding towards them, each holding the reins of a riderless horse. The two riders brought their mounts to a halt and Carbonne sucked in a deep breath.

'Alain, you and Rocheteau are to return to the Luxembourg with us immediately. Captain Milliere wants to see you. He says it's important.'

The room was on the second floor of the palace. It was

high ceilinged, as were all of those within, so the sound of Lausard's and Rocheteau's boots echoed loudly as they entered. Lausard recognised two of the occupants immediately. Captain Milliere sat behind a small desk, a bottle of wine and a goblet close to him, and Lieutenant Royere was perched on a corner of the desk, sifting through a pile of papers. It was the third man, a dark and swarthy individual with a pinched face and dressed in civilian clothes, who caught the sergeant's attention. He was standing with his back to one of the windows, swaying gently back and forth. Despite his civilian dress, he wore a sabre that clinked against the floor every time he moved. Lausard also noticed a pistol stuck into his belt.

The sergeant nodded a greeting to Royere then both he and Rocheteau saluted the two officers.

'Take a seat,' Milliere said, motioning towards the chairs before the desk.

The two dragoons accepted the offer.

Only now did the stranger move towards the desk. He poured himself some wine and ran appraising eyes over the two green-jacketed newcomers.

'This is Minister of Police Fouché,' Milliere explained, gesturing towards the swarthy man. 'He has something he would like to discuss with you.'

'What's the charge?' said Lausard.

Fouché grinned.

'I have not come to arrest you, Sergeant,' he said in a strident voice. 'Not yet, anyway. Though I would not be the first to do so, would I? You *or* your corporal.' He glanced at Rocheteau. 'Thieves, were you not? Arrested in ninety-four. Imprisoned in the Conciergerie.'

'You appear to know more about *us* than we do about *you*.'

'It is my business to know about people. The more I know, the fewer secrets can be kept from me. I do not like secrets.'

'Why are we here?' Lausard demanded. 'Are you to retry us for crimes we were accused of so many years ago?'

'I need your help,' Fouché admitted. 'As you may be aware, since General Bonaparte became First Consul certain misguided factions have sought to disrupt the peace his appointment has brought to France. Resistance has been encountered in several departments of the Pas-de-Calais, the Yonne and the Pyreneés Orientales. Also, there has been considerable opposition in Rennes and in the Jura. These pockets of resistance have been dealt with for the most part but it appears that some of their sedition may well be spreading to Paris itself.' The minister sipped at his wine. 'Four officers from different regiments have been murdered during the past week, in various areas of this city. Two colonels and two majors. A member of the First Consul's staff was also badly wounded in an incident just the other day. My sources lead me to believe that the men responsible for these atrocities are either Jacobins or possibly even Royalists. These men must be found and stopped before they succeed in corrupting the minds of some of those in Paris who are opposed to General Bonaparte.'

'Do you fear some kind of rebellion from the people?' Royere asked.

'The people know that General Bonaparte has their interests at heart,' Fouché said dismissively. 'But some may be fooled into believing the poisonous propaganda spewed out by his enemies.'

'We have heard of no such opposition,' Rocheteau commented. 'I didn't know that anyone had been killed.'

'The information has been suppressed,' Fouché told him.

'I ordered that it was not to become common knowledge. This kind of incident spreads disaffection.'

'What has this to do with us?' Lausard asked.

'The information I have leads me to believe that these conspirators are operating from a base in this area,' Fouché explained. 'In and around the Faubourg Saint Antoine, Saint Victor and Saint Marceau. They are led by two men, Louis Parquin and Marcel Rossoleil. Both fanatics.'

'If you know who these men are and where they are hiding, why don't you simply arrest them?' Lausard demanded. 'Isn't that your job?'

'These men are devious. They know Paris well. They hide in her sewers and her backstreets like rats, emerging only to perpetrate their crimes and then they disappear again, like phantoms. I need someone who knows the areas *they* know. Someone who can hunt them down. I need someone like you, Sergeant Lausard – and your men. Men intimately acquainted with the gutters and the rubbish that fills them.' He smiled crookedly. 'Criminals to catch criminals.'

'We are not criminals any longer, we are soldiers. Why can't your gendarmes catch these assassins? Are they so incompetent that they need the help of thieves, forgers, rapists and murderers?'

Fouché shot Lausard an angry glance. 'The competence of my men is not in question. You have been selected for this task because you are better suited to it. Better to lose half a dozen criminals than six of *my* men.'

'And what if *I* do not agree to this?' Captain Milliere interjected. 'Sergeant Lausard and his men are valuable members of my squadron. Why should I allow you to send them on a mission that may cost them their lives?'

'Where is your loyalty to the First Consul? Would you stand by and allow revolution to blossom in Paris itself? I am asking these men to perform a service for their country and their leader.'

'They have served their country, bravely, as soldiers for the last three years,' Milliere persisted.

'Captain,' Lausard interrupted, holding up his hand. 'I feel the minister wants us not for our expertise but because we are expendable. It would not be the first time we have been chosen for just such a reason.'

Fouché held Lausard's gaze but made no attempt to answer.

'You are professional soldiers,' he said finally. 'Disposing of a few Royalist or Jacobin sympathisers should be easy for you. Unless of course you feel some kind of sympathy for them. Is that why you are so anxious to avoid this mission?'

'Don't try your tricks on me,' Lausard sneered. 'Save your rhetoric for those who are fooled by it. It belongs with politicians, not with soldiers. We will find these men for you.'

Fouché smiled triumphantly. 'I want no survivors. When you track them down, kill Parquin and Rossoleil and all those who support them. For this country to attain true greatness there must be no divisions among its people. There must be no oppostion to the First Consul.'

'I thought a free country allowed *both* sides to express their opinion. Wasn't freedom the rallying call of the revolution? And yet when others seek to exercise that right they are to be slaughtered,' Lausard said. 'Perhaps you and I have a different interpretation of freedom. This is Paris, not Rome. Years ago, Rome owed its greatness to the creation of consuls. Is that what you expect to happen here?'

Fouché regarded the sergeant quizzically then sipped at his wine.

'You do not speak like a man who has spent his life in the gutters of Paris,' Fouché said at last. 'Your opinions are not those of one who has been forced to scrabble for crumbs in the streets. Where did you acquire your education?'

'Does intelligence frighten you, Minister? Is your view of all common men so damning that you presume them to be idiots?'

'My father was a sea captain. I know about hardship. I know about the common man, as you call him, and you, my friend, are much more than that. Perhaps there are some secrets in your background I should know about. What are you hiding from me? What is the true nature of the man I see before me?'

Lausard's expression gave nothing away. 'What you see before you is a soldier,' he said evenly. 'A man who was once a thief and a prisoner. A man who had lost his self-respect until the army gave it back to him. You see a uniform, Minister. You will never understand the man inside it. Not you or any other of your kind. You wear a sabre and a pistol but it doesn't alter the nature of the man I see before *me*. You belong in an office, behind a desk. Do not presume to tell me or any other man who has risked his life on a battlefield about loyalty. That word sounds hollow on your tongue because you will never know its true meaning.'

Fouché's face was scarlet with rage.

Lausard got to his feet and turned to face Milliere.

'If there is nothing else, Captain,' he said quietly, 'I will select the men for this mission and prepare them.'

'You may leave, Sergeant,' the officer dismissed him.

Fouché watched as the two dragoons made their way towards the door. 'Remember,' he snapped, 'when you find these subversives, kill them all. They are enemies of the state. You should consider them *your* enemies too.'

'This is a free country, is it not, Minister?' Lausard said, pausing at the door. 'Allow me to pick my own enemies. Some are closer than others.' He smiled at Fouché, then closed the door behind him.

Thirteen

'I never thought I'd be sorry to take off that uniform.' Rocheteau was looking down at his ragged clothes. He wore a faded, threadbare jacket and wooden shoes. His torn trousers were held up by a piece of string. His five companions were all attired in similarly wretched garments. Delacor in particular, convinced that his clothes were infested with lice, scratched almost unceasingly at his armpits and groin.

Charvet meanwhile had pushed straw into shoes that were several sizes too big for him. Giresse rubbed at his knee, exposed by a hole in his culottes. And Roussard was shivering in the thin, frayed shirt he wore. He rubbed his hands together as the chill wind swept mercilessly along the narrow streets.

Lausard wandered ahead, seemingly oblivious to the cold and the fact that his breeches had most of the backside missing. They had been crudely patched, as had the elbows of his shirt, but he appeared unconcerned and strode on, his eyes scanning the cobbled street. Occasionally he looked up at the grey buildings that surrounded them, which seemed to crowd in on the men menacingly. He thought how alien they now seemed; five years ago, they would all have called them home.

'How the hell are we supposed to find these bastards anyway?' Delacor muttered, still scratching frenziedly at his groin. 'It'll be like trying to find a needle in a haystack. I say we go back and tell that "pekinese" Fouché that we heard Partin and Rossolov have left Paris.'

'Parquin and Rossoleil,' Lausard corrected him. 'We'll find them. Besides, we were given a mission and we will complete it.'

'What does it matter? Who cares if a few Royalists want to take pot-shots at officers? Let them.'

'They are *our* officers in *our* army. And by finding them, we are doing our duty. It is a matter of pride, Delacor. Something I wouldn't expect you to understand.'

The six men continued up the narrow street in silence. They approached an inn, outside which several men and women were standing talking. A small baker's stall had been set up on the opposite side and the meagre selection of loaves and biscuits had already been consumed by those citizens fortunate enough to have the money to pay for them. Children, many without shoes, crowded around the stall as if determined to pick up any crumbs that may fall to the wet cobbled street.

Lausard led the dragoons towards the inn, pausing before they entered, aware of the curious stares directed at them.

'We don't belong here any more, Alain,' Charvet said quietly. 'And they know it.' He looked around at the civilians in the street, who continued to gaze. 'We are strangers in our own city.'

The sergeant ignored the comment and led his men into the hostelry. It smelled of smoke and he noticed a large stove in one corner, pieces of damp wood stuffed into it randomly. There were two or three tables. Around one, men were playing cards. The bearded man behind the bar shot them a cursory glance and continued cleaning the glass he was holding.

Lausard crossed to the bar and ran a hand through his hair.

'Drinks for myself and my friends,' he said loudly. 'Unless that bastard Bonaparte has banned the consumption of liquor.'

The barkeeper eyed him cautiously then poured six measures of brandy from a bottle nearby.

'To the end of tyranny,' said Lausard, raising his glass in salute. As his men joined him in the toast, the sergeant looked around at the other occupants of the inn. None had looked up. 'Will anyone else join us in a toast? Is there any other man here who would like to see an end to that dictator Bonaparte?'

There was still no answer.

The dragoons drank, pushing their empty glasses towards the barkeeper for a refill.

'What about you?' Lausard asked the man. 'Will you raise a glass to the death of that tyrant?'

'You should be careful what you say,' the barkeeper murmured quietly. 'Talk like that can get a man killed.'

'By whom?' Is this place the home of Corsican sympathisers? Are we surrounded by loyal subjects of the *First Consul*.' Lausard emphasised the words with theatrical disdain.

'The Minister of Police has spies everywhere,' the barkeeper continued, his voice still low.

'To hell with them,' Lausard snarled. 'To hell with Bonaparte and to hell with those who support him.'

'What have you got against Bonaparte?'

'We were in his army, all of us. We fought in Italy. We

followed that Corsican runt to Egypt and what thanks did we get? He promised us six acres of land. All he gave us was misery. He would have left us to rot out there just as he has so many of our companions. That is why we escaped.'

'Are you deserters?'

Lausard nodded. 'None of us will fight for that bastard again,' he grunted. 'Although we would gladly take up arms *against* him. He is destroying this country and no one can stop him.' Lausard raised his glass again. 'To the end of tyranny.'

The other men echoed the toast.

'Where are you from?' the barkeeper asked.

'Here in Paris. We left with nothing and we have returned to nothing. No homes. No work. We sleep in the gutters. We survive on what we can steal. Bonaparte has forced us into this.'

The barkeeper regarded the six men warily. 'If I had work for you to do I would offer it,' he said apologetically. 'It must be difficult for you returning here after having been soldiers.'

Lausard nodded. 'We want only what is ours by right,' he said finally. 'What that Corsican bastard denies us. I say the sooner he is removed from power the better.'

The sergeant tossed several coins on to the bar top, then he and his men turned and walked away.

The door slammed behind them. As it did, the barkeeper glanced across at a tall, thin-faced man in a striped shirt who had been sitting playing cards. The tall man waited a moment then slipped outside. He saw Lausard and the others making their way along the street, still exchanging comments loudly. He watched them through narrowed eyes for a moment longer then stepped back inside the inn.

* * *

Lausard had realised after less than ten minutes that he and his men were being followed. He had allowed the charade to persist as they crossed the Pont Neuf to the other side of the Seine then crossed back again further downriver. They had moved amongst the narrow streets, the crowded markets and the squares thronged with people. Wherever they went they vented their mock rage against Bonaparte and his Consulate. They had voiced opinions loudly, many of which had brought disapproving gazes from those who heard them.

And all the time Lausard had been aware of their pursuer. A man not suited to such treachery, the sergeant had mused, as he contemplated the man's inability to secret himself when it looked as if one of the men had spotted him. Lausard wondered who this man was. Why he was following them? His suggestion that it may well be one of Fouché's own spies, out to ensnare Jacobins or Royalists had brought howls of laughter from his companions.

The afternoon was sliding slowly into a premature evening, forced there by the dark, rain-sodden skies, and Lausard knew that they had to find shelter for the night. Giresse remembered that there used to be a brothel in the Rue Saint Antoine, which had, of all things, a stable next to it. It would provide the shelter they needed.

'I have sampled the delights of both the whorehouse *and* the stable in my time,' the horse thief confessed as they continued their journey.

The others laughed.

Lausard chanced a quick glimpse behind. Their pursuer was still there. No more than a hundred yards away, anxious not to lose sight of his quarry.

'Well, sleeping in wet straw can't be any worse than sleeping in these stinking clothes,' Delacor rasped, scratching himself.

They reached the brothel. It was still there; the stables were not.

Giresse looked on with disappointment.

'You fool,' snapped Delacor. 'Your mind is playing tricks on you.'

'It is more than two years since I was here,' Giresse protested.

'Who the hell would build a stable in the middle of a street?' Delacor insisted.

'Officers of the Royal Army,' Giresse informed him. 'They needed somewhere to leave their mounts while they were riding something else next door.'

More laughter greeted his remark.

'How did you manage to get inside a whorehouse used by army officers?' Rocheteau was curious.

'I was on intimate terms with several of the ladies who worked there. They were only too happy to entertain me.'

'It's a pity we haven't got enough money to spend some time in there now,' Charvet mused.

'Go and steal some,' Roussard suggested. 'You were a thief, weren't you?'

'I was arrested for gambling in a church, not stealing,' Charvet corrected him indignantly.

'Why should we have to steal money, Roussard,' Rocheteau pointed out, 'you used to *make* it, didn't you?'

The forger grinned.

'So, Alain,' Charvet asked, 'where do we spend the night?'

'Just keep walking,' Lausard told them, ducking into a doorway.

The men did as they were instructed, only Rocheteau hesitating momentarily. He tapped the hilt of the knife wedged into his belt. Lausard shook his head and motioned for the corporal to continue.

Lausard pressed himself back, swallowed by the shadows. He heard footsteps drawing closer.

He steadied himself.

A youth no more than twelve passed by and the sergeant let out a weary breath. As the boy moved on, Lausard sank back into the enveloping gloom of the doorway.

He heard more footsteps, but these were hesitant.

Again Lausard watched.

He recognised the man who stood before him. It was the same man who had been following them for most of the day.

Lausard snaked out both arms from the darkness and dragged the man back into the doorway, almost lifting him off his feet. He clamped one powerful hand around the man's mouth and chin; the other he used to grip the back of the individual's head like a vice.

'If you even breathe without me telling you too, I'll break your neck,' Lausard hissed. 'Do you understand?'

The terrified man tried to nod.

'When I take away my hand, don't make a sound until I tell you,' Lausard ordered, carefully releasing his grip on the man's jaw.

They stood together in the darkened doorway, Lausard able to hear the laboured breathing of his pursuer.

'Do you work for Fouché?' snapped the dragoon.

The man shook his head.

'Then why were you following us?' Lausard continued. 'Why should I believe you? That bastard has spies everywhere. I should kill you now.'

The man tried to turn around. 'No,' he bleated. 'I heard the things you said. About Bonaparte. About the Consulate.' He was speaking quickly, afraid he would not be given the opportunity to finish what he had to say. 'There are others who feel as you do. Others who oppose Bonaparte's dictatorship.'

'You're lying,' snarled Lausard, fixing his hand around the man's jaw once again. 'You're a spy.'

The man squirmed in his grasp. 'No, no!' he yelped. 'Listen to me.' He stepped away as the sergeant released his grip. 'If you are truthful in what you say about hating Bonaparte and his regime, then you should put that hate to good use. Help overthrow him.'

Lausard stood glaring at the man, thoughts churning in his mind. One in particular seemed luminous. Was this man who stood quivering before him one of the very men he sought?

'Bonaparte is too powerful,' he said finally. 'How do you propose to overthrow him?'

'Moves have already begun. Here and in other parts of France. The assassination of leading officers, the attack upon Bonaparte's aide de camp – they are but the beginning. Men like you and those who accompany you are the salvation of this country. Men like you will help rid us of Bonaparte's dictatorship. Unless your words were simply empty ravings.'

Lausard took a threatening pace forward. 'It is *you* who speak with empty words,' he snarled.

'No. Come with me. I will lead you to others who feel as you do. I will take you to meet the men who will see this country free again.'

'And why should I trust you? You could be leading us into a trap.'

'I am telling you the truth. I swear it.'

'Very well. Take us to these men.'

The cellar was lit by two torches, which gave off light and fumes in similar proportions as they burned. The whole chamber smelled of damp and Lausard could hear dripping water. A consequence, he assumed, of being so close to the Seine. The underground vault was large and there was a number of straw mattresses, two wooden tables and some chairs within it. Lausard was aware that many men were present but in the almost palpable gloom he could only guess how many. He and his companions stood close to one of the tables, watching as the man who sat behind it poured himself some wine and sipped at it.

Louis Parquin was in his early thirties. A squat, almost brutish man with a square jaw and a neck so short it seemed as if his head grew straight from his shoulders. The clothes he wore, like his companions and like most of the residents of Paris, were little more than rags. A deep scar ran from his hairline to the bridge of his nose.

Lausard studied the man, at the same time taking in his surroundings. Especially the position of the other men. Should any fighting start, he wanted to be sure he and his companions would not be caught in this cellar like rats in a trap. He cast a military eye over a civilian environment.

'I understand your suffering,' Parquin said finally. 'The whole of France has suffered under Bonaparte.'

'You cannot understand what we went through as soldiers,' Lausard told him. 'Your reasons for wanting an end to Bonaparte are different to ours.'

'The reasons are not important. The fact is we agree that this tyrant should be replaced. And so do many others.'

'But replaced by what? If you remove Bonaparte what do you expect to happen? Do you want the Directory reformed? Do you want the Bourbons restored?'

'We want what is right for France. And for *us*.'

Lausard turned as the newest voice came from behind him.

The newcomer was a year or two younger than Parquin.

He was a tall, elegant-looking man, with a shock of black hair that cascaded as far as his shoulders. He ran appraising eyes over Lausard and, as the newcomer passed close to him, the sergeant noticed that he had a pistol wedged into his belt.

The man had not given his name but Lausard suspected he was Marcel Rossoleil and as he spoke that suspicion grew in the sergeant's mind. He was soon convinced that he now faced the two men he and his comrades had been sent to kill.

'Every day we gather more men,' Rossoleil said. 'More men who are willing to oppose Bonaparte.'

'And what would you do?' Lausard asked. 'Form an army and fight him in the streets? Would you send bakers, inn-keepers and barrel makers against troops who have conquered half of Europe?'

'We are not fools. We will fight him from the shadows where our strength is. We will jab away at him as hunters jab at a wild boar, until he falls.'

Lausard laughed bitterly. 'Bonaparte is an elephant and you are ants. Do you really think that killing one or two of his officers every now and then will cripple him? Will the assassination of a handful of colonels and majors bring this Corsican to his knees? No.'

'When we strike again we will strike at more influential targets,' Parquin assured him. 'At generals. At Bonaparte himself. If we can kill *him*, then his regime will crumble. Like a snake. Strike at the head and the body dies.'

'And how do you propose to do that?' the sergeant persisted. 'How many men and weapons do you have? And of those men, how many have the necessary knowledge to strike at professional troops with any guarantee of success? You are speaking not of shooting a colonel of hussars but of murdering the ruler of a country.'

'Men like you could do that,' Rossoleil said flatly. 'You were professional soldiers, were you not? Use that knowledge to aid us.'

'So how many men *do* you have?' Lausard was determined to discover the real strength of his opponents.

'Three or four hundred,' Rossoleil told him. 'Spread out across the city. But the numbers grow every day.'

Lausard laughed. 'There are over fifteen *thousand* troops in and around Paris alone,' he said, shaking his head.

'I said we would not confront them directly,' Rossoleil retorted irritably.

'And what equipment would you use against Bonaparte?' Lausard pressed. 'Where are your cannon? Your horsemen? Your muskets? Or would you fight him with daggers and clubs?'

'We have about fifty muskets,' Parquin said. 'In the right hands they could be as effective as fifty cannon. We find the right place to strike and we use all our power in that one place. We kill Bonaparte and as many of his generals and staff as possible.'

'And where do you expect to find them gathered so conveniently for you?' the sergeant chided.

'He has meetings with his advisors every day,' Rossoleil informed the dragoon. 'When he travels he is usually escorted by a detachment of cavalry or a unit of grenadiers. Sometimes members of his staff travel with him. He is not a difficult man to find. We have also thought of attacking his home in the Rue Chantereine.'

'What you speak of is suicide,' Lausard told the men.

'I would be willing to give my life if it meant an end of that tyrant,' Rossoleil snapped.

'Then you are a fool. If you or Parquin die, do you think any of these men will continue your crusade?' Lausard made an expansive gesture with his hand towards those who remained in the deep shadows of the cellar. 'If you do not want to live under Bonaparte then leave the country. It would be simpler.'

'I will not be driven away by that Corsican,' Rossoleil told him.

'Then you will die,' Lausard murmured. 'You and all those who oppose this regime.'

Rocheteau looked to his sergeant, his hand straying to the belt of his trousers where he gently touched his knife. He wondered if the time had come for the dragoons to strike, and yet he, like Lausard, could not be sure of the numbers they faced inside that tomb-like cellar. He felt a hand brush his arm and turned to see Charvet shaking his head gently.

'So were all your words meaningless?' Parquin asked, gazing directly at Lausard. 'You spoke with passion of your hatred for Bonaparte. Would you walk away without even *trying* to oppose him? You said yourself he had left you and your companions with nothing. Where is your pride? Or did Bonaparte take that too?'

Lausard locked stares with the older man.

'Are you with us or not?' Rossoleil added.

The silence inside the cellar was menacing. The only sound seemed to be the crackling of the burning torches.

Rocheteau again touched the hilt of his knife, his heart thudding a little harder inside his chest.

Delacor slid his hand beneath his long shirt and felt the handle of his axe.

Giresse and Roussard were both looking in the direction of an archway close to them. Three men stood in the shadows there, but propped against the damp stonework were two muskets.

The moment dragged on into an eternity. It was as if

time itself had frozen. The dragoons were waiting for a sign from Lausard, but when that signal might come they had no idea.

'Do you speak for just yourself or also for the men with you?' Rossoleil persisted, finally breaking the silence.

'We are as one on this matter,' Lausard said quietly. He glanced surreptitiously at the other dragoons.

Rocheteau knew that the time was near.

'So,' Parquin asked, 'what is your answer?'

'With us or against us?' Rossoleil demanded.

'Against you,' Lausard told him, through gritted teeth.

Rocheteau pulled the knife from his belt and flung it at the man nearest to him, smiling with satisfaction as the blade buried itself in his chest. The scream of agony reverberated around the cellar and it was the signal all the men had been waiting for.

From the shadows, figures rushed at them but the dragoons were prepared.

Delacor pulled the axe free and caught his assailant a devastating backhand blow that sheared off a portion of the man's lower jaw. He fell back clutching his bloodied face, and Delacor finished him off with a blow to his skull.

Lausard shot out a hand and pulled the pistol from Rossoleil's belt before the other man had time to react. He pressed the barrel to the rebel's face and squeezed the trigger.

The hammer slammed down but there was just a spark as the flint grazed the frizzen. The weapon wasn't loaded.

Lausard used it as a club and slammed it against the forehead of his opponent, knocking him backwards, falling upon him and raining blows upon him. Blood spilled out in a wide pool all around Rossoleil's shattered head. But Lausard kept hammering the pistol down, even though he could barely keep a grip on it, the weapon being so slick with blood.

Roussard and Giresse succeeded in reaching the muskets, Roussard swinging his up to his shoulder and firing.

The roar inside the cellar was deafening.

The heavy lead ball caught one of the men in the forehead, smashing through bone and brain with ease and bursting from the back of his head. He dropped like a stone.

Giresse found that his weapon was not loaded but he flipped it in his grip and used it as a club, driving the metal-braced butt into the face of an opponent. Teeth spilled from the man's mouth as Giresse struck him, and the dragoon ignored the blood that spattered him.

Charvet used his fists to fend off two attackers, downing one with a savage right hook. The other he grabbed by the neck, lifted off his feet and flung to one side, pulling a long knife from the man's belt as he did so. With lightning speed and consummate skill, he slid the blade across the throats of both opponents.

Parquin, horrified by the savagery and unexpectedness of the attack, toppled backwards away from the table then leaped to his feet, sprinting towards the steps leading out of the cellar.

'Finish the others,' shouted Lausard, leaping from the motionless body of Rossoleil and hurtling after Parquin, who was already halfway to the stairs.

By now some of the other denizens of the cellar were beginning to seek a way out. Rocheteau pulled one of the flaming torches from the wall and swung it hard at an escaping man, slamming it into his face.

The man screamed as the flames seared his flesh, and he staggered around blindly, clutching his scorched face. By now his clothes had caught fire and they burned freely, filling the cellar with a sickly sweet odour of scorched flesh and giving off more light. The dragoons could see that those men not already dead were trying to escape the murderous confines of the cellar any way they could.

Parquin reached the top of the steps and crashed through the door, aware that Lausard was close behind him.

He finally reached the street and spun to his left, hurtling along the narrow cobbled thoroughfare. Lausard burst from the building close behind him.

Within seconds, Rocheteau had joined Lausard in the chase, having left the remaining dragoons to ensure that all those in the cellar were dead.

Lausard's heart thudded hard against his ribs and his breath rasped in his throat as he ran, but he could see that the distance between himself and his fleeing quarry was closing. Every so often, Parquin would chance a terrified glance over his shoulder and he too could see that the dragoon was gaining. Ahead was the Pont Neuf and, as he ran frantically towards it, Parquin slipped. Lausard saw him stumble then fall, skidding on the slippery cobblestones. The sergeant was upon him in a second, grabbing him as he tried to rise, seizing him by the back of the head and slamming his face hard against the ground. Parquin groaned and tried to fight back but the initial blow had stunned him. Lausard drove his head against the cobbles again and again. After several blows, Parquin was barely moving. Lausard rolled him over on to his back then stepped away, gazing down at the battered face, now a mask of blood.

He was aware of movement close by him and realised that Rocheteau had finally caught up. The corporal stood there panting, looking down at the pulverized features of Parquin. His gaze strayed to Lausard, who was staring blankly at the dying man, his own face set in hard lines.

'The others are all dead,' the corporal said, sucking in deep breaths.

Lausard nodded, turning away.

'What about him?' Rocheteau insisted, pointing at Parquin.

Parquin was making gurgling noises as blood ran back down his throat. One of his eyes was staring wide, the other was a mess of congealed blood and torn tissue.

'Leave him,' Lausard said. 'He won't live until morning.'

Rocheteau slid the knife from his belt and took a step towards the dying man.

Lausard shot out a hand to stop him.

'Leave him! We've spilled enough blood tonight. It seems that all we've done since we returned to France is kill those we used to call our countrymen.'

Parquin let out a long, sibilant breath. His head flopped to one side.

'Perhaps we should take his body back to Fouché,' Lausard rasped. 'Show the bastard that we have completed our mission. Let's go back to the cellar and collect all the bodies. How many have we killed tonight? Ten? A dozen? More? Well, I for one will not raise a hand against another Frenchman tonight. This is over, Rocheteau. We have done as we were ordered. I thought we had escaped these streets and these gutters but they sent us back here as murderers.'

'Do you think they *would* have tried to kill Bonaparte? If we saved his life isn't that the most important thing?'

Lausard began walking away, his words almost lost in the chill night air. 'Does it really matter any more?'

Fourteen

Not for the first time in his life, Alain Lausard experienced the feeling that time had somehow lost its meaning. Days and weeks, and finally months, had taken on a monotony and routine that had seen them blend into one.

Every day began with a bugle call summoning the soldiers from their makeshift beds. They cleaned their equipment, tended their horses and performed training manoeuvres. Sometimes at night they were allowed out into Paris itself, and on those few occasions the men had made the most of their temporary freedom. They had sought out the inns they'd known from their former lives in the capital, and they had drunk themselves into oblivion. Giresse and Delacor and a few of the others had sought more earthly pleasures among the prostitutes of Chaillot. For the most part these excesses were ignored by officers. As long as the men's ability as soldiers was not impaired then most aberrations were excused. Lausard realised the volatility of the situation; so many fighting men without a fight to test their skills, feeling like prisoners in the city many of them had grown up in. As winter had drawn on, estimates had varied about exactly how many troops were in the capital. Guesses put it anywhere between fifteen thousand and thirty thousand.

December turned into January, January into February, and Lausard began to experience feelings he'd felt before. The march prior to the intial invasion of Italy a couple of years earlier and the days of heat and suffering in Egypt had made him wonder whether time could be lost as easily as misplaced belongings; now he felt the same, as his and so many more regiments waited for orders to move out of Paris. Every day Lausard awoke to the sound of the trumpet, hoping this would be the day that brought an end to such a stultifying living and allowed him to do that for which he had trained. He craved a campaign. Of course there were many around him, indeed some in his own squadron, who were only too happy to continue this life of monotony. As long as they were safe they were delighted. Lausard could understand these feelings but he had no room for them in his own mindset. However, as February became March and leaves began to reappear upon the branches of the trees, Lausard wondered how long it would be before he too became content with a life of predictability and boredom.

News of developments in Egypt reached the troops via the newspapers. Lausard had read of a battle at a place called Heliopolis, which had, the papers reported, been another glorious victory for General Kleber. Celebrations had been held in his honour, and Lausard and his men had enjoyed an extra ration of brandy.

Lausard had also read on a number of occasions of military activity closer to home. He read of the loss of Italian cities, which he and his men had helped to conquer three years earlier, to the Austrians. He had read proclamations issued by Bonaparte asking for the support of the nation against these transgressors and now when he woke each morning he expected to find officers waiting with orders to move out. To finally advance to confront an enemy they knew only too well.

When the order finally came, Lausard was overjoyed. His life, already meaningless in his eyes, had purpose again and, in his case at least, the journey across France was made in high spirits.

Now, as he stared at the leaping flames of the campfire, he felt that the physical and mental stagnation of the past three months was finally over.

He looked around at the camp, which stretched as far as he could see in all directions; infantry, cavalry and artillery all thrown together on one vast plain. Lausard watched as several demibrigades were drilled, forming square from column and then back again, under the watchful eyes of their officers. Several squadrons of chasseurs were performing manoeuvres before a general he recognised as Lannes. Campfires, dotted all around the site, glowed orange in the late evening and sent up clouds of smoke into an already overcast sky.

Lausard had taken his usual solitary stroll around the campsite, impressed by the beauty of the surrounding countryside. There was a wooded height off to the north, and beyond it a breathtaking view of the countryside and Lake Geneva. The lake looked like a huge stain on the landscape, the water choppy as the wind whipped across it. The city itself was clearly visible several miles away.

Troops had been arriving for most of the day and as Lausard and his men sat around their campfire, another column of infantry marched past, many looking tired and hungry, and eyeing the dragoons' fire enviously.

'Half of the army are old men, the other half are children,' said Delacor, looking around as he chewed on a piece of mutton.

'What's this place called?' Tabor asked.

'Lausanne,' Bonet told him. The former schoolmaster was holding a copy of *Le Moniteur* that was several days old. He scanned it carefully then handed it to Lausard.

'These newspapermen call for us to restore glory to France,' the sergeant said.

'It's a pity they don't come and help us do it,' Rocheteau commented, as he stirred the pot of broth with his bayonet. The iron pot was suspended over the fire on two swords that had been tied together. He inhaled the aroma, dipped his metal dish into the pot, then sat down next to Lausard and began eating.

'Where do you think they will send us, Alain?' Bonet asked.

Lausard could only shrug. 'To Italy, to Prussia. Who knows? The Austrian army is in both places,' he said quietly. 'Where we go next is not in our hands. It is for Bonaparte to decide.'

'There are two divisions of the Austrian army before us,' Napoleon Bonaparte announced, gesturing towards the maps spread out on the table. 'We know that General Kray commands more than a hundred thousand men in the Black Forest and upper Danube area. General Melas has perhaps eighty thousand men in northern Italy. Our main objectives must be the destruction of these forces and the capture of Vienna itself.'

Eugene de Beauharnais stepped forward and stood beside his step father, looking down at the maps and the troop positions etched upon them.

'Would it not be true to say that our success depends not just upon the performance of our own men but on that of those under the command of General Moreau?' Eugene said.

'Moreau is a very able man,' Bessiéres replied. 'Do you doubt his abilities, Eugene?'

'He is too cautious,' Bonaparte interjected. 'But I need his support both as a general and as a political ally.'

'What has politics to do with our position here in Switzerland?' Berthier demanded.

'After the war is won there will be peace,' Bonaparte reminded him. 'The purpose of making war is to win peace. Once I return to Paris I want no opposition from Moreau.'

'If he was going to offer opposition surely he would have done it before now,' Eugene said.

'Possibly,' Bonaparte mused. 'But I feel that I am not yet sufficiently firm in my position to come to an open rupture with a man who has numerous partisans in the army, and who lacks only the *energy* to attempt to put himself in my place. It is necessary to negotiate with him as a separate power.'

'Moreau suggested we attack the Austrians through the Rhine salient,' Bessiéres reminded his commander.

'I shall carry out this plan, which he fails to understand, in another part of the theatre of war,' Bonaparte retorted. 'What he does not dare to do on the Rhine, I shall do over the Alps.' He pointed at the map, the other officers drawing closer. 'Moreau will launch a subsidiary offensive between 10th and 20th April, with the object of pushing Kray back towards Ulm. While he makes these preliminary moves, three divisions of the Army of the Reserve will cover him. Once moved to Geneva they will be within equal striking distance of either Schaffhausen on the Rhine or the Saint Gotthard Pass. The remaining thirty thousand men will move towards Zurich during the final days of April.' Bonaparte sipped at his wine.

'What are our numbers?' Bessiéres asked.

'Two hundred and eighty thousand split between five main field armies,' Eugene informed him.

'Recent intelligence would seem to indicate that Melas has been reinforced,' Berthier observed. 'He has also been promised an additional twenty thousand men by the king of Naples and ten thousand British troops too.'

'The Aulic Council moves slowly.' Bonaparte was dismissive. 'What they plan to do and what they actually achieve are two different things and neither Kray nor Melas can make a move without the instruction of those senile old fools in Vienna. This war will be over before they realise it is lost.'

'It will be as it was four years ago,' Bessiéres commented.

'Let us hope that we are blessed with victories as we were then,' Berthier intoned.

'We were not blessed,' snapped Bonaparte. 'We achieved our objectives because we had more able troops and better commanders. Men who fought for a belief. They still have that belief but now they are better trained and equipped.'

'Half a million francs in gold, three hundred thousand rations of brandy and four hundred and thirty thousand rations of biscuit have already been despatched by mule train to Lake Geneva,' Eugene mused. 'Not to mention one hundred thousand pairs of boots and forty thousand uniforms. Our men had little in the way of such rudimentary necessities during our last campaign in Italy.'

Bonaparte tapped the maps once again. 'Once Moreau has driven Kray back and cut the Austrian lines of communication, half of the Army of the Reserve will march for Italy, using either the Saint Gotthard or the Simplon passes. The rest of the army will be left to hold Switzerland. Moreau will then detach General Lecourbe's 4th corps to join us in the Po valley. It is a hundred and ninety-two miles from Zurich to Bergamo, no more than twelve days' march.'

'And what if Lecourbe and his men cannot cover the distance in that time?' Berthier challenged. 'Twelve days is an optimistic calculation. If Moreau neglects to detach the corps at the right time then your plan will fail.'

'Where is your faith, Berthier?' Bonaparte said, a gleam in his eyes. 'Once Lecourbe has joined us we will catch Melas like a rat in a trap, sever his communications and cut him off from any possible hope of reinforcement. And with Massena's men to his front and ours to his rear he will have no chance.'

'Providing Massena can hold Genoa. He is undermanned in that area on the left wing. Fewer than thirty-six thousand men are attempting to hold a line fifty leagues in length, including seventy miles of Ligurian coastline, and he faces attack from the Austrians from the landward and the British fleet from the seaward.'

'There is no man I would rather have commanding there than Massena. He will hold for as long as is necessary. I know he will.'

'I hope your faith is well founded,' Berthier said quietly.

'Can we also be sure that Moreau will beat Kray on the Danube decisively enough to push him back twelve days' march?' Bessiéres enquired. 'Anything other than a decisive victory will most certainly prolong the war.'

'Why are you all beset by such doubts?' Bonaparte said, looking around at his generals. 'Has my judgement ever been wrong before?'

'It is not your judgement that is in question,' Bessiéres replied. 'It is the capabilities of men you entrust with tasks so crucial to the success of this campaign.'

'If I could command on every front, in every theatre of war then I would. But with the responsibility of leadership comes the necessity to delegate. And I have chosen men I trust. Moreau and Massena will not fail us. I believe that or I would not have placed them in command of such vital areas.

You should have more belief in the ability of your brother officers, my friend. Should anyone voice doubts about your own skill as a commander I trust you would be similarly aggrieved.'

'I pray for the sake of the army and for the sake of France that your faith is rewarded,' Bessiéres murmured, holding the gaze of his superior for a moment.

'And what of our other enemy?' Berthier mused. 'The Alps? Taking men, horses and equipment over them could be our undoing. We command soldiers, not mountain goats. It will not be easy.'

'No one expected *any* part of this campaign to be easy, Berthier,' Bonaparte reminded his officer. 'But do not underestimate the determination of our men.'

'So, how do we surmount these accursed rocks?' Bessiéres asked.

'I ordered comprehensive reconnaissance of the major Alpine passes in December last year,' Bonaparte informed the cavalry commander. 'There are three main routes we may consider. The first is by way of Geneva and the Great Saint Bernard Pass, but it is narrow and some of the route is impassable for cannon. The second is through the Simplon. This leads almost directly to Milan and it outflanks the western river lines defending the left bank of the Po.' He paused and looked at the watchful faces of his generals. 'The Saint Gotthard is the farthest east of all the passes but it is probably the best. It is large enough to accommodate a whole army and its lines of communication. I feel that using a combination of the Simplon and the Saint Gotthard will best suit our needs.'

'And assuming we negotiate these rocks successfully,' Bessiéres persisted, 'what then?'

'When we arrive in the valley of the Po I will move the

Army of the Reserve, by rapid marches, to occupy Stradella, which is on the main road from Piacenza to Alessandria. The distance there between the Po and the Appenines is less than twelve miles. Stradella occupies the only usable road along the Austrian lines of communication. If they want to reopen those lines then it has to be by way of Stradella. This is perfect for us. The enemy cavalry could achieve nothing against its stone cottages and their superiority in artillery would be less effective there than anywhere else.'

Bonaparte stepped back, a smile on his lips. He ran a hand through his hair and waited for some kind of reaction from the other men. When none was forthcoming he continued.

'Melas has over one hundred thousand men in the field; Massena should tie down at least a third of them while he defends Genoa. That leaves Lecourbe with his twenty-five thousand and you, Berthier, with fifty thousand to face the remainder.'

'And what if Melas decides to bypass Genoa?' Berthier asked.

'He dare not. The Aulic Council would have him shot if he allowed the Austrian lines of communication in north Italy to be cut. He must dispose of Massena. It is the thorn in his side.' Bonaparte held a pin over the area of the map that marked Genoa. 'For myself, if necessary, I will lead the army beyond Stradella until I can destroy Melas once and for all. I will fight him here, on the plain of the Scrivia.' He drove the pin into the map.

The place he had speared was a village called Marengo.

Lausard moved the curry comb evenly over the flanks of his horse. The bay neighed once or twice, and flicked its head up and down contentedly as the sergeant continued his task. He had removed the horse's bridle, in readiness for sponging its muzzle and eyes, a task he would perform once the animal's coat had been satisfactorily brushed. Like the other horses of the squadron, his mount had been fed and watered. Fodder was unexpectedly plentiful and so too was fresh water. Equitation and general care of mounts had improved vastly during the previous four years. The cavalry had come a long way from the notorious days of the old Royal Army, when horses were so badly cared for. Lausard had heard older cavalrymen say that enemy troops used to joke that they could smell the French cavalry coming because of the horses' saddle sores. It was just one of many things that had changed under Bonaparte. Of course there had been the odd loss during the journey from Paris. Two animals had gone lame and been shot. Many others, Lausard's included, had thrown shoes on the roads from Dijon to Lausanne. But these had been easily replaced by the regimental farriers. In fact, Lausard couldn't remember when the condition of so many horses had been so good. But, he feared, their well-being, like that of the men he fought alongside, would doubtless deteriorate once the campaign began. For the time being, however, all seemed to be in good order.

He glanced across at Tigana, who was happily combing his horse's mane, whispering into the animal's ear as he worked. The big Gascon loved horses and they responded to his kind ways. His knowledge of them was limitless and Lausard continued watching him for a moment.

Rocheteau was kneeling to inspect his mount's hooves. He moved quickly around all four, removing some small stones with his pocket knife before patting the animal on the neck.

Tabor was chewing on a carrot. He took a bite then offered the rest to his mount as he brushed it.

Karim had already brushed his horse using the regulation

equipment and now Lausard watched, fascinated, as he repeated the process using only the flat of his hand, caressing the animal tenderly. Aware of the sergeant's prying gaze, Karim turned and smiled.

'A rider and his horse should be as one,' he explained. 'That is what the Mamelukes always taught me. If a horse trusts the man who rides it, then it will perform miracles for him.'

'Miracles are just what we might need, my friend.'

'Sergeant Lausard!'

The sound of his name made Lausard turn. He saw Gaston heading towards him. The young trumpeter, his scarlet surtout undone to reveal a thick shirt beneath, continued to head in the direction of the NCO.

'There is an issue of rations and cartridges,' Gaston explained. 'The quartermasters are distributing them now. Nine days' rations and forty cartridges to every man.'

'Rations,' Joubert said, grinning. 'Thank God for that; perhaps now we can all get a decent meal.'

'It's mainly biscuits,' Gaston added apologetically.

'And cartridges?' Rocheteau said quietly. 'We're obviously going to need them. Do you think the time has come, Alain?'

Lausard didn't answer. He patted his horse's neck then set off back towards the area where his squadron waited.

'Captain Milliere said that we are to take our place in the advance guard commanded by General Lannes,' Gaston continued as they walked. 'Our objective is a place called Aosta. Twenty-five miles from here.'

'Across those damned mountains,' Karim murmured.

'How the hell are we supposed to get horses over them?' Rochteau wanted to know. 'I heard some engineers say that there is a village called Saint Pierre and that beyond it the tracks are impassable to guns and heavy vehicles. How will we get cannon over?'

'The horses are our only problem,' Lausard reminded him. 'Let the engineers concern themselves with guns.'

'We will *all* be concerned if we reach Italy with no artillery support,' Rocheteau pointed out. 'You can be sure the Austrians will have it in strength.'

As Lausard strode purposefully through the massive encampment he glanced towards the menacing snow-capped peaks of the Alps, thrusting upwards towards the heavens, threatening to tear the clouds that shrouded them. A cold wind was already blowing from that direction.

Fifteen

Lausard cursed as his horse slipped on the icy slope. The bay whinnied alarmingly as its back legs skidded, and it took all of Lausard's expert horsemanship to prevent the animal sliding backwards. He knew that one such slip could cause untold chaos. The dragoons, as well as the troops who moved behind them, were on a track barely wide enough to take three men riding abreast. Since the column had set off before dawn that morning, the slope had grown more precipitous the higher they had climbed.

Lausard patted his mount's neck, urging it on, his breath frosting in the freezing air as he spoke. The sun had attempted to crawl into the sky from behind the unforgiving mountains but it had soon retreated back behind the dense banks of cloud. With that cloud had come first rain, then sleet and finally snow, small flakes driving like needles into the faces of the men, reducing visibility – a further hazard to their already perilous journey.

Lausard pulled up the collar of his green cloak and ducked lower across the neck of his horse in an effort to shield himself from the stinging white curtain that blanketed everything. It covered the rocks and filled crevices in the narrow track. Every so often a man or a horse would step into one of these natural traps. Four horses and more than ten men had already broken bones because of this new menace. Up ahead, Lausard could see Captain Milliere and Lieutenant Royere forcing their mounts up the ever-more treacherous slope. A layer of ice was beginning to form now, the snow freezing beneath the feet of the troops as they toiled on.

Close behind, he saw one of the eight-pounders being hauled by a group of grenadiers. The barrels, each weighing in excess of fifteen hundred pounds, had been placed in troughs made from hollowed out tree trunks. Ten infantrymen were on each side, holding on to stout sticks which had been put through ropes to act as makeshift traces; they were guided by gunners as they dragged their precious cargo along the narrow defiles. In addition, two men carried each axle tree, two more carried a wheel, four toiled under the weight of the upper part of the caisson, eight were burdened with the heavy ammunition chest and eight more men carried the muskets of their companions. Rumour had it that Bonaparte had promised six francs and two extra rations a day to any man who recovered items of equipment left behind during the perilous journey. Lausard had heard that elsewhere up to a hundred men had been harnessed to each piece in order to drag it over the mountains, working like mules to ensure the safe passage of the cannons. Sledges on rollers were also being used but these, Lausard feared, would become incredibly dangerous on the increasingly slippery slopes. As if to reinforce his misgivings, the wind blew with incredible ferocity, whipping snow into his face and causing his horse to duck its head. Like its rider, its breath clouded in the air as it panted and snorted with the strain of trying to keep its feet on such a treacherous surface.

The sergeant could see that the pathway was becoming narrower, but even more disturbing was the deep precipice to their left. Lausard watched as some small boulders, dislodged by the scrabbling horses, broke away and tumbled into the yawning gorge below. It was a number of seconds before he heard them strike more rocks below. He could only guess at how high up they were. He glanced behind at the rest of the column, struggling along, desperate to keep control of their mounts, only too aware of the fate that awaited them should they fall. There would be no chance of survival.

And still the snow came. Slashing into the men as if it were razor sharp shrapnel. Even beneath their thick gauntlets their hands were chilled to the bone. Many had wrapped rags around their faces to try to protect themselves from the icy blasts. Hidden as he was beneath his helmet, which was itself covered by its waterproof cloth cover and a scarf, only Karim's eyes were visible. He kept his gaze straight ahead, not allowing his concentration to waver.

As the column rounded a curve, Lausard saw a vast expanse of white ahead. Snow clung to everything: the sides of the mountains, the pathways and boulders that littered the way. He couldn't begin to imagine how deep it was. The pathway widened somewhat into a plateau, which seemed to connect two of the tall peaks. Lausard saw Captain Milliere pause before leading his horse on through the snow. The animal sank as deep as its flank. As more troops passed through, the snow was gradually flattened and blinding white walls began to build up on either side of the men. The snow was now falling even more thickly and Lausard had to wipe his face every few yards. His horse whinnied but he calmed it with a pat on its neck, chancing a glance at his companions. Rocheteau, Bonet, Delacor and Sonnier all rode with their heads down. It seemed only Karim was actually looking where he was going.

Lausard could now see clearly the grenadier units hauling the eight-pounders close behind, straining under the incredible weight. The men hauled the weapons through the snow, slowing their pace as they drew close to the edge of the precipice, ignoring the shouts of engineers, officers and gunners urging them on. The sergeant watched as a man lost his footing, rolled over once and screamed in terror, as he realised how close to the edge he was. Several of those nearby let go of the ropes they held and dashed to his aid. But two slid on the ice and both toppled over the side. Their screams echoed through the snow-choked air as they hurtled to their deaths.

Rocheteau looked around, glanced at Lausard and shook his head, tucking his chin down again as another withering blast of freezing wind struck them.

Up ahead, Captain Milliere had brought his horse to a halt and was pointing towards the thick snow, Lieutenant Royere was leaning close to him, nodding occasionally. Also present was an engineer known to the men as Garet. Every unit in the army had been assigned at least one engineer in order to aid their passage over some of the more lethal obstacles the Alps presented. Lausard saw the officer beckon to him and prodded his horse with his spurs to urge it on.

'It may not surprise you to know, Sergeant Lausard, that we have a problem.' Milliere was forced to shout to make himself heard above the howling wind. He pointed to an outcrop of rocks about fifty yards ahead, which formed a ledge about halfway up one of the sheer rock faces; the ledge was packed with fallen snow. 'General Marescot, the army's chief engineer, warned of the danger of avalanches. I fear we may be riding into one.'

'What choice do we have, Captain?' Lausard lowered the scarf from his mouth slightly.

'General Marescot recommended the firing of cannon to bring down and clear such dangers,' Garet told him. 'Unfortunately, that is not possible now.'

'Why can't we use one of the eight-pounders?' Lausard questioned. 'It wouldn't take the gunners long to reassemble a piece and discharge it.'

'The pathway here is too narrow,' Royere argued, his voice muffled by the thick cloth wrapped around his face. 'It would not support the carriage of such a gun.'

'We can pass through,' Milliere said, looking up at the ever-growing mass of snow, 'taking the chance that it won't collapse. Or we can try to displace it with an explosive charge. Have you an opinion, Sergeant?'

'Forgive me for saying so, Captain, but I suspect that you have already made a decision and that my opinion counts for very little. I suggest you need someone to plant the charge.'

'It would be foolish to even *think* about continuing, with such a potentially dangerous obstacle ahead,' Garet insisted. 'If it falls then it could wipe out an entire squadron.'

'Garet will plant the charges,' Milliere said. 'Pick two of your men to help him, Sergeant.'

'*I* will help him. I would not ask any of my men to perform a task that I would not do.'

Milliere nodded then pulled his scarf back up around his mouth.

Lausard raised a hand and signalled to Rostov. The Russian guided his horse carefully towards the waiting group of men, saluting the officers when he reached them.

'We have work to do, my friend,' Lausard told him, swinging himself out of his saddle. He offered the reins of his horse to Lieutenant Royere, who nodded and took them. 'Take good care of him, Lieutenant. I trust I shall want him back very soon.'

Royere also took the reins of Rostov's mount and he and Milliere rode back to join the dragoons, who looked on with a combination of bewilderment and concern.

'If we plant the charges beneath that outcrop,' Garet explained, pointing to where the snow lay most heavily on the cliff face, 'it should clear the way.'

'How do we get up there?' Lausard asked. 'It must be thirty feet high.'

'And the rest,' Rostov observed, looking over the side of the precipice to the appalling drop below.

Garet reached into his pack and pulled out a grappling hook. A long length of rope was attached to it, which the engineer began unravelling. He also removed a small box and set it atop a boulder. Lausard guessed it was the charge. A fuse, wrapped in waxed paper, was protruding from one corner.

'It's a number four fuse,' Garet explained. 'Four pounds of flour powder, sixteen pounds of saltpetre and eight pounds of sulphur. It will burn for just over sixty seconds. I'm using a number four because it has a very fierce spark, due to the camphor in it, which will ensure that the snow does not extinguish it.'

Lausard nodded. 'How can you be sure it will ignite?'

'Twists of thread at the outer end,' Garet said, as if that explained everything.

'And will two charges be enough?'

'One should be sufficient. The second will probably bring most of the mountain down too.' Garet smiled.

Lausard watched as the engineer, a squat, powerfully built man in a blue overcoat and knee-length boots, swung the grappling iron around his head in ever-increasing circles. Finally he flung it, smiling when it caught first time on the rocky ledge. He tugged on it, ensuring it would take his weight, then he looked at the two dragoons.

'We'll carry the charges,' Lausard offered, taking the other small box from Garet. Then he and Rostov watched as the little engineer began hauling himself up the rope. It swayed alarmingly in the savage wind but Garet continued upwards, snow lashing him mercilessly. When he reached the rock overhang he waved at the dragoons, signalling for them to follow.

Lausard stuffed the charge into the pocket of his tunic and gripped the rope, dragging himself up with his powerful arms. The ascent was tortuous and the sergeant closed his eyes more than once to protect them against the driving snow. Below him, Rostov also began to climb. Five feet up, the Russian's hand slipped on the rope and he almost lost his grip, but he held on and continued upwards. As he moved higher he tried to stop himself looking down, wishing to avoid the sight of the jagged, ice-encrusted rocks hundreds of feet beneath him.

Garet was waiting on the ledge. Snow was packed like a wall against the cliff face, slabs of it already beginning to slide away and scatter in the air.

'We haven't got much time,' the engineer muttered as Lausard joined him. 'Plant the other charge there.' He motioned to what appeared to be the far extent of the ledge, about thirty feet from where they stood.

More snow suddenly came free, hurtling over the rocky outcrop and disappearing into the chasm below.

'You have sixty seconds, once it's lit,' Garet reminded Lausard and he pushed a tinder box into his hand.

Rostov scrambled up to join them.

'Once I see that yours is lit, I'll ignite mine,' Garet told them.

Lausard and Rostov made their way along the ledge with as much speed as possible. Where the rock wasn't already covered by snow, it was sheathed in a thick layer of ice that made even walking hazardous.

Lausard finally stopped beside some small boulders and pushed the charge in amongst them. Despite the icy wind he could feel perspiration clinging to his back; he told himself it was from the exertion of the climb. He retrieved the flints from the tinder and struck them together, Rostov cupping his hands to shield them from the biting wind. Lausard kept chipping away, tiny sparks flowering between the flints. But as he pushed the flints closer to the dry pieces of wood and thread, the wind continued to batter them. He rasped something under his breath, striking the flints even harder. They sparked. The tinder flamed. For precious seconds it blazed, but then the wind extinguished it. He tried again. And again. From above, they heard a loud roar and several more slabs of frozen snow hurtled from the rock face. Lausard knew there wasn't much time. At any moment the entire white wall could come crashing down, sweeping them away.

He redoubled his efforts, striking the flints together furiously.

A spark.

Then another. He pushed the stones closer to the tinder and watched as it caught. The flame glowed brightly and Rostov cupped his large hands even more closely around it, watching the yellow flare. Lausard pushed it into the tinder, fanning the growing fire with one hand. Moving quickly, he held it against the fuse.

It lit first time, crackling loudly as it ignited.

Lausard slapped Rostov on the shoulder, urging him to move away as quickly as possible. The big Russian needed no prompting and spun round. The sergeant glanced back at the burning fuse then followed.

Sixty seconds.

He counted as he ran.

Suddenly there was another flurry of snow from the white mass, some of it spilling across their path.

Rostov slipped.

Lausard saw his companion overbalance and clutch at empty air. He realised that the Russian was going to fall. He hurled himself forward but he couldn't grab Rostov in time.

He toppled over the ledge.

But, in a final desperate attempt to save himself, Rostov shot out a hand and by some miracle Lausard grabbed it.

Lausard gritted his teeth, evey muscle in his body straining to hold the weight of his comrade. Rostov kicked his feet uselessly in the air as he held Lausard's hand, knowing that to let go meant certain death.

Behind them the fuse continued to burn.

Fifty seconds.

Lausard tried to bring his other hand over to get a better grip on Rostov's arm but, as he did so, he felt himself sliding closer to the edge, dragged down by the weight of the other man. It felt as if his shoulder was on fire and he knew that he could not hold the Russian for much longer. Furthermore, Rostov's gauntlet was beginning to slip off. Lausard dug his fingers even deeper into the Russian's arm and tried to pull him up, but it was useless.

'Garet!' he called out. 'Help me.'

The engineer, who had seen what had happened, was already at his side and took hold of Rostov's arm and began to pull.

Forty-five seconds.

Rostov began to rise as the combined strength of Lausard and Garet drew him nearer to the rim. Both men pulled with all their strength and Garet leaned forward and grabbed hold of the big Russian's cloak, using it to haul him to safety.

Thirty-five seconds.

Rostov hooked one leg over the lip of the ledge and rolled over, his breath coming in racking gasps. But they knew they had no time to wait. All three men hurtled towards the rope, Garet reaching it first, sliding down in one practised movement. Lausard pushed Rostov ahead of him and the Russian gripped the rope, allowing himself to slide down.

Thirty seconds.

The sergeant looked down at the deep snow below him.

It took him only a second to make up his mind.

The snow would break his fall.

Wouldn't it?

He jumped.

Garet and Rostov, already racing back towards the waiting column, turned to see Lausard launch himself into the air. He plummeted the thirty feet in an instant, landed in a deep snow drift then hauled himself from it, his body coated with white flakes. He blundered on, knowing that there were mere seconds left now. If only he could cover another few yards. Surely the snow on the rock face wouldn't fall immediately. He would be granted another few seconds before the white wall came crashing down.

There was a deafening explosion above him as the charges went off.

Lausard ignored the blasts and kept running, ploughing his way through the deep snow until he felt icy rocks beneath his feet. Only then did he turn and look back.

The cliff face had disappeared beneath clouds of snow and reeking black smoke.

A moment later he heard a sound like bending saplings. A loud groaning that grew into a roar. The wind blew away the smoke and Lausard could see huge sheets of frozen snow sliding from the mountain. The snow crashed down, bulldozing its way down the side of the sheer face, carrying rocks, boulders and more snow with it. Like an unstoppable white tide, the avalanche roared down the slopes, crashed into the tightly packed glacial mass below and carried it onward with a deafening whoosh.

Lausard stood gasping as he watched the rock face being swept clear by the deluge. Trees and lumps of ice the size of a man tumbled along in the wake of the blast-born blizzard. The sergeant finally turned and trudged back towards the waiting dragoons, who had watched mesmerised as events had unfolded before them.

Rostov looked at the sergeant and opened his mouth to speak but Lausard extended his hand for the Russian to shake. He saw the gratitude in his companion's eyes. No words were necessary.

Garet also shook hands with Lausard, smiling as he watched the dragoon swing himself into the saddle. The sergeant brushed snow from his cloak and wrapped the scarf around his mouth once again. His horse pawed the icy ground and tossed its head, as if relieved that its rider had returned. Lausard patted its neck.

The column moved on.

It seemed as if the worst of the blizzard had passed. For the last thirty minutes, the ascent had been a little easier, as the dragoons were spared the onslaught of the freezing snow. Lausard was grateful for this since the mountain paths on which they travelled were so narrow in places that just two horses at a time could traverse them. He could only imagine what kind of problems the infantry behind them would encounter, dragging the artillery pieces over the perilous terrain. The sergeant wondered how many men would fall victim to the elements and the landscape before they even *saw* their first Austrian.

'Does anyone know where the hell we're supposed to be going?' Delacor's muffled voice pleaded. 'I didn't know the Austrians were hiding at the tops of these stinking mountains.'

'We'll probably all freeze to death before we see them,' Sonnier replied.

'Do you know where we are, Alain?' Rocheteau asked.

'The Great Saint Bernard Pass,' Lausard told him, glancing up and spotting a dark shape amidst the startling whiteness of the snow. 'That,' he said, pointing at the shape, 'must be the hospice.'

'What is it?' Rocheteau asked.

'It's a monastery. The monks who live there tend to travellers.'

'Who the hell would want to live up here?' Delacor hissed. 'They must be insane.'

'They are men of God,' Moreau told him. 'You should afford them the reverence they deserve.'

'Shut up, your holiness.'

'Judging by the height of these mountains, they must be able to shake hands with God,' Rocheteau observed and, momentarily forgetting the cold, a number of the other men laughed.

'The hospice is over eight thousand feet above sea level,' Bonet informed his colleagues. 'It has been here for many years. A haven amongst all this.' He made an expansive gesture with his hand.

'It looks as if someone has been here before us,' Lausard observed. 'There are wagon tracks.' He nodded in the direction of several deep ruts in the snow. 'The artillery caissons that were sent on ahead obviously managed to make it through.'

'And the engineers too,' Rocheteau added, noticing that the road had been widened and several paths had been cut through the rocks that formed a barrier along the approaches to the hospice.

Indeed, as the dragoons drew closer to the building, they realised that they were able to ride four abreast once more, even though the ascent was very steep. Lausard and several others put spurs to their mounts to force them up the precipitous incline, and, despite their whinnies of protest, the animals carried their riders almost effortlessly up the slopes.

The ground began to level out and Lausard could see more clearly the outline of the hospice; a dark intrusion against the glaring white background of snow and the menacing bulk of the mountains.

As the dragoons slowed down, they noticed figures moving about outside the buildings. The figures were garbed in dark clothing and some were accompanied by huge dogs, which followed them around as meekly as puppies.

'What are those monsters?' Roussard pointed at one of the dogs, which was wandering unhurriedly and unconcernedly towards the approaching cavalrymen. It had little difficulty walking on the snow with its huge paws.

One or two of the horses shied away from the massive dog but the rest seemed unconcerned by its presence. Lausard looked down as the dog seated itself on the cold ground and watched disinterestedly as the column passed. Up ahead, Captain Milliere and Lieutenant Royere had already dismounted and were shaking hands with several of the dark-robed monks, who had emerged to greet them. Milliere signalled to the column to halt, some of the horses pawing the frozen ground impatiently.

Rocheteau shivered as the icy wind began to blow with renewed ferocity.

'What now?' he wondered aloud.

Lausard had no answer. Like his companions, all he could do was sit upright in his saddle and wait. And for the next ten minutes that was precisely what he and the rest of the dragoons did.

The wide corridors inside the Hospice of Saint Bernard were wide and easily accommodated men who wished to sleep. Many of the dragoons took advantage of the opportunity. As the wind howled outside, its strident sound mingled with the grumble of much snoring within.

Lausard sat up, his back propped against his saddle, chewing on a piece of cheese supplied by the monks. Once the troops had been ordered inside the hospice, the monks had brought a bucket of wine for every twelve men and each individual trooper had received a quarter of a pound of Gruyere and a loaf of bread. It was a more than welcome supplement to the men's meagre rations. Some had saved part of the issue. Others, like Joubert and Delacor, had devoured all but crumbs and both now slept contentedly, wrapped in their cloaks, on the stone floor.

Lausard looked around at the men of his squadron, either huddled in groups talking or sleeping, their numbers filling the corridor from one end to the other. Every one of them, himself included, had been relieved to find shelter from the elements, no matter how short their reprieve. Captain Milliere had given orders that their stay was not to exceed six hours. Their horses too had been fed and groomed, and although there was nowhere to shelter them, each of the animals had been covered by a stable cloth to keep it warm.

'You should not be eating that food and drinking that

wine,' Moreau addressed Karim, who was sipping some of the liquor from his canteen. 'These men serve *our* God, not yours.'

'It was men who offered me these supplies, not Gods. If these same rations had been supplied to you in the name of Allah, all praise to Him, would *you* have refused them? I think not.'

Lausard chuckled. 'He has a point, Moreau. Perhaps you would be better off staying here and joining these men, instead of continuing on with us.'

'You may be right,' Moreau announced piously. 'My true vocation lies in the saving of lives, not in their destruction. I feel that is how God would wish me to spend my life. Perhaps I *should* remain.'

'And be shot for deserting?' Rocheteau pointed out.

Laughter erupted amongst the men.

'It is a sad thing when the desire to work for God is punished by the threat of death,' Moreau said.

'You do as much work for your God fighting the Austrians,' Lausard told him. 'After all, God is on the side of France, isn't he? I'm sure Bonaparte has spoken to him personally to assure us of victory.'

'Bonaparte is as much a heathen as you or any of the men in this army,' Moreau snapped. 'He feels himself superior to God.'

'God cannot move troops on a battlefield with the speed and skill Bonaparte uses.' Giresse grinned.

'More blasphemy,' Moreau groaned. 'And in a house of God too. You will pay the ultimate price for your lack of respect.'

'If any of us pays the ultimate price it will be because of an Austrian bullet, or sword, or roundshot,' Lausard retorted. 'Our deaths, when they come, will have nothing to do with

God but with other *men.* And these holy men who offer us shelter and food, do you think they care for the outcome of our war? Do you think it bothers them who rules Europe? Who is going to bother them up here? If the Austrians had passed through they would have treated them with the same kindness.'

'Because they serve God and not a country or an ideal,' Moreau countered.

'And what ideals do we serve?' Lausard demanded. 'The advancement of the Republic? Of the First Consul himself? What is our purpose as soldiers, Moreau? Do you know? Did any of us *ever* know? We joined this army because it offered us a way out. An escape from the guillotine. After four years, do not begin to confuse the reasons we are wearing these uniforms.' He ran a hand along the arm of his green tunic. 'I, for one, fight because I am ordered, not because I agree with the politics that drive this conflict.'

'My understanding is that we fight the Austrians in order to regain land they have taken back from us since ninety-six,' Rocheteau offered. 'Land *we* helped to win.'

'That is true,' Lausard echoed. 'It is a war, like any other, of conquest. We will fight on until the Austrians are defeated. Until Italy is in French hands again. After that, the decision is Bonaparte's. Should he decide that the war ends, then so be it. If he desires that it should continue, then we will follow him.' He fixed Moreau in a steely gaze. 'If there are no enemies left then there can be no more wars. It is a very simple equation.'

'So, Alain, you would have us slaughter our enemies to ensure they could not oppose us again?' Rocheteau asked.

'If that is the answer then yes. There is a ridiculous supposition that war is alien to civilization. That is not so. War is destruction, *not* possession. It *is* standing booted over dead soldiers *and* civilians if necessary.'

'And if *we* are the ones to die . . . ?' Rocheteau's words hung in the air.

'Then we must accept that too,' Lausard told him.

'Do you care so little for your own life?' Carbonne enquired.

'I've told you before. When life offers so little for a man, why should death hold any terrors?'

Some of the men turned as they heard footsteps coming down the corridor. Two of the monks were moving slowly along the lines of dragoons, distributing biscuits from a small sack. Lausard noticed that many of the men were kissing the hands of the holy men, others kneeling before them in supplication. Lausard watched as they drew closer. Moreau dropped to his knees and grabbed the hand of the nearest monk, kissing it.

'Thank you, Father, for all you have done for myself and my comrades.' He crossed himself vigorously.

'We did no more than God would have expected of us, my son,' said the older of the two men. 'If we can offer even the most meagre of comforts then we are doing His will.'

Lausard got to his feet and shook hands with both of the men.

'Thank you,' he said quietly.

'Do not thank us, my son, thank God.' It was the older monk who spoke again. 'We are merely His instruments upon earth. Offer your thanks to the Almighty, not to his servants.'

'It was *you* who gave us food, not God. It is *you* I thank.' Lausard looked down at the biscuits the monks had given him. 'It was you who baked these, not your God.'

'Have you no faith, my son? It was God who guided you to us. It is God who will protect you when you leave here and journey down the mountain. Why can you not accept His love?'

'Do not speak to me of love, Father,' Lausard insisted. 'All that I ever loved was taken from me years ago when my family was murdered. If God is willing to protect me now, why would He not protect my family then?'

'Do not abandon your saviour. He would not abandon you.'

'He already has. In the meantime, I thank *you* and your companions for your kindness.'

The monk held his gaze for a moment longer then moved on.

Moreau genuflected again as the holy men passed by. 'They are saints,' he said quietly.

'They are good bakers too,' Rocheteau chuckled, munching on one of the biscuits.

'My father would have been proud of these,' Charvet added. 'And he was a master baker.'

'I wonder where they get their ingredients,' Rocheteau mused, wiping crumbs from his chin.

'There are villages throughout this range of mountains,' Bonet informed the corporal. 'Tiny settlements of perhaps no more than five or six buildings. Those who live there farm the lower slopes. There is a village called Saint Remy quite near here. It stands close to a frozen lake. I believe we have to cross it, don't we, Alain?'

Lausard nodded, contentedly eating one of his biscuits. He wrapped the others in a piece of linen he'd taken from his jacket, laid them carefully with his other rations, and wrapped up the entire haul before storing it in his portmanteau. All food would have to be conserved. Like his companions, Lausard had no idea when they would be issued with rations again. The same was true of drinking water. Troops had been given an extra ration of vinegar to mix with any melted snow water they might be forced to drink. The consumption of such fluid in its normal state could cause terrible digestive problems; Lausard had already seen a number of cases of dysentery in his squadron.

Something else he'd witnessed since the men had entered the hospice was troopers eager to remove their boots, which was something he had decided against and had warned those close to him to avoid. In the warmth of the building, he warned, their feet, which had been encased in freezing boots for so long, would swell. Lausard wondered if any of the men who had removed their footwear would actually be able to replace it when the time came. And that time was close. Six hours' rest Milliere had said. No more. Lausard chewed slowly on his biscuit and lay back against his saddle. Outside, the wind continued to howl.

The snow had returned with a vengeance. It blasted into the faces of the men as they descended the almost perpendicular slopes that led away from the hospice. It also buffetted them from behind and, it seemed, from both sides, despite the shelter offered on one side by the mountain itself. Lausard felt as if he was trapped inside his own personal whirlwind. Like his colleagues, he was walking, leading his horse by its reins down the treacherous pathway. At the head of the column, moving unconcernedly through the blizzard, was one of the monks. Flanked on either side by Captain Milliere and Lieutenant Royere and accompanied by one of the huge dogs, he strode on through the snow and freezing wind, occasionally pointing towards pathways with the stout wooden cane he carried. Monks led each of the three dragoon squadrons towards the banks of the Dora Baltea; the river that began as a trickle high in the Alps, and grew, with the accumulation of melted snow, into a raging torrent and finally gushed into the Po, close to Chivasso in northern Piedmont. The dragoons, like the troops who followed them and those units that had gone before, were to stay close to the Dora Baltea. Using it as a guide until they were safely on the plains fifteen miles to the east of Turin. There the bulk of the advance guard would assemble once any Austrian opposition encountered en route had been brushed aside. The remainder of the army would follow close behind. Lausard thought how simple the plan sounded; it probably looked similarly unspectacular on paper. The reality, as Lausard had experienced many times before, was a different matter.

He saw the land suddenly flatten out into a white mass of drifted snow and it was with relief that he heard Milliere give the order for the dragoons to mount up. The officers shook hands with the monk, who stood to one side, watching with a slight smile on his face as the snow-covered troops filed past. Many saluted the holy man; others crossed themselves; some even risked the wrath of their officers and NCOs by leaping quickly from the saddle, shaking the priest's hand and then remounting.

Lausard nodded in the direction of the monk as he passed.

'God be with you all,' the monk intoned as the men passed, repeating the words over and over. With one hand he stroked the dog's head as it sat patiently watching the steady stream of men and horses.

'I hope He is,' Sonnier murmured. 'I really do hope He is.'

Lausard guided his horse on, surprised at how flat the land was beneath the animal's hooves. He glanced down and saw that the brushing of snow was lighter here and he realised that many of the animals were having difficulty keeping their footing.

'The frozen lake.' His voice was almost engulfed by the wailing wind, which, despite its power, didn't seem as bone-chillingly cold in the valley.

'I hope the ice can stand the weight,' Rocheteau commented, a note of concern in his voice.

'What I can't understand is, if the world is round, why is a frozen lake flat?' Tabor interjected.

'Just shut up and keep riding, idiot,' Delacor berated him.

'No, my friend, you have a point,' Bonet intervened, patting his large colleague on the shoulder.

'And do *you* have an answer, schoolmaster?' Delacor demanded.

'Actually, it isn't something I've ever thought about,' Bonet confessed.

'Then you shut up too,' Delacor rasped. 'You talk too much as it is.'

Suddenly they were distracted by a loud crack, which reverberated around the valley and echoed in the men's ears. The noise resembled a cannon shot.

Lausard looked up at the snow-encrusted rocks.

'Another avalanche?' Giresse pondered.

The sound came again. Louder this time. Now more of the men began looking around in bewilderment, concern etched on their wind-blasted faces.

'It could be the engineers ahead of us clearing the passes of snow,' Rocheteau suggested.

Lausard was unconvinced.

When it came the movement nearly sent Lausard toppling from his saddle.

The world lurched violently to one side and it took all of the dragoon's expertise to remain in the saddle.

Lausard looked down and saw water bubbling across the ground. Fresh clear water. He knew immediately what was happening.

At the top of his voice he roared the warning: 'The ice is breaking!'

Sixteen

Even as he shouted the warning Lausard saw more cracks appear in the frozen covering. All around him, men who had heard his words put spurs to their mounts, desperate to get away from the source of danger but not really knowing which way to ride. Lausard knew that trying to lead the men off the ice in orderly groups would not only be impossible but also extremely dangerous. There was no way of knowing how badly the ice was cracked, whether it was going to give way and, if it was, how quickly it would dissolve beneath the weight of hundreds of men and horses. He feared that the churning hooves of so many frightened animals, driven on by equally terrified riders, could only accelerate the damage.

Behind him he saw Charnier from the third squadron driving his mount on at full gallop over the slippery surface, two of his companions hurtling after him. More men tried to spur their animals away from the potential danger but had less success. Four men from the second squadron collided as the leading horse lost its footing on the icy surface. They crashed down in an untidy heap, the added impact on the already unstable ice exasperating the problem. Horses, desperate to get to their feet flailed madly with their hooves, and one of the men went down in agony as his left knee was shattered by an iron-shod hoof.

Tigana's horse reared and almost unseated the Gascon but he gripped the reins and maintained control of the animal.

The ground lurched once more.

Lausard grabbed the bridle of Gaston's horse and tugged the animal to one side, the young trumpeter hanging on grimly as his mount struggled to retain its footing.

'Move!' Sergeant Delpierre bellowed, but the men ahead of him needed no prompting. Ice and snow flew up into the air as the horses were driven on in all directions, nobody certain where the shore was, or, indeed, the depth of the freezing water beneath them. Their immediate concern was that if the ice broke completely, they would all end up in the freezing water and, given the temperatures, there was little hope for any creature swallowed by it.

Lausard slapped the rump of Gaston's horse and the animal bolted, followed by several more terrified animals. There was another loud crack and, this time, Lausard saw a rent in the ice open up. It ran across the frozen surface, chasing the hooves of the horses, and the two edges began to separate. Realising the danger, Lausard put spurs to his mount but, as he did so, a wall of white rose before him. One section of the ice was tipping like a plate. Lausard yanked hard on his mount's bridle and swung it round, turning it in a wide arc. When he was about ten feet from the rising ice, he urged the bay forward, digging in his heels to force it into a jump.

The horse landed with a whinny of fear and slid down the slope that had been created on the other side of the huge rent. Lausard was thrown from the saddle. He hit the iron-hard ice with an impact that knocked the wind from him. He tried to roll to one side, aware that his horse was sliding towards him, threatening to crush him. By now, dozens of other terrified animals were also sliding, skidding or falling in his direction. Those dragoons who remained in the saddle had very little control over their horses and could only cling on and pray. Two men were crushed by horses as Lausard looked on. Another man was kicked in the forehead by a flailing hoof, the impact shattering his skull. Blood began to stain the white surface, mingling with the water as the lake continued to open like a huge mouth, ready to swallow all those upon it.

Suddenly Lausard felt strong hands lifting him from the ice and he looked up to see Karim on one side and Charvet on the other. They rode quickly and the sergeant raised his legs clear of the ground. He knew that he could hold on only for a matter of seconds. The grip of his companions was not strong enough to hold him either and he felt himself slipping. He hit the ground hard, rolled over twice and struggled slowly to his knees, his head spinning, a thin ribbon of blood trickling from just below his cheek. He wiped it away, realising that it had been caused by a lump of shattered ice, one of many that had been hacked away by the churning hooves of the terrified horses. But the blood didn't bother him. He was free of the frozen lake and that was all that mattered. Karim swung his horse back and looked down at the sergeant, who nodded.

Behind him came a loud crash and Lausard heard the screams of more than a dozen men and horses.

The ice rose like a castle drawbridge then split in two. All those on it fell into the freezing water below. The incredible shock caused a number of the troopers to black out immediately. They sank, weighed down by their equipment. Others fought to keep their heads above water and, in the confusion, dragoons were buffeted and kicked by their own mounts and those of their companions. Men fought with each other as they tried to reach the ice, but all the time the breath was being torn from their lungs by the icy water. The horses fared little better, and the water was churned white as legs, arms, hooves and feet splashed frantically to escape the deathly embrace of the lake.

A number of riderless horses bolted past and Lausard grabbed the bridle of one. A big grey. He held tight to the reins, bringing the horse under control, then he swung himself into the saddle. Whoever had ridden the grey had clearly been shorter than Lausard and he had to bend his powerful legs in order to slip his boots into the stirrups. But all that mattered now was that he was back in the saddle and hurtling towards other members of his squadron, who waited on what was obviously the shore of the frozen lake.

Behind him, the ice had split in two or three more places but only that one crack had proved fatal. He could see equipment spilled across the surface: boots, portmanteaus, shabraques, swords, helmets, gauntlets and even one or two cloaks blowing in the icy wind. On the other side of the split one riderless horse pawed the ice helplessly, as it stood over a dragoon lying face down on the freezing surface, still gripping his reins in one rigored hand. From his sodden uniform, Lausard guessed that the man must have fallen into the lake and then somehow managed to drag himself out again. The cold had obviously killed him. The combination of the freezing water and the sub-zero temperatures brought by the wind and swirling snow was as lethal as any roundshot.

Up ahead, some of the dragoons had already begun to make their way down a narrow defile and Lausard could hear the splash of water close by.

'How the hell will the men who follow us get over that stinking lake?' Delacor wanted to know.

'The engineers will be able to bridge it,' Lausard assured him.

'Unless the whole mountainside collapses under them,' Giresse observed. 'How many men did we lose? Ten? Twenty? This weather and these mountains will kill more of us than the Austrians.'

'We're on the way down from now on,' Lausard assured him. 'It will be easier. We follow the Dora Baltea all the way into Piedmont.'

The sound of the river grew louder.

The raging waters of the Dora Baltea river looked black, their darkness heightened by the contrast of the white-flecked banks. The river roared and hissed like a monstrous snake as it wound its ways down the slopes, and Lausard couldn't help but be impressed by its sheer power.

They had been following the raging waterway for more than an hour now, keeping close to its west bank, but never too close, for the ground was eroded and unstable. Rocks and lumps of mud were regularly swept into the rushing torrent and carried away with frightening ease. Three dragoons and their mounts had already been lost to the savage waters. The snow had stopped. The light coat that covered the banks had fallen some time ago and only the chill in the air allowed it to remain. More than once, Lausard thought that the air was getting a little warmer, but he knew there was still some way to go before they reached the foothills of the Alps and emerged into the more welcoming environs of northern Piedmont.

Joubert chewed on a biscuit as he rode, collar turned up against the wind and the spray of the river.

'You should save those biscuits, fat man,' Rocheteau told him. 'We've got a few miles to cover yet before we reach Italy.'

'The land of fine wines and grapes,' Roussard recalled wistfully. 'No more of this melted snow to drink.' He took a sip from his canteen, swilled it around his mouth then spat it out.

'Fine wines and fine women,' Giresse added.

'We'll have more important things than wine and women to contend with once we reach our destination,' Sonnier remarked. 'God knows how many Austrians will be waiting for us.'

'Let them wait,' Rocheteau sneered. 'We have nothing to fear. We've beaten them before. Or have you forgotten? They ran from us at Arcola. Melted away at Lodi and fled at Rivoli. The same thing will happen again.'

'You sound very sure of that, my friend,' Karim murmured. 'Might the Austrians not wish for revenge? You may find them even more formidable adversaries this time.'

'What do you think, Alain?' Bonet interjected. 'Will the Austrians make more of a fight of it this time?'

'They made a fight of it *before*, didn't they? How many thousand dead did we leave behind to prove it?' Lausard shook his head gently. 'They will be ready for us but it should not matter.'

He glanced ahead to see that the leading dragoons were moving cautiously on to a wooden bridge that spanned the two banks of the Dora Baltea. The move to the opposite side was unavoidable, as the narrow track on which the troops currently moved was being eroded by the encroaching mountains on the west bank. The bridge looked firm enough and the dragoons led their mounts unhurriedly over the single span. Many of them could not help looking down at the dark, rushing water beneath and contemplating what chance they would have should the bridge collapse.

'Do you think it will take artillery?' Rocheteau mused, the sound of hooves echoing on the wooden slats.

Lausard nodded. 'I hope so.'

As the leading squadron crossed the bridge, the sergeant noticed Lieutenant Royere astride his horse, glancing alternately at a map and then at the sky. Clouds were gathering, but not with the same premonitory darkness that had shrouded the skies over the mountain tops and passes. Rain now looked to be a bigger threat than snow, something to be welcomed by the troops. It would wash away the last of the snow and make their passage through the lower passes and foothills easier. As Lausard drew close, Royere motioned him across.

'We have no idea how far up these passes the Austrians have penetrated,' Royere said. 'Some light cavalry, a detatchment of hussars, were despatched on reconnaissance earlier today but so far we have heard nothing.'

'Perhaps that would indicate the Austrians are closer than you thought, Lieutenant,' Lausard observed.

The officer nodded, then smiled. 'How is it that you always make me feel somehow inadequate, my friend? Surprisingly enough, that possibility *had* occurred to me too.'

Lausard grinned broadly. 'That was not my intention, Lieutenant. Merely an observation. If the hussars did not return then it is possible they have encountered Austrian troops. Probably their own outposts. They will be as anxious as we for intelligence reports. Either that or our cavalry has pushed on farther in an attempt to find the Austrians.'

'Well, whatever the outcome, I need you to take some men, find out what is going on and report back. General Lannes is insistent that the enemy's whereabouts are known at all times. And, like you, I do not relish walking into an ambush.'

'Would you presume to find Austrian troops this far into the Alps?'

'It's possible. The thinking behind this manoeuvre was that no one would expect us to attack using these Alpine passes but, if the Austrians consider all our options, there is little else for us to do. The element of surprise may not be as great as General Bonaparte has assumed.'

'They cannot be words of doubt from such an enthusiastic Republican as yourself, surely, Lieutenant,' Lausard smiled. 'Have you cause to question your First Consul?'

'In case it had escaped your notice, my friend, he is *your* First Consul too.'

The smile did not leave Lausard's face. 'Are you still a Republican, Lieutenant?'

'It is in my blood, Sergeant, as cynicism is in yours.'

Lausard nodded, saluted and prepared to wheel his horse away.

'If you encounter the enemy, do not engage them,' Royere said. 'I want reports, not casualties.'

'Who says they would be *our* casualties, Lieutenant?'

The collection of buildings was so small that 'village' seemed rather too grand a title for it. Lausard surveyed the cluster from his horse, using the telescope. There was what looked like a large wooden barn and several other buildings, which Lausard could identify only as stables. All had flat roofs trimmed with thick slates, and the rain that had been threatening to fall for the past thirty minutes was now cascading from these roofs like miniature waterfalls. The sound of the falling rain was, as it had been for their entire journey down the mountain, accompanied by the ever-present roar of the Dora Baltea.

Lausard watched as Karim rode slowly back up towards the waiting dragoons, guiding his horse with effortless skill along the narrow pathway leading back from the buildings.

'There are lots of tracks,' the Circassian reported. 'Thirty or forty horses. Made no more than an hour ago.'

'We'll go down and check the buildings,' Lausard instructed.

'I hope there's food,' Joubert said hopefully.

'As long as there aren't any Austrians,' added Roussard.

Lausard raised a hand and motioned the small group of men forward. They urged their mounts towards the buildings, ears and eyes alert for the slightest sound or movement. As he rode, Lausard thought back to his conversation with Lieutenant Royere. Surely, this was too far for Austrian troops to venture. After all, according to the map he carried, there was still more than half a mile to travel before they reached the bottom of the Alps. Nevertheless, the hairs at the back of his neck prickled. Lausard sensed that there were troops nearby. He felt a hand tug at his sleeve and looked round to see Karim motioning towards the wet ground and the many hoof prints he had spoken of.

'They could be our own men,' Lausard said.

Karim nodded, but as he did so he pulled his razor-sharp sabre from its curved scabbard and rested it against his shoulder.

Sonnier slid his carbine from the boot on his saddle and checked that the pan was dry. He, like the other men, had wrapped wax cloth around the firing mechanism even before they began their ascent of the mountains and now he smiled as he saw that the precaution had been worthwhile. Satisfied, he slipped it back into position and waited.

Delacor slid one hand inside his cloak and allowed his fingers to brush against the handle of the axe jammed into his belt.

Lausard looked around, the rain dripping from the peak of his covered helmet. He held up two fingers for all his men to see then pointed at each of the flat-roofed wooden dwellings. The men understood. They split into pairs and immediately made for each appointed place.

The sergeant, accompanied by Karim, slipped from the saddle and headed towards the barn, the largest of the buildings. Karim held out an arm to restrain Lausard as they drew closer to the large double doors. There were more hoof prints in the mud but also the indentation of boots. Lausard pulled out two pistols and put his weight against the doors. Karim mirrored his actions, the sabre now across his chest. The sergeant nodded and pushed against the doors. They swung open and both men immediately sought the safety of the thick shadows.

'*Vive La République!*'

The shout came from the top storey of the barn and Lausard looked up to see a dark figure heading for the ladder there. He recognised the oil-skin-covered fur kolpack, the dark blue, fur-trimmed pelisse, with its intricate gold lacing, and the dark blue, leather-lined overalls, all worn over a pair of fine Hungarian-style boots. The man climbing down the ladder was a French hussar. He jumped the last three feet and turned to face the dragoons. Lausard saw the great long plaits of hair he sported; one alongside each ear and another at the back of his head. He also boasted a thick, bristling moustache that curled up proudly at the ends.

'Feraud,' the man announced. 'Captain, third hussars.'

Lausard saluted. 'Was it your unit that was sent out as reconnaissance this morning, Captain?' the sergeant enquired.

Feraud nodded and clicked his fingers. As he did, a magnificent black horse emerged from the shadows, concealed as if it had been a part of the darkness itself. It stepped into view, a graceful and lithe component of the umbra. Feraud patted its neck and planted a kiss on its muzzle.

'My horse injured itself on the rocks,' Feraud explained. 'I thought it had gone lame. I sent my men ahead while I tended to this fine creature.' He patted the horse once more.

'How long ago was that?' Lausard pressed.

'Less than an hour. What are you men doing here?'

'I fear we are on the same mission as you, Captain. To search for any signs of Austrian troops and report back as to their strength and dispositions.'

'Since when has that kind of work been the job of dragoons? Does General Lannes doubt the ability of my men?'

'There was some concern about the well-being of your unit, Captain. No one knew if the Austrians had penetrated up into these passes or not.'

'If they had I can assure you that myself and my men would have dealt with them quite easily.' Feraud glared at the sergeant and found his gaze held. 'You may return to your regiment and advise them that the task of reconnaissance is being more than adequately carried out, as usual, by light cavalry.'

'My orders are to investigate these passes, Captain,' Lausard insisted. 'That is what I intend to do.'

'I have already told you, there is no evidence of Austrian troops. Do you question my word?'

'No, Captain, I do not but I have been given orders and I intend to carry them out.'

Feraud took a step closer to the NCO.

Lausard didn't move.

Karim looked on silently.

'I am ordering you to return to your unit, Sergeant.'

'I've told you, Captain, I already *have* orders from one of my *own* officers. I will not return to my squadron until those orders are carried out.'

Feraud's right hand fell to the hilt of his sabre and the barn was filled with a loud metallic hiss as the blade was drawn and pushed towards Lausard's face, the tip inches from his nose.

But as Feraud stood gazing at the sergeant he heard an unmistakable sound. It was the click of a pistol hammer being drawn back. The officer looked down to see the weapon aimed at his stomach, gripped tightly in Lausard's fist.

'You dare threaten me, you insolent bastard!' Feraud snapped.

'It is no more of a threat than your sabre is to me, Captain, but have no doubt that I will use it to defend myself if you force me to.'

Both men stood motionless and defiant, then a smile creased the hussar's face and he swung the steel away, sliding the razor-sharp weapon back into its scabbard.

'Such impertinance. You should have been a hussar.' Feraud grinned.

Lausard gently eased the hammer of the pistol down and jammed it into his belt.

'Rider coming in!'

The shout from outside caused them both to turn and walk towards the doors of the barn. They saw a blue-uniformed hussar ride into the centre of the clutch of buildings, looking around him at the dragoons. The rider then spotted Feraud and rode towards him, bringing his horse to an abrupt halt. The animal skidded slightly on the wet ground, its breath clouding in the air. It was heavily lathered and Lausard guessed that it had been ridden at some speed for quite a distance.

'Any contact?' Feraud demanded.

The hussar shook his head. 'We found tracks in the foot-hills. It looks as if their cavalry patrols have been out. No sign of any men though.'

'Ride back, tell Sergeant Boulet to return and give me a full report,' the officer instructed, watching as the trooper saluted then tugged on his reins and galloped off in the direction he had come. Within a matter of moments he was enveloped by the rocks and trees once again, the sound of his horse's hooves gradually echoing away into silence.

'And what of your orders now, Sergeant?' Feraud looked at Lausard. 'Do you wish to follow my man? See with your own eyes what he has just told me?'

Lausard shook his head.

'Then leave. Tell your officer that there are no Austrians here. You will know soon enough when you meet them.' Feraud flicked at the plaits that hung from either side of his head. They looked like extensions of his kolpack, hanging like great furry brown tails.

The other dragoons formed up in a column behind Lausard, two abreast. They were watched by Feraud as they rode back up the slope.

'Who the hell was *he*?' Delacor asked.

'No one,' Lausard murmured, pushing his pistols back into the holsters on his saddle.

'He looked as if he had the right idea,' Rocheteau said. 'Staying there in the warm while his men ride ahead. Bastard officers.'

'What would you do in his place?' Lausard asked. 'Call it a privilege of rank.'

'But our officers wouldn't do that,' Bonet protested.

'All officers are different. All *men* are different. We might all be the same if we had the chance.'

'*Lieutenant* Rocheteau,' the corporal said grandly, a smile on his face. '*Captain* Rocheteau. *Colonel* Rocheteau. Perhaps even *General* Rocheteau. It has a ring to it, doesn't it?'

'Why stop there?' Lausard enquired. 'What about *First Consul* Rocheteau?'

The men laughed.

* * *

Napoleon Bonaparte sipped at his wine and stood with his back to the huge fire. Outside the Hospice of Saint Bernard the wind was whipping across the frozen landscape with increased ferocity, screaming around the buildings like some crazed demon.

The remains of a simple meal of bread, cheese and chicken stood on the table. Eugene de Beauharnais picked at the contents of his plate. He was wrapped in the dark blue cloak of a grenadier. Bonaparte stared off into the distance, his eyes lit only by the candles that burned on the table, and yet still they darted back and forth with each fresh thought. Eugene wondered if there was ever a waking moment when his stepfather was not immersed in frantic musings. Outside, the sound of troops moving past the hospice seemed to be made by invisible men; it was impossible to see them in the blackness.

The door opened and one of the monks entered, nodding a greeting at the First Consul, who was shaken from his pondering.

'I thank you again for your kindness,' Bonaparte said. 'Towards myself, my staff and my men. Rest assured, you will be handsomely rewarded for your services.'

'We are rewarded by God. We have no need of material gratitude.'

'I insist on paying you for the provisions you have distributed to my men. Unfortunately, our baggage train, which carries our gold, has yet to reach here. I trust you will accept a note of honour that may be redeemed? A promissory note signed in my name as First Consul of France.'

'Your generosity is gratefully accepted. Can I fetch you more food?'

Bonaparte watched fascinated as the holy man went about his business. 'Why do you serve us, Father?' he asked finally.

'We represent all that you find worst about mankind, all that your holy teachings deny. We are soldiers. Our business is war. Conquest. Subjugation if necessary. And, most of all, we bring death with us. It is against all the laws of your God and yet you still treat us with kindness. How can you reconcile that with your beliefs?'

'We do not have to agree with your values in order to offer our aid. We are here not to judge but to carry out God's will. We would help you if you were soldiers or woodcutters, hunters or traders. You are all God's children and we are here to help those who need us, regardless of their nature.'

'Does it concern you that so many of the young men you have helped these past few days will die in the coming weeks?'

'They go to God. If it is His will, then so be it. But I would be lying to you if I did not confess some regret at their passing.'

'I feel the same. I grieve for every son I lose,' Bonaparte said, his voice low.

'Then why fight?'

'There is no other way, Father. But I would not expect you to understand *that*.'

'Is life so meaningless to you that you can spend your days waging war? Watching men die?'

'It is precisely because life *means* so much to me that I do wage war,' snapped Bonaparte. 'The campaigns I fight have a purpose and every one of the men under my command would happily die in the service, and for the betterment of his country. You *have* no country. It is something else I would not expect you to understand.'

'I have God, that is all I need. When I stand before Him on Judgment Day, I can only pray that He forgives my small sins. I should pray for *you*. That He can forgive you for bringing the worst sin of all to His world. The sin of war.'

'I do not need you or any of those like you to pray for me. Destiny is in the hands of men, not God. I am following my own destiny and I will continue to do so, no matter what route it takes.'

The monk looked at Bonaparte, nodded and left the room.

'I appreciate their help,' Bonaparte said to his stepson, 'but I have no need of their piety.' He sipped at his wine.

Eugene sat quietly at the table, staring at the food on his plate, occasionally gazing into the leaping flames of the fire.

'Do you ever think about death?' he asked softly.

Bonaparte seemed taken aback by the question. 'There have been times during my life when I have faced death but I cannot ever remember contemplating my own mortality in the depths of the night, if that is what you mean. Why, does the thought trouble *you*, Eugene? Do you fear for your own safety in this coming campaign? You have never given me cause to think that you act with anything other than selfless courage. If I had an entire division like you, our troubles would be over very quickly.'

The younger man looked up at his stepfather.

Bonaparte crossed to him and placed a hand upon his shoulder.

'I suspect that the serenity of these surroundings and the sanctity of our hosts have caused you to become melancholy,' he said gently. 'You have nothing to fear from death. And these monks are more concerned about what happens *after* it. They long to meet their God. Why should *they* have any fear of death?'

'And when *we* meet Him, how will He judge us?'

'It will be a long time before either of us stands before God. But when I do, I will face Him as an equal.'

Eugene smiled. 'You think yourself a God now?' he remarked.

'Those who believe in God believe He has the power both to give and to take life, do they not? As the commander of an army, that is something I share with him. In this campaign, those who die may do so because of *my* commands. Not God's.' He sipped his wine and, like Eugene, gazed into the dancing flames of the fire.

Seventeen

'Austrians.'

Lausard lowered the telescope and handed it to Rocheteau, who peered through the glass at the troops deploying in and around the houses of the small town in the valley ahead. He watched for a moment longer then returned the telescope to Lausard, who trained it on the detachments of cavalry also swarming Aosta. He could pick out hussars in light blue and dark grey uniforms. There were mounted jagers in grey and even a handful of Polish lancers, the pennants on their fifteen-foot-long pikes fluttering in the breeze. Lausard counted fewer than two hundred mounted men; the bulk of the enemy force comprised infantry, as did the French force. As the dragoons sat on a slight rise overlooking the town, patiently awaiting orders, they could see several blue-clad demibrigades of infantry marching along the narrow road. The staccato rattle of drums rolled through the early morning air and sent a flock of birds flying high into the dull, cloud-choked sky. Lausard watched them disappear then returned his attention to the tableau unfolding before him.

'What cavalry they have are no more than scouts,' he

said, finally, handing the glass back to Rocheteau for the last time.

Bonet held out his hand for the telescope and the corporal handed it to him.

'There are some Hungarian troops down there with them,' said the former schoolmaster, as he scanned the enemy position. 'You can tell by the colour of their jacket facings.'

'Since when have you been an expert on enemy troops?' Delacor wanted to know.

'It pays to know your enemy,' Bonet murmured, looking around as he heard several horses galloping forward at speed. One of the riders was General Lannes; Bonet could see his gold-trimmed bicorn with its flowing white feather plume.

'He makes a good target for enemy muskets,' Rocheteau muttered, also spotting the general.

'Well, well,' Lausard muttered, watching a unit of blue-uniformed cavalry moving up alongside the French infantry. 'If it isn't our old friend, Captain Feraud.'

There was no mistaking the imposing figure who led the hussars, his huge moustache almost covering his face, his plaits bouncing as he rode. His magnificent black horse moved effortlessly over the rough terrain, looking as eager as its rider to get to grips with the Austrians.

Lausard knew how both man and horse felt. It was the moment he had been awaiting ever since they had left Paris. How long ago had that been? Weeks? Months? The long march to Dijon. The camps. Then the journey to Lausanne. More waiting. Finally, the terrible journey over the mountains. It had seemed like an eternity. But now, at last, it was over. He felt the hairs on his neck rise, not in fear but in anticipation. Around him, his colleagues looked on with feelings ranging from resignation to barely disguised fear. Not all shared his almost obsessive desire for combat. In fact, he doubted any of the other dragoons sought such murderous conflict with the same enthusiasm as he.

The men prepared themselves. All along the lines, horses pawed the ground. Some could barely contain themselves and it took all the skill of their riders to keep them under control.

Lausard watched Captain Milliere and Lieutenant Royere riding slowly back and forth in front of the waiting dragoons, their telescopes trained on the infantry now fast approaching the outskirts of Aosta.

Lausard's musings were interrupted by the sudden eruption of gunfire. The waiting Austrian infantry had fired a volley and, through the clouds of reeking smoke, the sergeant watched as they reloaded and prepared to fire again. But the next salvo came from the French who, having fired, increased the pace of their march. Another twenty yards and they halted again and, with incredible precision, poured more fire into the waiting Austrians. Like components in a well-oiled machine, the blue-clad troops continued to advance and fire. Advance and fire, each movement taking them closer to their objective. They seemed unworried by the volleys fired by the Austrians and unfazed by the blue-clad bodies that littered the slope leading towards the town, and advanced with the same robotic motion. Lausard could see their standards waving in the wind, and hear their wild shouts of '*Vive Bonaparte!*' The sound seemed to swell and rise on the wind until it filled the valley, only to be eclipsed seconds later by another explosion of musket fire. Dozens more men crashed to the ground but those who followed stepped over the bodies of their fallen comrades and continued on towards the waiting Austrians. After only four or five volleys, the valley was filled with choking, sulphurous smoke, banks of it driven by the strong breeze. Every now and then, a blinding eruption of muzzle flashes would illuminate the demibrigades who were now within striking distance of the waiting Austrians. More gunfire. More men fell to the ground but the French were carried on by their impetus and Lausard watched as they crashed into the first ranks of white-coated troops like some kind of unstoppable blue tide.

Some of the Austrians broke immediately but the majority held their ground and, through the drifting smoke, Lausard could see that the fighting had degenerated into hand-to-hand combat. Bayonets, musket stocks, knives, swords and even bare hands were used as the two sets of infantry locked together. Some of the French infantry forced their way through and the fighting spilled over into the streets of Aosta itself.

Lausard felt a hand on his sleeve and turned to see Rocheteau pointing towards a battery of Austrian horse artillery, which was thundering into position to the right of the French infantry. The brown-jacketed gunners were either riding the gun-team horses or clinging to the cannon trails as the three-pounders bumped over the uneven ground. Lausard watched as the first of the units came to a halt, the men leaping from their positions to unlimber the piece. The crew went to work. He watched as the first man mopped out the barrel then rammed home a canister placed at the mouth of the cannon by a second man. A third rapidly set the fuse in the touchhole and lit it. The entire movement was completed with breathtaking efficiency. They were so close to the French infantry that there was no need to aim the cannon. Seconds later, the barrel flamed and the three-pounder spewed out its deadly load of thirty lead balls, each weighing an ounce and a half. The discharge tore into the French infantry and scythed them down. While the first crew reloaded, their companions were preparing to add their own fire to the savage blasts now ripping into the demibrigades.

'Damned sausage batteries,' snarled Rocheteau, glaring at the blazing cannon. 'Where the hell is *our* artillery?'

Lausard said nothing, watching as more of the French infantry were mown down by the lethal fire of the battery. A dozen of the troopers tried to charge the three-pounders but a devastating salvo merely blew them away like wind scattering leaves. When the dense smoke rolled aside, the ground in front of the barrels was strewn with bloodied rags, all that remained of the infantry. From such close range, the effects of canister were horrifying. And Lausard could see that, in the areas close to the guns, the French advance had faltered slightly. But still the Austrian gunners continued to pour fire into their enemy's ranks.

'Horseman,' murmured Rocheteau glancing across towards General Lannes. From the high ridge occupied by the general and his staff, an aide-de-camp was galloping down the slope. He held something in his right hand and, as he rode across the front of the watching dragoons, they realised what it was. The ADC guided his mount towards Captain Milliere, who took the orders from him and scanned them. Lausard watched as the ADC gesticulated towards Aosta, waited a moment then wheeled his horse and galloped back towards Lannes. It was the turn of Captain Milliere and Lieutenant Royere to send their horses trotting back and forth before the ranks of cavalrymen and, as the order was given to draw swords, the air was filled with the familiar metallic hiss of over one thousand blades being pulled from their scabbards.

Gaston and the other trumpeters spurred forward, sounding the familiar notes of the advance. The sound seemed to fill the air, rising high into the cloudy sky, to be eclipsed a moment later by the jangling of harnesses and the steady rumble of thousands of hooves. The dragoons moved forward. First at a walk, then at a trot, the ground beneath them shuddering.

Lausard gripped the hilt of his sword more tightly and glanced around at his companions. Most had their eyes trained directly ahead, towards Aosta. He saw Moreau cross himself. Some of the men were sweating, as were the horses. Lausard detected odours he had grown accustomed to during the past few years: the smell of human and animal sweat; horse droppings; damp leather and oiled steel; and, through it all, the smell of trampled earth and grass. Every sense was sharpened. He could see colours more clearly, even pick out the features of some of the gunners as the dragoons drew nearer. They had spotted the oncoming cavalrymen by now and two of the cannons were being resighted to meet their attack.

There were now less than two thousand yards between the horsemen and their quarry. The sound of every single bridle seemed to ring in Lausard's ears, along with the beating of his own heart and the panting of riders and their mounts. It was said that men are never so alive as when courting death, and Lausard truly believed that. His wits were sharper and the adrenalin surging through his veins made his eyes feel as if they were bulging in their sockets. He saw a small detachment of cavalry, comprising hussars and a handful of lancers, forming up close to the Austrian guns. The pennants on those lances fluttered challengingly.

There was a deafening roar and two of the three-pounders opened fire. Lausard gripped his reins and saw one of the roundshot thud into the ground about twenty yards further ahead. The second struck a tree stump and split it in two before rolling harmlessly into a dried-up stream. The dragoons continued to advance, as the Austrian gunners expertly reloaded. Lausard saw the corporals of both cannon sighting the guns for the next salvo. At the same time, Milliere raised his sword and orders filled the air as the dragoons broke into a canter.

The second burst of fire was more successful.

The first roundshot ploughed into one end of the dragoons' leading rank, the solid lead ball scything effortlessly through men and horses. Men were blasted from their saddles, horses maimed or killed, while those nearby were sprayed with human and animal blood. Screams of agony ripped through the air. The second shot tore away part of Lausard's shabraque then caught a man in the rank behind him, killing him instantly and ripping into the troops behind, smashing the front legs of two horses and tearing off the arm of another trooper. The severed limb, still clutching the sword, spun into the air, spurting blood from the stump.

Captain Milliere bellowed for the dragoons to charge and the trumpeters blasted out the notes as the horsemen leaned forward over the necks of their mounts to protect themselves from the musket fire that was now beginning to pepper them from Austrian infantry to their right. The rumble of churning hooves filled the air and every other sound was drowned out as they hurtled forward like one vast unstoppable mass.

Lausard wondered if the Austrian gunners would have time to get off one last murderous salvo of canister before the dragoons reached them. He could see them frantically swabbing out their barrels and trying to ram home the new charges. But it was too late.

The dragoons smashed into the men as they tried to run for shelter. Lausard caught one of the gunners with a devastating backhand swipe and laid open his neck to the spinal cord. Other gunners were simply ridden over by the French cavalry. Lieutenant Royere directed his horse straight at the gunner with the ramrod, parried the man's desperate swipe and cut him downwards across the face, finishing him with a thrust that tore through his chest. All around, men were slashing madly at the gunners. Lausard rode on and cut the traces of the limbers to ensure that the cannon couldn't be hauled away later. One of the gunners, desperate to protect his team, pulled a pistol from his belt and fired at the sergeant. The ball cut a path through the skin on Lausard's left cheek and nicked his ear. He felt blood spilling down his face but he ignored it, thankful that the shot hadn't been an inch to the other side. He brought his sword down with tremendous power and severed the gunner's hand, striking again at his face and shattering his bottom jaw. Lausard wiped some of the blood from his own wound and spun round to see that the Austrian cavalry had now come hurtling down a small incline and were actually amongst the dragoons.

He saw a lancer drive his deadly spear into the chest of a dragoon but the metal tip of the lance jammed between the Frenchman's ribs and, as he fell screaming from his horse, the shaft was wrenched from the lancer's grip. Momentarily unarmed, the lancer reached for his sword but couldn't pull it clear of its scabbard in time. Rocheteau caught him across the eyes with a savage cut that blinded him and sent him cartwheeling backwards out of his saddle. Meanwhile, Karim deflected another lance thrust, knocking the spear aside then striking with his sabre. The sharp steel sliced effortlessly through the Austrian's neck and severed his head. The terrified horse bolted and the headless body, still upright in the saddle, was carried away, blood spouting from the stump of the neck.

Joubert found himself confronted by two Austrian hussars, one of whom fired at him with his carbine. The ball hit Joubert's horse in the neck and the animal reared, hurling the dragoon to the floor. He rolled over to avoid the dying animal as it fell, aware of other hooves slamming into the ground around his head. He pulled himself into a foetal position, grunting in pain as a horse brought its hind leg down on to his ribs, cracking two bones and tearing the wind from him. Tigana slammed the pommel of his sword into the face of the first hussar and pulled the man from the saddle. He parried a sabre stroke from the second Austrian but the blades of the two soldiers slipped apart and a quick movement from his opponent caught him unaware. The sabre cut easily into his forearm and he almost dropped his sword. The hussar struck again but Tigana blocked the stroke, pulled one of his pistols free and pressed it against the man's face, firing as he did so. There was a loud bang and a cloud of smoke and the Austrian fell from the saddle, a hole the size of a man's fist in his temple. Tigana, his arm bleeding badly, caught the reins of the horse and urged Joubert to clamber up into the saddle.

All around Lausard men fought on, some from the saddle, some on foot. Others, their mounts killed, ran about looking for fresh horses, not caring which side they were from.

Charvet slammed a powerful fist into the face of a hussar, and satisfied that the man was too dazed to defend himself, he drove his sword into the Austrian's stomach, watching as he slumped forward in the saddle.

Roussard shouted in surprise as his horse was stabbed in the side by a lance thrust, the animal whinnying in pain as it toppled over. Roussard realised with horror that his leg had caught in the stirrup and as the horse crashed down, he took the full weight on his leg. Pain enveloped the limb from ankle to hip. His dead horse kept him pinned to the ground and he could only look on helplessly as the lancer readjusted the pike in his hand and prepared to skewer him. However,

Bonet rode his mount into the lancer, cut through the shaft with one blow of his sword, then caught the Austrian with a ferocious backhand swipe that ripped open his throat and sent him reeling from the saddle. Bonet jumped down and tried to pull his companion free of the dead weight that trapped him, but the horse was too heavy. He shouted to Tabor, who also dismounted, and the two other dragoons watched as the big man gritted his teeth and lifted the carcass enough to enable Bonet to pull Roussard free.

'Can you stand?' Bonet asked, forced to raise his voice to make himself heard above the screams, curses and shouts of combat that surrounded them. Steel sang against steel and the sound of carbine and pistol fire added its own punctuation. He supported Roussard, who nodded none too convincingly and allowed himself to be helped to a riderless horse. Tabor practically lifted him into the saddle and both he and Bonet could see that Roussard's breeches had been torn in several places, his boots, like his tunic, spattered with mud. He sat uneasily in the saddle, his face pale. He had one foot in a stirrup, the other leg dangled uselessly on the opposite side of the saddle. If it was broken, they all knew the fate that awaited Roussard.

'They're running. Second squadron with me.'

The shout came from Captain Milliere and the dragoons saw that, indeed, the Austrian cavalry was wheeling away. Led by Milliere, the second squadron of dragoons thundered off in pursuit of the defeated enemy horsemen.

Lausard, his face still spattered with blood, ran his sword into the back of a fleeing hussar, wrenching the blade free as the man fell. He looked around and saw that Rocheteau and Delacor were already rummaging through the discarded equipment of two dead Austrian officers. Gaston had removed his helmet and was mopping sweat from his head and face.

He also wiped blood from a bullet hole in his hand, scrubbing away black powder. The bullet had passed through the fleshy part of his thumb but other than that he seemed unharmed. Moreau sat motionless in his saddle, his breathing coming in gasps, his bloodied sword still gripped in his fist. He had a wound to the left side of his neck. Part of his collar was hanging free, soaked in blood like one part of his tunic but the wound didn't appear to be too deep.

Karim was tending to a horse that had suffered a bad sword cut across its rump. The Circassian seemed more concerned with the suffering of the animal than with that of his companions. He looked over at Lausard and nodded. The sergeant raised a hand in acknowledgement. Then he looked up to see that General Lannes and his staff had left the rise where they had been positioned and were moving forward towards Aosta. The entire valley was shrouded in smoke and the crackle of musket fire still sounded intermittently. Lausard, breathing heavily, led his horse in the direction of the town and saw that the Austrians were falling back, pursued by the French demibrigades. On the ground leading to the town and in the streets themselves bodies lay where they had fallen, dead and wounded together. Those who could crawled about in search of water. The less fortunate waited for assistance which, in many cases, never came. He looked down at one of the prostrate French infantrymen. The youth was in his teens, his skin so smooth it had obviously never felt a razor. His eyes were still open and staring sightlessly at the sky.

'I wonder if he had a family?'

Lausard turned and he saw Lieutenant Royere walking his horse towards him.

'I wonder how many mothers have lost sons, how many wives have lost husbands today?' the officer continued.

'Your compassion is showing, Lieutenant. He died for your First Consul. Aren't you proud of him for that?'

'Even if the cause is a just one I take no pleasure in seeing so many corpses.'

'Nor I, but rest assured, Lieutenant, you will see many more before this campaign is over. Sons. Husbands. Brothers. Perhaps even generals.' He wheeled his horse and rode away, swallowed up by the choking banks of smoke.

Night brought with it intermittent showers of freezing rain that were unusual in northern Italy in the spring months. Lausard looked up accusingly at the sky as he sat huddled in his cape close to the smoky fire. The pieces of wood that the other dragoons had gathered sputtered noisily and gave off little light or heat. They did, however, belch forth grey smoke, which stung the men's eyes and made them cough. Some tried to sleep, wrapped in their cloaks and blankets on the damp ground. But all, except Joubert it seemed, were destined to suffer the curse of wakefulness. As usual, the big man was snoring loudly and Lausard marvelled as ever at his ability to sleep no matter where. For his own part, Lausard neither welcomed nor needed sleep. With it came the dreams he so dreaded, dreams of his murdered family. He had no use for such torment. To augment this, the day's fighting had left adrenalin surging through his veins so that he doubted he would have succumbed to sleep even if he'd been given a draught. He gently touched the wound on his cheek, as if to remind himself of the combat, and he looked around at those of his men who had suffered injuries.

For the most part, they had been lucky. The wounds suffered by Tigana, Gaston and Moreau had been hastily cleaned and bandaged. They had even been given a mouthful of brandy to ease their pain. That same brandy had been mixed with sugar and used to disinfect the wounds, since in the field hygiene was difficult at the best of times and as many men died of blood poisoning and infection as from bullets or bayonet thrusts. The severely wounded had been transported back five miles to a temporary field hospital, but Lausard didn't expect many to survive the journey, let alone the rudimentary treatment they would receive once they arrived.

Joubert's broken rib didn't appear to be causing him much concern, certainly not, Lausard reasoned, from the way he was snoring. The big man's bulk had saved him from worse injury. The luckiest of all those who had been injured during the day's fighting was Roussard. If his leg had been broken, as they had all suspected, it would most definitely have been amputation. But the trooper had been lucky enough to escape with severe bruising. Even now, he sat close to the fire massaging his thigh and knee, occasionally groaning with the discomfort. Charvet, who was puffing contentedly on a pipe he'd taken from a dead Austrian hussar, patted Roussard on the shoulder, and offered him a draw from the pipe.

'Why are we sitting around here?' Delacor demanded, his tone as always aggressive. 'We've beaten the Austrians. We should press on.'

'Why are you so eager to pursue them?' Sonnier enquired. 'I'm happy to wait until they order us to move on again. The longer we are here the less chance we have of getting killed.'

'Why *are* we sitting on our backsides getting soaked, Alain, when we could be chasing the enemy?' Rocheteau echoed Delacor, pulling the collar of his cloak more tightly around him.

'We have to wait for reinforcements. Chabran's division

is still making its way over the Little Saint Bernard Pass. Lannes clearly has orders not to advance too far without support. What happened here today was only a skirmish. If we chase the Austrians we might end up outrunning our own support. They could cut us off.'

'I agree.' Bonet nodded. 'Caution is called for in situations like this.'

'Since when did *you* become a tactical genius, schoolmaster?' Delacor sneered.

'History teaches us this principle. You only have to look at the campaigns of Caesar, Hannibal or Alexander to realise—'

Delacor raised a hand to cut Bonet short. 'We are not your pupils.'

Lausard could see Gaston pulling at the bloodied bandage that had been wrapped tightly around his hand. The young lad was inspecting the crimson stain that covered the gauze, occasionally wincing as he flexed his fingers.

'Your first wound?' Lausard asked.

Gaston nodded.

'You were lucky you didn't lose the whole hand,' the sergeant told him. 'Or at least a finger or two.'

'With the doctors we have, he's lucky he didn't lose his *arm*,' chuckled Rocheteau. 'They would amputate a man's head to cure him of lice.'

The men around the fire laughed. Even Lausard managed a smile. As he did he brushed his cheek again; another scar to add to the rest. But the deepest were unseen, gouged across his very soul. Again he looked up at the weeping sky, the rain dripping from the peak of his oil-skin-covered helmet. He sat a moment longer then got to his feet, his green cloak billowing in the wind.

'Get some sleep while you can,' he told those closest to

him. 'Once we start moving, it may be some time before any of us get a rest again.'

'What about you, Alain?' Rocheteau called after his companion. 'When will you rest?'

'Plenty of time to rest in the grave, Rocheteau!' Lausard moved slowly among the other troops camped beyond Aosta. The higher ranking officers, including General Lannes, were billeted in houses within the town, but the remainder of the advance guard were, like Lausard and his dragoons, forced to brave the elements. He passed lines of horses, draped in blankets to protect them from the cold and rain. Those badly wounded had already been destroyed and their carcasses used as meat.

Lausard passed dozens of campfires, all with men crouched around them. Infantrymen, artillery gunners and cavalry troopers crammed together. Some of the artillery gunners were taking advantage of their equipment to try to escape the worst of the weather. They lay beneath ammunition caissons, grateful for even the slightest shelter. A group of artillerymen was struggling to replace a damaged wheel on a four-pounder, the hammering causing some shouts of anger from those nearby trying to sleep. Lausard walked on, heading for a slight rise dotted with trees. The lower branches had been pulled from them to make campfires and, standing near the top of the ridge, Lausard looked back over the enormous French bivouac to see it shrouded in smoke as surely as the battelfield had been that day.

'There's nothing like bad weather to bring out the grumbler in us all, is there?'

The voice startled Lausard and he turned to see its source.

He recognised the man who stood before him immediately. The dark blue uniform swathed in a cloak of the same colour. The brown fur kolpack protected by oil-skin, and the huge moustache, looking somewhat bedraggled in the dreadful conditions. Captain Feraud of the third hussars nodded what passed for a greeting.

'Sergeant Lausard, is it not? I trust you are well. I saw your squadron in action this afternoon. They fought well.'

'I'm glad they met with your approval, Captain,' Lausard mused, a slight edge to his tone. 'I expected you and your men to be scouting ahead of us tonight. That is the duty of light cavalry, isn't it?'

'Not at night, Sergeant. You should know that. Horses stampede more easily in darkness. The infantry act as outposts at night. Besides, the enemy will take little finding now. They have only one road to retreat along.'

'They will not retreat forever. What happened today was inconsequential compared to the battles we will face when they confront us in any number.'

'Do you doubt our ability to defeat them, Sergeant?'

'I believe that our army could defeat anything put against it. We defeated the Austrians before; there is no reason why we should not do so again.'

'Your self belief is admirable, Sergeant. Let us hope it is not misplaced.'

'I have no reservations about my own abilities, Captain. *Or* those of the men who fight alongside me.'

'Are the fighting abilities of rapists, horse thieves, murderers, forgers and common criminals more worthy than those of ordinary soldiers?'

Lausard looked at Feraud through narrowed eyes.

'It is the business of a hussar to gather information, Sergeant,' the light cavalry officer told him. 'I know about you and your companions.'

'From who did you gather your information, Captain?'

'Does it matter?'

'Then why the interest in myself and those like me? It has no relevance to our abilities as soldiers. It is true that I and a number of other men in the first squadron were prisoners. But it was the Directory who freed us to help save France from circumstances *it* had created. That is how inept those lawyers were. They were forced to clean out the prisons of Paris, forced to call upon the services of men they themselves had condemned. We would have been as well riding into the Tuileries and putting those bastards to the sword.'

'Do I gather then that you were happy to see them fall? Men who saved your life?'

'I never asked them to,' Lausard retorted. 'My life was saved because they needed men and they gave no thought to where those men came from. They needed soldiers and that is what they got. Criminals to protect criminals. Do you not find the irony amusing, Captain?'

'And you and your men are still criminals. How can you be trusted?'

'Since I put on the uniform of a dragoon I have obeyed every order, no matter how idiotic. Those around me have also showed their worth. In Italy four years ago. In Egypt, and now here again. They have nothing to prove, Captain. A man should be judged on what he *is*, not what he *was*.'

A sneer flickered on Feraud's lips. 'So your allegiance is to our First Consul?'

'And yours, Captain? Where is yours?'

'Are you questioning my loyalty to General Bonaparte?'

'No more than you question mine. You know about *my* past, Captain. Is there something I should know about *yours*? You are quick to condemn me and those like me.'

'You and most of the first squadron are criminals,' Feraud insisted. 'Do you deny that?'

'And your men, Captain? Are they saints? Have they never

robbed or killed or cheated? Have you never taken food from dead enemy soldiers? Never used the horse of an enemy cavalryman when your own was killed or wounded?' He regarded the officer sternly. 'This entire army is composed of thieves and killers. Do not preach to me about the supposed inadequacies of myself or my companions. We are one unit among fifty *thousand* criminals.'

'I could have you shot for sedition.'

'I speak nothing but the truth, Captain. But if you wish to have me shot then proceed. If not, I will return to my unit.'

Again the two men locked stares.

'You show a lack of respect I would associate with one of your kind,' Feraud managed finally.

'My kind, Captain? What *kind* of man do you think me to be?'

'You are of the gutter. Born there and raised there. It is where you belong. You and those like you.'

Lausard smiled. 'You shouldn't always judge a man by his appearance, Captain,' he said, as he turned away from the officer. 'We both wear uniforms and we both obey orders. There may be fewer differences between you and me than you may think.'

'We have nothing in common, Lausard, other than we both fight for France.'

'That much *is* true, Captain,' the sergeant said without looking back.

Lausard headed back down the slope to his own unit. Once again he moved among the scores of campfires, the acrid smoke swallowing him as surely as the darkness. Had he turned, he would have seen that the hussar was still watching him. Standing motionless in the rain that continued to pour down.

Eighteen

The two shell bursts came simultaneously. The thunderous aerial blasts seemed to tear the very clouds apart and portions of the sky flared brilliant red and white. Lausard chanced a quick look up then ducked low, pieces of hot metal slamming into the ground close to him. One lump, the size of a man's fist, blasted off part of the rock he was crouched behind. Another, slightly smaller, caught a man close to him in the back, shattering his spine and rendering him helpless and shrieking on the wet earth. The sergeant looked across as the wounded man was dragged away, his screams soon eclipsed by a fresh salvo of artillery fire. More of the explosive shells came hurtling out of the sky, some exploding in mid-air, others erupting as they struck the ground.

'Howitzers,' Rocheteau snarled through gritted teeth. 'Bastards.' He was looking towards a massive stone structure that looked as if it had been hewn from the very mountainside. The monolith appeared impregnable and, for all he knew, probably was.

The Fort of Bard stood astride the single road that led down into the valley at the bottom of the mountain, surrounded on three sides by precipitous rocks that afforded it the kind of natural protection no engineer could ever have created. The village beneath it had been cleared of Austrian troops but those who had not fled had sought refuge inside the fort and they poured out their own fire at the attacking French troops, who had already assaulted the bastion more times than they cared to remember. Dozens of blue-clothed bodies were scattered over the approaches to the fort. Lausard and his men had fought on foot during the engagement, the terrain around the fort making it impossible for cavalry to function effectively. Now he sat with his back against a boulder looking towards the fort, watching as each fresh cloud of smoke from the embrasures signalled another howitzer shell or burst of canister fire from the cannon within. Sometimes he would count the seconds from the initial bang to the explosion as the ten-pounder howitzers lobbed out their deadly 824-pound loads with clockwork precision.

'How many of the bastards are in there?' Delacor ducked low as another aerial blast sprayed steel splinters over the sheltering troops.

'According to intelligence reports there are four hundred grenadiers of the Kinsky regiment,' Lausard murmured, 'and twenty-six cannon of various sizes.' He ducked as another shower of deadly metal came hurtling out of the sky.

'Including those stinking howitzers,' Rocheteau hissed. 'How the hell are we supposed to get past that?' He indicated the fort. 'We'll still be sitting here when the rest of the army comes over the pass.'

Even as he spoke a battery of horse artillery galloped past, their four-pounders bouncing around at the back of the limbers. Lausard and the others watched as the gunners quickly unlimbered the pieces and dragged them into position directly opposite the gate of the fort. Moving with incredible speed and precision, the men swabbed the barrel, loaded it with double shot and lit their fuses. The roar of the French cannon joined that of the Austrian bombardment and the sound was deafening, amplified as it was by the towering rocks all around.

With the sound still ringing in their ears, the gunners prepared to fire again. Infantrymen, sheltering as best they could, added their musket fire to the cannon blasts, but it was hopelessly ineffective and Lausard saw a number of NCOs giving the order to cease fire. The area around the fort was a sea of noxious fumes and it was practically impossible to see the cannon until they were illuminated by their muzzle flashes.

Lausard could taste gunpowder. He spat and watched the French gunners manoeuvring their pieces back into position after each shot; the recoil from the guns sent them hurtling backwards anything up to eight feet. As he observed the artillery duel, he scanned the area around the fort. A narrow road led past the fort through some jagged rocks and beyond to the gentler slopes of the foothills. But this road was right beneath the fort. Anything trying to pass would be an easy target. He glanced around and saw General Lannes standing in the mouth of a cave towards the rear of the French position, tapping a map agitatedly and occasionally shaking a fist at the defiant bastion. Lannes knew the importance of advancing quickly, of not being delayed by this apparently insurmountable obstacle. The general took off his bicorn and wiped his forehead with the back of his hand, watching as the French guns opened up again.

The first gun was reloading when it was hit by a howitzer shell.

The deadly projectile exploded almost as it struck the barrel. The blast was devastating. The two-pound charge inside the shell, coupled with the one and a half pounds of black powder inside the four-pounder barrel combined to create a monstrous eruption. The men standing close to the gun were blasted off their feet, their bodies thrown through the air, limbs torn off by the ferocity of the blast. The four-pounder barrel simply split in two, the brass mingling with the lethal shrapnel from the shell to create more devastation. More men were scythed down by flying metal and wood. An artillery corporal was decapitated by part of the metal-braced rim of one wheel, while a colleague of his was sliced in two by a huge lump of metal. Lausard covered his face with his upraised arm as a huge cloud of smoke billowed across the ground and enveloped the men. Immediately, more howitzer shells began to rain down, the sky now one enormous tapestry of detonations and smoke. Charvet hissed in pain as a needle-like piece of steel tore through the lobe of his right ear.

The remaining artillerymen in the battery hurriedly attached their guns to the limbers and, desperate to escape the fate of their companions, sped away from the ground in front of the fort. Wounded men tried to seek refuge behind the bodies of dead horses but with the constant hail of shot and shell they stood little chance. Corpses, both human and animal, already shredded by the withering artillery fire, were torn further with each fresh blast. The ground leading up to the fort was covered in blood, mingling with the mud.

To his right, high above, Lausard heard more cannon fire and glanced up to see that two French eight pounders had somehow been placed upon a flat rock above the fort itself. As he watched they poured round after round of canister into the bastion and after a few moments the Austrian barrage began to slacken.

The sergeant saw Lieutenant Royere scuttling towards

him, a wound on his right arm. His tunic had been torn by a piece of metal and that same missile had gashed his flesh, but he seemed oblivious to the blood seeping from the laceration. He kept low and finally slid across the slippery ground, catching his breath.

'How did they get those guns up there?' Lausard asked.

'The engineers set up some kind of winch,' Royere explained. 'The carriages were disassembled, hoisted up there then put back together again. They've been told to keep the Austrian gunners pinned down.'

'We can't pass the fort, can we, Lieutenant?'

'General Lannes thinks that the infantry can get through when night falls. That path is wide enough for men but not guns or horses. Not moving in any great numbers.'

'There has to be a way. What are we meant to do? Wait here until the Austrians starve to death or run out of ammunition?'

'As I said, it may be possible to get cannon through, and horses too if they were led. But it would be hazardous. I suspect General Lannes may try to gather enough artillery around the fort to simply blow it to pieces.'

'And how long will that take? The fort is part of the mountain,' Lausard hissed. 'The artillery could fire at it twenty-four hours a day for a month and not destroy it. If the infantry manage to pass through then they will be without guns *or* cavalry support. The Austrians will destroy them. Eventually they will begin to advance up the passes themselves. We will be trapped.'

'That is why the general knows he must get at least half a dozen artillery pieces through. It would make all the difference to the success or failure of the infantry who advance into Piedmont. He could then leave the remainder of the guns here to reduce the fort. But some cannon *must* be taken through.'

'Using *that* pathway, beneath the very noses of the Austrians! And how does he propose to do that, Lieutenant?'

'One of the artillery officers has an idea,' Royere said. 'If it works then General Lannes will have his guns.'

'And if it fails?' Lausard's words hung in the smoky air. 'Do we choose where we die? Beneath the Austrian guns or hemmed in against the rocks when their armies advance from the passes below?'

'There is a chance, Sergeant, that this idea will work but it will take men like yourself to ensure its success. Six guns and one squadron of cavalry is what General Lannes requests as support to the infantry who will pass beneath the fort tonight.'

'And cling like goats to the side of Mount Albaredo?' Lausard snapped.

'There is no other way, Sergeant.'

Lausard ducked as another howitzer shell exploded high above them.

'So tell me, Lieutenant,' he said, looking the officer squarely in the eyes. 'What *is* this idea?'

'Is this what they have reduced us to?' grunted Roussard, trying to hold his breath while he worked. 'I thought we were supposed to be soldiers. They have turned us into farmers.'

'Just shut up and keep working,' Rocheteau snapped.

'Yes, besides, what is wrong with being a farmer?' Rostov demanded.

'Indeed,' Tigana echoed. 'Farmers are honest and hard-working. I was proud to have worked the land.'

'My father had a farm and his father before him,' Tabor joined in. 'I was to have taken control of it too when the time was right.'

'You couldn't tell a pig from a goat, you half-wit,' Delacor rasped through the piece of material he had tied around his nose and mouth in an effort to lessen the foul stench that filled the air.

Lausard stood watching his men for a moment, then he continued with the work. He dug his gloved hand deep into the pile of horse droppings and then smeared the reeking brown matter on to the steel-braced wheel of the four-pounder. Tons of excrement had been gathered by artillery-men and engineers, some of it mixed with straw. The men were now up to their ankles in it. Elsewhere, other men were busy covering the hooves of their horses with the mixture. Cavalry horses and those from the artillery train were receiving the same treatement. The artillery were performing the same task on a couple of howitzers and eight-pounders. In the pitch black streets of the village, others were spreading more dung and straw along the narrow thoroughfares, pausing every now and then to look up at the towering edifice of the Fort of Bard, now silent in the impenetrable night. Lausard couldn't even see lights inside the bastion. He and his colleagues worked in almost total darkness, the only respite from the cloying umbra provided by a crescent moon that periodically forced its way out from behind the dense clouds. But light was the last thing the French wanted. If this hazardous manoeuvre was to be completed successfully, they needed the night as surely as they needed silence.

'We'll never get through,' said Delacor, continuing to smear droppings on the wheel. 'They'll hear us and open fire.'

'Not if you and everyone else keeps their mouth shut,' Lausard berated him.

'But what about their sentries?' Sonnier protested.

'They are secure inside their fortress,' Lausard reminded

him. 'They will not post sentries outside. They have no reason to.'

'I wish I shared your optimism, Alain,' Bonet said, kneeling beside his horse to check that its hooves were smothered sufficiently with dung. He looked towards the road that led through the village, covered as it was by the reeking carpet of dung and straw.

'Cover your boots too,' Lausard told those within earshot. 'Use this stuff or wrap them in rags. Anything to deaden the sound. And make sure any loose equipment like swords or carbines are well secured to your saddles. And remember, silence is to be strictly maintained at all times. Unless you want an Austrian bullet in you. And if I find any man breaking that silence, I will personally cut his throat. Clear?'

The men did as they were instructed, standing with their mounts, holding the reins, waiting for the order to move. Ahead an artillery caisson, four of its crew seated on it, was also waiting to begin the perilous journey beneath the walls of the fort itself. Then came the guns, their crews all trying to remain calm, to drive from their minds the reality of just how close the enemy was.

Lausard patted the neck of his horse then led the animal slowly along the road, surprised at how effectively the carpet of droppings muffled the sound. At the head of the small column, Karim, Lieutenant Royere and Captain Milliere already waited. The officers nodded a greeting and Milliere raised a hand in the darkness to signal the advance. He checked his pocket watch and saw that it was one minute after midnight. The leading troops moved off. The column advanced with excruciating but necessary slowness, the wheels turning easily on the dung, the sound of their metal rims muffled. Troopers walked with their mounts, leading them by the bits not the reins, anxious to keep the animals calm.

Lausard looked up and saw the Fort of Bard towering above them. As yet, it was silent. He could hear a steady thud and knew it was his own heart banging hard against his ribs. His pulse, he knew, was not the only one that quickened as the column moved inexorably along the pathway, beneath the fort and on towards the defile in the rocks that would lead them to a more easily negotiated and less dangerous route.

Gunners scurried ahead like worker ants, scattering more straw and dung along the route, anxious that no sound should be detected. The remainder of the column pressed on, ears alert for the slightest sound from above or from the rocks that hemmed them in on all sides. One of the horses pulling the caisson snorted loudly and its rider hastily rubbed its neck to calm it, desperate to ensure its nervousness did not communicate itself to the other animals harnessed to it, or indeed to the dozens in front and behind it.

The dragoons moved slowly but assuredly in the darkness, their breath frosting in the air. Moreau crossed himself and wondered if their collective exhalations might form some kind of warning cloud to the Austrians. A number were wearing rags wrapped around their noses and mouths, both to protect them from the cold and to spare them the foul stench of the droppings. But, Moreau reasoned, the smell was the least of their problems.

Karim had moved slightly ahead of the column, his horse treading lightly, his eyes scanning the narrow pathway. As the men passed beneath the fort, the defile was scarcely wide enough to allow the passage of the caisson; but the gunners led their team on, the wheels slipping slightly on the muck.

Lausard was the first to hear the shriek of metal on metal and he spun round, squinting in the gloom to find the source of the noise. Several artillerymen were gathered around one of the eight-pounders, two of them slapping grease on to the axle close to the off-side wheel. The squeaking continued for interminable seconds, amplified by the walls of bare rock, then it died away. The column moved on, with many anxious eyes turned in the direction of the fort now directly above them, but there was neither sound nor movement from within its walls. The sergeant wondered if the silence was a ruse. Were the Austrians actually aware of the French advance? Were they even now waiting further down the defile with cannon, ready to open fire on the artillery and dragoons? Common sense told him that wasn't the case. The infantry had already passed down that same route earlier. Any Austrians who had originally been in the village of Bard were either fleeing or safely ensconced in the walls of the fortress.

More horses neighed and their riders sought to quieten them, perhaps hoping that the animals would not sense their own unease.

Lausard felt a hand tug his sleeve and he looked round to see Karim pointing at the sky.

The moon had finally managed to break free of the clouds. It spilled its cold white light across the slowly moving column, illuminating it to anyone who should gaze down upon it. Lausard silently cursed the gleaming crescent. Another thick bank of cloud was approaching and he watched it for a second, willing it to move more quickly and wrap the moon in its stifling blanket once again. The column moved on, many anxious faces now turned towards that sickle of white light.

Lausard heard voices. They were speaking Austrian. They sounded only yards away and his right hand moved instantly to the nearest of his two holsters. Others too had heard the enemy words. Karim allowed his free hand to drop to the hilt of his sabre; Delacor closed one hand around the shaft of the axe jammed into his belt. Lausard heard the voices again. Soft, conspiratorial. Then, with relief, he realised that in these mountains and in the almost unearthly silence sound carried to an amazing degree; voices that seemed but yards away might be hundreds of feet distant. The voices must be coming from men on the fort's parapet, high above them. Nevertheless, it didn't stop his heart from hammering that little bit faster. The defile that would mean safety was still over one hundred yards away and, with the speed the column was forced to adopt, that distance may as well have been a mile.

Behind, the artillery pieces trundled on, their crews still scattering fresh dung and straw beneath their wheels. Lausard watched as Karim suddenly swung himself into his saddle, the movement spotted with alarm by Captain Milliere, who tried to hold the Circassian back. But Karim moved with uncanny assurance and walked his horse towards the defile, disappearing within the deep shadows cast there. Lausard kept his eyes on the passage between the rocks.

What seemed like an eternity passed and still the Circassian did not return. Lausard began to wonder if his own fears of an ambush had been so ridiculous. Then, with a silent sigh of relief, he saw Karim reappear. The Circassian rose in his stirrups and waved both hands first above his head and then towards the column, as if to urge it on. Lausard felt a hand on his shoulder and turned to see Lieutenant Royere smiling at him. Yet still there could be no increase in the speed of the advance. The column continued its tortuously slow pace beneath the fort, men treading carefully, all too aware of the close proximity of their enemy. Lausard wondered how long it would take the cannon and its escort to make the short but dangerous journey into the safety of the defile beyond. It was to be another hour before he had his answer.

Nineteen

'When will it ever stop raining?' Rocheteau groaned, looking up at the dark clouds, which seemed to perpetually hang over the French troops. 'This is Italy. I remember it being dry and warm. We picked grapes by the handful from vines we passed beneath. It was not like this.'

Around him, some of the other men grumbled in agreement.

The column moved with surprising speed considering the appalling conditions. The narrow roads had been turned to mud by the torrential rain of the past few days; the waters of the Po had been swollen so greatly that in a number of places the dark mass had threatened to burst its banks. To Lausard, riding along wrapped, as usual it seemed, in his green cloak, the journey down from the Alps along the narrow passes that bisected the mountains had been achieved with less difficulty than he had anticipated. Austrian troops had been successfully brushed aside at Ivrea, Chivasso, Pavia and Belgiosi. Lausard had revelled in the almost incessant routine of marching, fighting, bivouacking. The entire tableau repeated again and again as the French drove ever more deeply into the heart of Italy towards their objective.

He glanced at his own equipment and saw that there were several holes in his cloak, some made by Austrian bullets, one by a cuirassier's sword during the fighting at Ivrea. Part of his left boot top had been torn away by a fragment of shrapnel at Pavia and even his horse had sustained a number of injuries, the worst being a wound in its flank from a canister during a skirmish outside Belgiosi a few days earlier. Hardly a man in his squadron and, he suspected, in the entire regiment was without a wound of some description. But, for the most part, his companions had been lucky. Cuts, minor bullet wounds and bruises seemed to be the order of the day for most of them. Of course men had died, too many for him to count, but considering the size of the advance guard and the preparations of the Austrians, the string of victories had been quite breathtaking. And there had been moments of pleasure too. At Ivrea, they had discovered two hundred barrels of fine wine, as well as cheese and freshly baked bread. It had been a welcome supplement to their meagre rations. At Pavia, they had come across more than three hundred enemy cannon, mostly siege and some field pieces. A few of these had been suitable to add to the six original pieces that had been secreted past the Fort of Bard. Lausard couldn't remember exactly how long ago it had been since that perilous night. All he knew was that the bulk of the French army was now in Italy, massing at various points designated by Bonaparte. News had also reached them that the Fort of Bard had finally fallen after three weeks of siege. More cannon, employed in the destruction of the fort, were even now being transported into Italy to support the gathering French forces.

Bonaparte, they had heard, was in Milan. French forces

had been greeted there as liberators by a population weary of Austrian rule. Lausard couldn't help but think that the campaign was going well, but nagging away at the back of his mind was the awareness that despite the number of engagements he and his countrymen had already fought, they had yet to face the full might of the enemy. He glanced around at his companions, tired, wet and dirty, and wondered how many of them would survive. Would he himself live beyond that battle when, and if, it came? He glanced up again at the swollen clouds and brushed rain from his face. Ahead, perhaps a mile distant, the French light cavalry, including Feraud and his hussars, were performing their expected task, offering a screen for the main bulk of the force but also gathering information about enemy strengths and dispositions. At the head of the column the infantry demibrigades marched, in places sinking up to their ankles in mud. Behind them came the artillery, their teams of horses struggling to drag the guns across the ever more treacherous terrain. Many of the gunners trudged alongside their pieces; those more fortunate rode the carriages and traces. Then came the dragoons and a handful of other cavalry, mostly chasseurs, the hooves of their horses churning the already pulverzied earth. The geysers of mud sprayed up around the men, occasionally splashing them, adding more dirt to their already filthy uniforms.

'Perhaps God is punishing us for what we have done,' Moreau opined, crossing himself.

'What have we done that your God would object to?' Delacor snapped. 'If He does not like the way we fight then that is His bad luck.'

'What have we done this time that is any more terrible than before?' Lausard added. 'We have done what we were ordered to do. Orders given by General Lannes, not by your God. We have killed Austrians, our enemies. Men who would kill *us*. That is all. Just as we killed Italians, Egyptians and Mamelukes before them.'

'How do you think God treats those who kill Frenchmen?' Roussard snapped, his gaze directed at Moreau. 'Enough of our own men have died in this campaign so far.'

'You should never have left those monks up in the mountains, Moreau,' Rostov interjected. 'It seems you would be more confortable in a habit than a uniform.'

The other men chuckled.

'That has always been the case,' Moreau said wistfully.

'How can men live as *they* do?' Charvet mused. 'Cut off from the world and their fellow man. It must be a very lonely life.'

'They have God with them, how can they be lonely?' Moreau retorted.

'I would need more than God,' Giresse said. 'I would need the company of some good women.'

There was more laughter around him.

'They probably don't get much to eat up there either,' Joubert offered, a note of concern in his voice. 'I would not want to go without food, even if it was in the name of God.'

'Perhaps they have the right idea,' Lausard intoned. 'What is so wonderful in this world to make a man want to be a part of it? What wonders did any of *us* see before we became soldiers? A life in the gutters of Paris and then the inside of a prison cell, with only the promise of death on the guillotine to release us. This world we know has only ever had death and suffering to offer. Those monks may be more intelligent than we think.'

'Could you live alone, Alain?' Rocheteau asked.

'I have been alone for many years, ever since the death of my family. Men can still be lonely even when they are surrounded by comrades. Sometimes the loneliest man is the one in the centre of a room full of people.'

'I felt like that after my wife died,' Rocheteau confided. 'I had no one. But the feeling passed. I still miss her but I am no longer alone.'

'You lived alone in the desert, Karim,' Bonet said. 'Did you ever crave the company of others?'

'I had escaped enslavement thanks to Allah, all praise to Him. Every day for me was to be savoured. No one truly appreciates freedom until it is taken from them.'

'And so with life,' Bonet commented. 'None of us appreciates how lucky we are to be alive until we are facing death.'

'Death holds no fear for me,' Lausard told his companion. 'Because life offers me nothing any longer.'

'Are you saying you *want* to die, Alain?' Bonet looked puzzled.

'Death comes for us all eventually, Bonet. For soldiers. For politicians. Even for First Consuls. When death comes perhaps one would do well to embrace him, not fight him. I have nothing to live for but this uniform. If necessary, I will die in it. Death on the battlefield is my only chance to regain the one thing in life I still hold dear. My honour. That is so with many other men. Not just in this regiment but in this army.'

'Well, I don't want to die on some stinking battlefield,' said Sonnier. 'I want to live to be a hundred years old and then die peacefully in my bed.'

'I want to die in bed too,' chuckled Giresse. 'Surrounded by ten beautiful women. That *would* be a death worth waiting for.'

There was more laughter.

'I would happily die after eating the finest meal ever prepared,' Joubert offered. 'Roast duck. Onions in oil. Omelettes made with twelve eggs and filled with succulent slices of ham.' His stomach rumbled protestingly.

'When I die I know I will be with God,' Moreau said. 'I just pray that he will forgive me for what I have done.'

'Then do something for me, will you, your holiness?' Lausard said. 'If you die tomorrow, ask your God to stop this rain.'

Another chorus of laughter echoed around the dragoons.

The rain continued to fall.

Twenty

'I do not believe it.' Napoleon Bonaparte's, voice was a low, harsh whisper. 'I *refuse* to believe it.' He brandished the piece of paper in his hand angrily at General Bessiéres. 'You do not understand German. You have misunderstood this communication.'

'It is correct,' Bessiéres sighed. 'Genoa has fallen. General Massena has surrendered.'

Bonaparte looked again at the piece of paper then screwed it up and hurled it across the room. 'We cannot be sure of the accuracy of such information.'

'General Murat intercepted these communications two days ago near Alessandria,' Bessiéres reminded him, retrieving the discarded note. 'They were destined for the Aulic Council itself. Why should Melas lie to his own commanders? What reason would an Austrian general have for inventing such a story? He has nothing to gain by it.'

'Melas knows he cannot defeat Massena,' Bonaparte continued angrily. 'He knows that the Aulic Council wanted Genoa captured. He is merely lying to save his own position.'

Bessiéres held up the letter and handed it to Eugene de

Beauharnais, who was standing close by, eyes fixed on his stepfather's furious countenance.

'*You* read it, Eugene,' Bessiéres said. 'Perhaps from your mouth the words will take on the truth they already embody. A truth which we must face.'

Bonaparte spun round and glared at Bessiéres, his eyes blazing.

'The letter says that Melas ordered the siege of Genoa to be lifted on 2nd June,' Eugene began. 'In order to concentrate his forces against the army from Germany. I assume that is the army of the reserve. It was then that General Massena requested negotiations.'

'There is another letter here dated 5th June,' Bessiéres continued. '"The capitulation of Genoa, begun on 2nd June by Commander in Chief Massena, was completed yesterday. By this morning, the place should have been evacuated by the enemy. The garrison will be escorted as far as the foe's outposts, and from there will be free to recommence operations."' Bessiéres shrugged.

Bonaparte paced agitatedly for a moment then turned, resting both fists on his desk, looking first at Eugene, then at Bessiéres. He glanced down at the map before him.

'I counted on Massena; I hoped he would hold Genoa. But if they starved him out, I had already sworn to retake Genoa on the plains of the Scrivia,' he said quietly.

'We should thank God that he held out for as long as he did,' Bessiéres offered, glancing at more of the papers before him. 'Word is that his hair has turned grey. That he and his troops were forced to put down the starving population by force. At the end his men were on a ration of flour mixed with sawdust, starch, hair-powder, oatmeal, linseed and cocoa. And still the Austrians feared he would try to fight his way out.'

'Massena,' Bonaparte murmured, a slight smile on his lips. 'It is an instance where one man is worth twenty thousand. The Austrians dare not leave him where he was for fear he would cut their lines of communication should he break out. He has bought us time and we will use that time to our advantage.' His eyes were still fixed on the maps before him. 'So Massena and his men are to be repatriated behind the river Var, if we are to believe those Austrian communications. Three or four days' march from here. Once that is done, Massena and his men can take the field again.'

'It will take time for him to reorganise his troops,' Bessiéres said. 'We cannot count upon his as an effective fighting force.'

'But the Austrians do not know that,' Bonaparte snapped.

'We must only hope that they do not use Genoa as a refuge or centre of operations now,' Eugene offered. 'If that was the case they would be protected from the sea by the British. It would be impossible for us to starve them out.'

'I doubt that Melas would do that. He would be hemmed in by the Ligurian Alps on one side and the Appenines on the other with no way out. He may be cautious but he is no fool. However, we must guard against that eventuality.'

'So, what are we to do?' Bessiéres wanted to know.

'The fall of Genoa is the spur for us. We must now assume the offensive. We have close to eighty thousand men in northern Italy, including those of Massena. The Austrians have around ninety thousand. Our objective must be to advance on Alessandria. We must compel the Austrians to fight under any conditions. Melas may well seek the safety of the north bank of the Po or, as Eugene suggests, he might, if he dares, retire into Genoa itself.' Bonaparte ran a hand through his hair then crossed his arms and stood contemplating the maps.

'I will instruct Berthier to move from Pavia and engage the Austrians before him. General Lannes will be instructed to march for Voghera, halfway between Stradella and Alessandria. Including his cavalry, Lannes has eight thousand men under his command. He is to be supported by Victor, Monnier and Gardanne. A further sixteen thousand men. Generals Murat and Duhesme, who between them have ten thousand men, will make corresponding moves. In this way we will apply pressure to Melas.' At last he stepped forward and ran a slender finger over the maps, his speech increasing in speed. 'General Moncey and the Italians should place a unit north of the Oglio. A second detachment should continue the blockade of the citadel at Milan. A third, for the defence of the Ticino, should march up the left bank of the Po, keeping up with the main army so as to be able to assist any moves from one bank to the other. And lastly, in the event of the enemy crossing the Po, this force should be ready to retire before him to join with all the men who may have arrived at Milan and undertake the defence of the Ticino. We will move our own headquarters ahead to Stradella.'

The other men looked on, nodding silently as the deluge of instructions and objectives poured forth from their commander.

'It is a radical change of intentions,' Bessiéres remarked.

'What choice do we have?' Bonaparte countered. 'To some extent, the movements and dispositions of the Austrians dictate our own manoeuvres. But they will not expect us to take up the offensive. The element of surprise is still in our favour.'

Bessiéres was shaking his head. 'I hope that all of these instructions are carried out. There may be some who become lost within this labyrinth of orders.'

'Do you doubt your fellow generals, my friend?' Bonaparte asked, a slight smile on his lips.

'I merely fear the worst. Many of these men have little or no experience of cooperation with one another. That, combined with the suddenness of the move on Stradella and the abrupt concentration of so many units. And then there is the matter of supplies . . .' He allowed the sentence to trail off.

'I wish that you shared my faith. These orders and the movements they precipitate must be carried out with a boldness and determination that only men under my command could offer. Your concern is unfounded. Trust me.' The words were spoken with such conviction, Bessiéres found it hard to do otherwise.

'I have my orders and I intend to carry them out. France will not hang *me* for failing in my duty to the First Consul.'

Lausard looked up as he heard these words and he saw General Lannes and several staff officers pass within yards of the dragoons. The officer, dressed in a dark blue jacket trimmed with gold, was riding a magnificent bay that he guided skilfully over the flat terrain.

To the relief of Lausard and all the men in the advance guard, the rain that had plagued them for so long had ceased and the bright sunshine and a strong breeze were now conspiring to dry out land previously sodden by the downpours. Also welcome, after weeks of travelling over mountains, valleys, hills and uneven terrain, was the level ground. Lausard was aware that the advance guard was on the plain of the Scrivia, which on one side extended as far as the Alps and on the other was bordered by a chain of hills covered with gardens, farms and richly cultivated fields. Off to the north, the lofty summit of Mount Monviso rose dramatically into the clear sky like some snow-topped pyramid.

'This is good ground for cavalry,' Karim observed, glancing down.

'And food, too, by the look of it,' Joubert said delightedly, as the dragoons found themselves approaching a dense expanse of mulberry trees. As they passed through, many of the men snatched the fruit from the branches and pushed handfuls into their mouths.

'This is the Italy I remember,' Rocheteau chuckled.

Beside him, Lausard also pulled down several bunches of the berries and chewed contentedly on them, but his eyes never left Lannes and the other officers, who were now close to the head of the column, riding between the infantry and the artillery. The sergeant could see the general gesticulating ahead, sometimes wildly. A moment later, Captain Milliere and Lieutenant Royere wheeled away from the general and headed towards the dragoons.

'We have orders from General Lannes.' Milliere spoke. 'He has been commanded by Bonaparte himself to push on to Casteggio. But the entire advance guard is running short of supplies. Ammunition most importantly. We have also been instructed to find places to ford the river ahead.'

'But I thought that light cavalry patrols had already been despatched this morning, Captain,' Lausard queried. 'I saw them leave myself. Hussars and chasseurs.'

'That is correct. But there has been no contact with them since they left the column. It is our turn now. General Lannes fears that the Austrians may be closer than was first thought *and* in greater numbers.'

'Those peacock bastards the hussars are no use for anything other than strutting around waxing their moustaches,' Delacor sneered.

'And because of their failure we must put our lives at risk again,' Sonnier intoned wearily.

'Lieutenant Royere will lead the second squadron, I myself will take command of the first,' Milliere said. 'I want both units in formation now.' He rose in his stirrups and signalled to the dragoons to follow.

Gaston and two other trumpeters sounded the strident notes instructing which manoeuvres were to be executed; the troopers responded with consumate accomplishment and precision. They guided their mounts skilfully to the left, moving in threes, to form another column alongside the main one. As they headed off at the trot, Lausard glanced around and saw the marching infantry and artillerymen watching the green-coated dragoons. General Lannes himself saluted the horsemen as they passed. The sun glinted on their brass helmets, the horsehair manes attached to the crests trailing behind them as they rode.

Apart from several shallow defiles, which Lausard guessed were dry stream beds, the land was indeed flat and as the dragoons rode, it rose only occasionally into gentle slopes and ridges that the horses had no trouble negotiating. The column gradually spread out into open order as it crossed the featureless terrain, men keeping their eyes open for any sign of movement around them. Karim scanned the far horizon for any hint of dust clouds and even Milliere used a telescope to sweep the area ahead for any sign of troops, enemy or otherwise.

It was Karim who spotted the tracks first.

'Cavalry *and* infantry,' he said, pointing down towards an area beyond them that had been churned up by the passage of many feet and hooves. 'I can't say whose. But they passed here recently. Perhaps three or four hours ago.'

'The infantry must be Austrian,' Lausard murmured. 'All of ours are still back there.' He hooked a thumb over his shoulder in the direction of the distant column.

They approached another gentle slope and instinctively the dragoons slowed their mounts. The slope was covered by thickly planted trees – good cover, Lausard thought, for any enemy infantry lurking within. His hand brushed against the hilt of his sabre. Sonnier and a number of the other dragoons loosened the thin strap that held their carbines in place, preparing for any eventuality. Even above the jangling bits and hooves of so many horses, Lausard was aware of the unearthly silence that hung over the trees. He squinted in an effort to catch any sign of movement.

The single horse bolted from inside the woods and hurtled towards the dragoons, its head flailing around wildly, its tongue lolling from one side of its mouth. Its muzzle was flecked with foam and the animal was badly lathered. It was also injured. Lausard could see a savage gash running along one flank. The cut, which Lausard guessed had been made by a sword or bayonet, had almost severed the girth strap but the saddle was still in place, the dark blue shabraque beneath it flapping as the horse continued to leap and cavort before the watching dragoons. As the animal drew nearer, Lausard shot out a hand and grabbed its bridle, tugging hard, the bit cutting deep into the frantic animal's mouth. Its eyes rolled in the sockets but the pain was enough to calm it temporarily and Lausard could see that the saddle was spattered with partially congealed blood. He and Captain Milliere exchanged glances then the officer looked towards the woods once more. Lieutenant Royere galloped across to join them, also glancing at the horse as Lausard finally let go of its bridle. The bewildered animal remained where it was, ducked its head and began chewing on the grass.

'I will take twenty men into the woods on foot,' Milliere said. 'The remainder of the first squadron will also dismount and prepare to fight on foot. The second squadron will remain in the saddle. Divide them into three units, Lieutenant, and cover the east and west sides of the wood. If there are any enemy troops inside the wood we will withdraw, tempt them out and fight them in the open.' Milliere then turned and looked at Lausard. 'I want you and your men with me, Sergeant. Give the order to fix bayonets.'

Lausard did as he was instructed and the twenty dragoons closest dismounted, pulled their carbines from their saddles and snapped the bayonets into place at the end of the Charleville barrels. Milliere took his own weapon down and checked the firing mechanism, then, handing the reins of his horse to another trooper, he walked to the front of the waiting men and waved them forward.

Lausard and his colleagues had fifty yards of open ground to cover before they reached the woods. They were only too aware that the terrain offered no cover of any description; it couldn't have been flatter had an engineer levelled it. Should there be any enemy troops hidden within the maze of densely planted trees they had ample time to load, aim and fire any number of volleys at the defenceless dragoons. Even Lausard felt his heart thudding that little bit faster as he advanced.

The dragoons' swords bumped against their boots as they walked, their pace brisk but not hurried. Five or six feet ahead of the broken line, Captain Milliere moved purposefully, eyes ever alert for any sight or sound from the woods. With the other dragoons now in position, Lausard realised how even more unnatural the silence was. He couldn't even hear birds singing. To his right Karim walked with his shoulders slightly hunched, prepared to throw himself to the ground should they be fired upon. To the left, Rocheteau stalked forward, eyes narrowed. Beyond them, the other men moved on, gripped by a mixture of anxiety, impatience and downright terror. Lausard could see the emotions etched clearly on their faces. The realisation that the Austrian muskets they could be facing were widely acknowledged as the most reliable currently in use by any army, only served to heighten Lausard's trepidation. Wielded by troops every bit as well trained as those of his own country, the weapons were constructed from heavier and more robust parts, the weight helping to absorb more of the fearful recoil when the piece was fired. A metal fireshield around the pan prevented flames erupting from the touchhole should too much powder be used. The pan-cover was contoured on the underside to form a water-resistant seal, making the weapon less susceptible to damp. And the lock had fewer screws and therefore required less attention. It was, in every way, a superior weapon to the Charleville and, as the tree line came closer, Lausard began to wonder just how many of these muskets were now aimed at him and his unit. He could feel sweat beading on his top lip and he knew that it was not all due to the rise in temperature.

They were twenty yards from the trees now.

Lausard licked his lips. If the Austrians were indeed waiting to open fire then they were ensuring that the dragoons were close enough so that none escaped.

He quickened his pace.

Sonnier raised his carbine slightly, prepared to swing it up to his shoulder should the time come. He hoped he would have the chance to use it.

Charvet's powerful hands gripped his Charleville so tightly that his knuckles turned white. The sun glinted on the sharpened tip of the bayonet.

More than once, Roussard closed his eyes briefly, as if to block out the flashes of fire and the clouds of smoke that could, at any second, explode from the woods.

Moreau was silently murmuring a prayer as he advanced.

There was now less than ten yards between the dragoons

and the trees. Surely, Lausard mused, if there were Austrians hidden within, they would have opened fire by now.

Five yards.

The men could virtually see into the gloomy confines of the woods. Lausard was sure he could see something but what it was he could not say.

A branch snapped loudly.

It was like a thundercrack in the silence.

'Someone's moving in there,' Rocheteau whispered, taking a step closer to the sergeant. But Lausard didn't answer. His attention was riveted on the woods. Captain Milliere had reached the trees by now and he paused as he passed the first of them, followed swiftly by the other dragoons. The floor of the wood allowed what looked like easy passage for infantry and cavalry. There was a distinct lack of undergrowth and it was only the thick canopy of leaves high above that made the woods appear so dense and impenetrable.

Lausard moved up to within a couple of feet of Captain Milliere. Karim wandered a few yards ahead, glancing down at the mossy earth, checking for tracks. He raised his hand and beckoned Lausard and the officer over. There were several large puddles of blood spattered across the earth. Lausard noticed some splashes on the trunks of nearby trees too. Then, as he glanced around, he saw the first of the bodies.

Clad in their familiar blue dolman jackets and blue-grey pelisses, Lausard could see immediately that they were French hussars. He could also see that there didn't appear to be any survivors. The corpses, some shot, some stabbed or slashed, lay in untidy heaps. Many were slumped close to or across the carcasses of their horses. There was a number of chasseurs among them too. The dragoons moved among the men, Karim and Bonet checking the bodies for any signs of life. But their search was futile. Finally, in the cloying silence,

Lausard heard a sound he recognised – of flies buzzing expectantly around the dead.

'So this is what happened to the light cavalry,' Captain Milliere mused, looking around at the dead Frenchmen.

Lausard nodded distractedly, kicking at the scorched shreds of paper that littered the floor of the woods, which he recognised as the remnants of waxed cartridges.

'But this isn't *all* of them,' he said. 'There were at least three squadrons despatched. Nearly seven hundred men.' He surveyed the carnage. 'There are no more than two hundred here.'

'They must have split up to cover a wider area,' Milliere insisted. 'These poor bastards were the unlucky ones.'

'Then where are the rest of them, Captain? Why has there been no contact with *any* of the light cavalry detailed by General Lannes this morning?'

Milliere had no answer.

'Captain, over here! There's one still alive.'

Both Lausard and the officer spun round to see Rostov and Tigana kneeling beside a figure. They were helping the man upright, allowing him to rest against the fallen bulk of his horse. Even from a distance, Lausard could see that the man's uniform was covered in blood, his face, too, obscured by a mask of crimson. But as he drew nearer and saw the hussar accepting a drink from a water bottle, the sergeant recognised the three plaits of hair reaching past the shoulders, the broad frame and the distinctive bushy moustache curling up at either end.

'Feraud,' he said under his breath.

'Do you know this man, Sergeant Lausard?' Captain Milliere wanted to know.

'Our paths have crossed once or twice.'

The dragoons gathered around the hussar officer, Milliere

kneeling beside him, glancing at the blood that seemed to cover every inch of his uniform. Feraud was gasping for breath and clutching at his left side. There was a deep gash just above his right eye, the blood having mingled with that already covering him.

'What happened here, Captain?' Milliere demanded.

'Austrians,' Feraud gasped. 'They ambushed us. They must have seen us coming. We had broken off from the main force. They were waiting. My men didn't have a chance.'

'Are you the only survivor?'

'They took some prisoners *and* the horses. My horse was killed. It fell on me. I cracked my head when I went down.' He touched the gash above his eye. 'I must have been unconscious while the fighting was going on.'

'You were very lucky, Captain,' Lausard said evenly, his gaze meeting that of the hussar. 'Are you wounded?' He nodded towards the blood that coated the light cavalryman's uniform.

'That's not *my* blood. Most of it is from my horse.'

Feraud was helped to his feet where he wavered slightly. Lausard moved to aid him and the officer shot out a bloody hand to steady himself. As he did so he met the sergeant's eyes once again.

'Had you received any contact from the other units before you were attacked?' Milliere pressed. 'Or learned anything of the Austrians' movements or dispositions?'

Feraud shook his head. 'We saw nothing of them until we were attacked but they must be close even though they still appear to be retreating. We had seen ammunition caissons and supply wagons on the road.'

'Joubert, Carbonne and Tigana. You take Captain Feraud back to the main column, let him make his report to General Lannes,' Milliere ordered.

'And what do we do, Captain?' Lausard asked.

'We were ordered to bring back supplies. If Captain Feraud is right about the wagons he saw, then we have a chance of capturing some from the Austrians ahead of us. We go on.'

'And end up like these poor bastards?' Delacor gestured at the dead hussars.

Milliere ignored the comment and set off back out of the wood, the other dragoons following.

'Someone should bury them,' Moreau said mournfully. 'They have a right to *some* dignity in death.'

'Then you stay and do it, your holiness,' Rocheteau hissed. He turned and looked at Lausard, who was watching Feraud hobbling along, supported by Joubert and Carbonne.

'They say that any hussar who lives beyond the age of thirty is a blackguard,' mused Lausard. 'Those men back there, in the woods, have at least found the death they wanted.'

'Either that or their luck just ran out,' Rocheteau replied.

Lausard nodded, his eyes still on Feraud. 'Some men are blessed with good luck,' he said quietly. 'But then again the devil looks after his own, doesn't he?'

Rocheteau looked puzzled but said nothing. He followed Lausard out of the wood.

Lausard counted six wagons in the slowly moving procession that trundled its way across the shapeless landscape. All were driven by grey-uniformed men and accompanied by infantry; Lausard estimated there were fewer than a hundred foot soldiers. On either side of the column rode several dozen hussars. The crocodile moved unhurriedly, unaware that the two squadrons of dragoons were closing in on them.

Led by Captain Milliere, the French horsemen moved forward at a trot, gradually increasing their pace to a canter as they drew closer. Milliere shouted the order to draw swords and, as he did so, trumpeters sounded the signal and the entire mass of green-clad riders accelerated into a gallop. The noise was deafening: the jingling harnesses, the shouts of the men, the snorting of the excited horses, the sound of their hooves. And, as ever, Lausard smelled a gloriously familiar scent: the mingling sweat of horses and men, leather and damp cloth; the more pungent odour of droppings and the stink of oil from so many swords.

The rain, which had begun to fall again during the last hour, did nothing to hamper the advance of the dragoons and they hurtled towards their prey with relish, some of them bellowing oaths as they waved their swords at the startled Austrians. Lausard spotted a slight rise ahead of the fleeing enemy troops and a narrow defile cutting through it; he assumed the Austrians were heading for it in an attempt to escape the onrushing tide of horsemen now thundering towards them. Some of the infantry fired their muskets at the dragoons but Lausard just saw puffs of smoke; he could hear nothing but the deafening and all-enveloping rumble of hooves. Small geysers of earth erupted ahead of the charging dragoons as the musket balls fell short. Now, both the Austrian infantry and cavalry began racing headlong towards the rise, many of the foot soldiers even discarding their weapons in an effort to outrun the tide of horsemen. Some of the hussars fired from their saddles and Lausard was aware of a dragoon nearby crashing to the ground as his horse was hit by a bullet.

The leading rank of dragoons reached the supply wagons and swarmed around them like crows around carrion. Lausard caught one of the drivers with a powerful backhand swipe of his sword and sent the man reeling, his chest gashed by the blade. Milliere despatched another driver with a thrust to the stomach. Sonnier cut down an infantryman then pulled his carbine from its boot and shot another of the drivers.

Elsewhere, the dragoons were finding little resistance from those Austrians who had not already fled. In fact, Lausard noticed that many of the enemy troops were raising their arms in surrender. Delacor seemed unimpressed by the gesture and caught one of the would-be prisoners across the face with a savage blow. Others were simply ridden down by the pounding hooves of the dragoons' horses. Some of the hussars drew sabres and tried to fight back but it was an uneven contest. Bigger men on bigger horses, the dragoons had the advantage in every respect. Karim used his sabre with devastating power and skill, slicing easily through the arm of his opponent at the elbow, severing the limb. His second blow cut through the hussar's shako, splitting it cleanly in two and carving effortlessly into the skull beneath. The body toppled from the saddle and the Circassian turned his horse, looking for another opponent.

Rostov blocked a sabre stroke with his sword, grabbed the arm of his attacker and hurled him bodily from his saddle, waiting until his opponent rose before cutting him down with a blow that sliced off an ear.

Giresse leaped from his horse on to the driver's seat of one of the wagons, grabbed the reins and tugged hard on them to halt the terrified horses. Lausard grabbed the harness of the off-side lead horse, aiding his colleague as he turned the team.

Other dragoons were following his example and three of the wagons were already in French hands.

There were still a few individual ongoing combats but for the most part the Austrians were fleeing.

Milliere looked towards the escaping men and smiled.

Seconds later, the smile froze on his lips.

The first wave of Austrian cavalry crested the low ridge and poured down it like a tidal wave, breaking immediately into a gallop. The ground shook beneath the weight of such massive horses and their heavily armoured riders.

Lausard also saw the devastating charge begin, his eyes riveted on the troops thundering towards him and his countrymen. The high-crested black helmets, the white tunics covered at the front by a lacquered black metal breastplate, and the blood red shabraques that flapped wildly as the men charged.

'Cuirassiers,' Lausard hissed, mesmerised by the oncoming waves of heavy cavalry. He could only guess at how many there were. Five hundred. Perhaps even a thousand. They swept forward, swords already drawn, their lines almost perfectly straight even as they charged. The huge horses pounded the earth to dust as they thundered onwards. They were flanked by detachments of lancers and dragoons, resplendent in their green jackets, the pennants of the lancers fluttering menacingly in the breeze.

'Withdraw!' roared Captain Milliere, barely able to make himself heard above the deafening thunder. Gaston blasted the notes on his trumpet but even they seemed to be eclipsed by the sound of the oncoming heavy cavalry. Many of the French cavalry managed to turn their mounts but it was too late. The first wave of cuirassiers crashed into them like a battering ram.

Men and horses were knocked over by the sheer force of the impact, many crushed to a bloody pulp by the thousands of churning, heavy hooves. Lausard found himself facing an Austrian officer, the red velvet edging of the man's cuirass and the black fur saddle skin marking out his higher rank. The officer struck at Lausard with his sword and even as Lausard fielded the blow he felt the impact reverberate up his arm. But the Austrian weapon was heavier and more difficult to manoeuvre, even in the hands of an experienced man. Lausard pushed away the superior sword and struck back with his own. The officer lifted his pallasch, blocked the strike and brought the lethal hatchet-pointed blade down again; this time, the sheer power of the weapon caught Lausard out. The blade hacked open his sleeve and cut deeply into his right arm, blood bursting from the wound. But Lausard gritted his teeth, ducked low over the neck of his horse and drove his sword forward with devastating speed and accuracy. The blade caught the officer in the throat, above the ruff of the cuirass, and opened a large hole from which blood spouted wildly.

Lausard barely had time to enjoy his victory when two more cuirassiers came at him. He caught one across the chest but the sword simply clanged against the steel breastplate and skidded off. The first of the men cut at him, missed and hacked open the left flank of his horse, the animal rearing in pain. Lausard struck again as his mount brought its forelegs down. He jabbed at the back and side of his adversary and skewered him between two ribs. He was about to wrench his sword free when the second Austrian aimed a powerful blow at him.

Karim appeared at his side as if from nowhere. He hacked off the man's hand at the wrist and finished him with a cut across the throat.

Lausard pulled a pistol from his holsters and shot another cuirassier in the face from point-blank range.

Captain Milliere fired into the head of a horse, the dead animal crashing down, bringing several others with it. He rode over their riders, slashing down at them.

Rocheteau joined him, suddenly aware that the Austrian heavy cavalry had downed over two dozen of the dragoons.

Outnumbered and taken by surprise, the French fought madly to extricate themselves from the crush of men and horses.

Giresse, still on the driver's seat of the wagon, hauled a sack of grain from the back of the transport and hurled it at a cuirassier, knocking him from his horse. He reached for his sword and managed to parry a savage blow only for another enemy horseman to slash him across the back of the calf with a blow that not only sliced effortlessly through his boot but also cut deep into his flesh. Lausard shouted to him, guiding his horse closer to the wagon, extending an arm. Giresse knew what he must do. He jumped from the wagon, Lausard's good arm helping him up on to the back of the animal. He linked his arms around the sergeant's waist and clung on as Lausard spurred the animal away from the scene of furious fighting.

All along the line, the dragoons were falling back, trumpeters using all their lung power to blast out the notes of recall. As Lausard looked back he saw dozens of green-clad bodies lying motionless, many mauled where they had been ridden over repeatedly.

Just ahead, two cuirassiers were pursuing Tabor and another dragoon. One of the Austrians struck a powerful blow against the dragoon's side, and the man toppled from his horse with a scream. Lausard spurred forward and drove his sword into the unprotected back of the cuirassier. Blood spread rapidly over his white tunic and he slumped forward in his saddle, his horse veering into that of his companion. Tabor took his chance, leaned across from his saddle and grabbed his pursuer by the head. Using his tremendous strength, the big man twisted his opponent's head to one side, breaking the Austrian's neck as easily as a man would snap the neck of a chicken. As Lausard drew up alongside Tabor, he noticed he was bleeding from a wound close to his right eye, the blood coursing down his face making it difficult for him to see. But he, like the other dragoons, rode on, anxious to escape.

The cuirassiers, their horses exhausted by the charge, had eased off their attack, but the Austrian lancers and dragoons still pursued the fleeing French. Lausard witnessed several of his fellow troopers being speared in the back as they fled. He drew his remaining pistol and fired over his shoulder at the lancers, the pain coursing along his arm making it feel as if the entire limb was on fire. Giresse clung to him, desperate not to fall from the horse. Suddenly Rocheteau galloped up alongside them, leading a riderless horse by the bridle. Giresse leaped into its blood-flecked saddle and rode on without even slipping his feet into the irons.

Lieutenant Royere, his uniform spattered with blood, had drawn about fifty dragoons into a line to meet the charge of the lancers, and as they came within twenty yards, he gave the order to fire. There was a loud roar as the Charlevilles spat out their lethal loads and more than a dozen lancers went down. A thick blanket of smoke billowed over the field and, as the dragoons frantically reloaded, Lausard saw that the lancers had wheeled and were heading back towards their own lines. French dragoons, many of them wounded, some even without horses, were making their way back towards their colleagues, who had formed up in two ragged columns. Some of the troops spurred forward to help their fellow soldiers. Lausard saw Sergeant Delpierre ride past, his face disfigured by two savage cuts, one of which had almost blinded him. One of his fingers had been crushed beneath a horse's hoof but he held on to his reins and gathered more men around him.

'That was no patrol,' Rocheteau gasped, wiping perspiration from his face. He looked at Lausard, his blood-splashed sword still gripped in his fist. 'Where the hell did they come from?'

'The Austrians must be much closer than anyone suspected.' Lausard winced as he touched his arm; it was starting to feel numb. He knew it needed treatment quickly. There was always a chance of infection setting in.

'Take this,' Karim said, pushing a small canteen towards him. 'It's brandy.'

Lausard nodded and accepted it. Like the other men, he knew that alcohol was the best disinfectant for wounds. He unscrewed the top, the scent filling his nostrils, then he took a mouthful. The rest he poured on to the open wound. Excrutiating pain filled his senses and it was all he could do to prevent himself passing out. He sucked in several deep breaths and remained in the saddle, teeth gritted, the blood rushing in his ears. He clenched and unclenched his fist around the hilt of his sword, each fresh contraction bringing pain.

'What a waste of good liquor,' he managed through clenched teeth.

'We must get back to General Lannes,' Captain Milliere said agitatedly. 'If the main Austrian force *is* nearby, then he must be told as soon as possible.'

'The nearest village of any size is Montebello,' Lieutenant Royere offered. 'That way.' He motioned into the distance. 'To the north-west is Alessandria. Beyond the Bormida river.'

Off to the north came a sound like rolling thunder. A moment later they heard it again. Lausard knew immediately what it was. Cannon fire. It became more insistent until it gradually welded into one continuous roar.

'My guess is that the general *already* knows how close the Austrians are,' Lausard said, looking in the direction of the cannonade. 'And if he didn't before, then he does now.'

The artillery fire continued.

Twenty-One

The candles were burning low, their small plumes of orange flame casting deep shadows across the tent. Outside, the rain, which had returned like some unwelcome guest, continued to pour down. The officers could hear it beating against the tarpaulin and against the already sodden ground.

'Where are these accursed Austrians?' General Joachim Murat asked. 'It is as if they have been spirited away.'

'They are in retreat, surely,' Bessiéres said. 'Otherwise we would have found them.'

'What news from the light cavalry patrols?' asked General Desaix.

Murat could only shrug. 'They have found no trace of the enemy.'

'How can this be?' Napoleon Bonaparte hissed. 'Melas has over thirty thousand men in the field. How can that many troops leave no trace? Perhaps your cavalry are not performing their duties properly, Murat.'

'You are welcome to ride with them and see for yourself,' Murat countered irritably. 'If there had been any Austrian troops in the vicinity, my cavalry would have found them.'

'We have heard nothing for five days,' Bonaparte snarled. 'Since Lannes and Victor beat Melas at Montebello.'

'They are still retreating,' Lannes offered. 'They mean to avoid direct battle. As we speak, Melas is withdrawing to Alessandria.'

'But we have no proof of this,' Bessiéres argued.

'I agree with Lannes,' Bonaparte interrupted. 'I fear that Melas is determined *not* to face us. But I also believe now that his chosen haven is not Alessandria but Genoa itself.'

'You insisted that could not be,' Bessiéres reminded his commander.

'There are only two places where they can seek refuge now,' Bonaparte continued. 'Alessandria or Genoa. We can at least prevent him from reaching Genoa. Desaix, you, my friend, will march with Boudet's division towards Rivalta and Novi and cut the main highway between Alessandria and Genoa. If the enemy tries to break out north of the Po then Lapoye and Chabran's troops will prevent them cutting our lines of communication.' He paced back and forth agitatedly. 'But my conviction is still that they mean to run rather than fight. We have done everything possible to force Melas into a battle and yet still he has avoided one. We crossed the Scrivia, he did nothing to counter our advance. Lannes beat him at Montebello, he was content merely to retreat. What will it take to make this old man fight?'

'Perhaps he is following the orders of the Aulic Council,' Desaix suggested. 'If it has instructed him to withdraw then he is constrained. We will not achieve the battle we seek.'

The men turned as the flap of the tent was opened, the sound of the rain momentarily amplified. Beyond the entrance stood two grenadiers, rain dripping from their huge bearskins. They remained at attention, seemingly oblivious to the foul conditions.

General Gaspard Gardanne swept off his bicorn and ran a hand through his hair as he entered the tent, aware that all eyes were upon him. Rain was dripping from his blue cloak, mud clung to his boots and he was breathing heavily. He ignored the inquisitive looks and made straight for the wine on the table before him. He downed two huge swallows before wiping his mouth with the back of his hand.

'The Austrians have crossed the Bormida and destroyed the bridge behind them,' he said flatly. 'Further intelligence leads me to believe that Alessandria is only lightly held.'

'Then Genoa *is* their target,' Eugene de Beauharnais added. 'They have no wish to fight here, only to escape.'

Bonaparte stroked his chin thoughtfully and began pacing back and forth.

'What other proof do you need?' Murat demanded. 'If the bridge across the river has been destroyed then Melas *cannot* attack or *be* attacked. He has put the river between himself and us for a reason.'

'It makes no sense,' Bonaparte insisted. 'If he has men close then there would be no reason to run. Supposedly he has reinforcements under General Ott nearby.' He turned to face Gardanne. 'Are you *sure* that the bridge was destroyed?'

'What is it you doubt?' Gardanne said defensively. 'My word or my eyesight?'

'I want the area reconnoitred again,' Bonaparte insisted. 'I want further confirmation. Murat, send some light cavalry to inspect the area more closely.'

'We are less than three miles from Alessandria,' Gardanne protested. 'Melas could not hide an army of thirty thousand men between there and Marengo.'

'The troops could be concealed within the city itself,' Bonaparte countered.

'But even if they are, how are they to fight us when they

are separated from our forces by the Bormida?' Murat wanted to know.

'And I told you that my intelligence indicated Alessandria was only lightly held,' Gardanne added. 'Thirty thousand men constitute more than a mere garrison.'

'Send the light cavalry,' Bonaparte ordered. 'Do it now.'

Murat nodded and headed out of the tent.

Gardanne turned to follow. 'It would appear you no longer require *my* presence either,' he grunted. 'As my judgement *and* my powers of observation seem to be in doubt, I feel I would be better served resting out of this rain rather than remaining here to be insulted.' He pushed through the flap and strode off into the rain-soaked night.

'We have so much information and yet each piece seems to contradict the other,' Bonaparte mused. 'I have been brought intelligence reports that appear to indicate Austrian cavalry movements towards the Po. That hardly constitutes a retreat, and yet Austrian prisoners report that Melas has sent a force to Acqui. If *that* is true then it would seem to support the idea that he is running for Genoa.'

'Whose word would you take?' Desaix demanded. 'That of a captive enemy or that of one of your own generals? What reason do you have to doubt Gardanne? There is every likelihood that Melas ordered the bridge over the Bormida destroyed. You yourself said you were convinced he was determined to avoid a battle. Would that not confirm your own suspicions?'

'My suspicions are still groundless, still unsubstantiated by facts. For five days we have had no contact with the Austrians. Who knows what thoughts are going through the mind of Melas?'

'And if the bridge over the Bormida *has* been destroyed,' Desaix insisted, 'what then?'

'Then we pursue Melas until we catch and destroy him. Hopefully, with your troops and mine acting together, there will be no escape for him. But he must be stopped *before* he reaches Genoa. Go now, my friend. Rejoin your men. The next time we meet let it be on a field of victory.'

Desaix pulled his cloak more tightly around him, arranged his bicorn on his head and saluted, before stepping out into the night.

'In view of the information we have,' Bonaparte addressed the remaining officers, 'I feel that detaching Desaix from our main force is a prudent and well-advised measure.'

'Even with the possibility of so large an enemy force being near?' Bessiéres asked.

'Melas does not want to fight. Not here,' Bonaparte insisted quietly.

'The ground would suit him,' Lannes argued. 'The Austrians have a superiority in cavalry. You know that this area is perfect for them. Melas will know that too.'

'He will not fight.'

'You're very sure of that?' Bessiéres intoned. 'I hope for the sake of the army that you are right.'

'I will spend the night at the Villa of Torre di Garofoli rather than return to Voghera,' the Corsican said. 'I want to be near my men while the situation remains so uncertain. But before I retire, I wish to view this area again myself. Ride with me.'

'With what purpose?' Bessiéres wanted to know. 'What do you expect us to see?'

'I cannot trust other men's eyes, I trust my own. Perhaps *I* will see an enemy no other has yet seen.'

Lausard flexed the fingers of his right hand, relieved that he felt only slight stiffness in both them and his forearm. The wound had been so deep it had taken the past five days to even begin healing. He had changed the dressing himself twice a day, occasionally bathing the wound in water so hot he could barely stand it. But he knew the potential implications should it become infected: fever, gangrene and the inevitable loss of the limb. A shortage of bandages had meant that he had had to wash the same ones over and over, adding vinegar to disinfect them. But he had persevered and had been relieved to see that the wound had responded to his rudimentary treatment. Lausard thought how lucky he was not to have lost the use of his hand, so savage had been the attack. The bruises he had sustained to his thighs during the crush of horsemen were all but gone. Many of the other troopers had suffered similar injuries, but they were to be expected among cavalrymen. Rostov had damaged a knee quite badly during the exchange and he still limped as he wandered across towards the huddle of drenched dragoons, who sat around in the rain with their heads bowed. Orders had been given that no fires were to be lit and the stink of damp clothing pervaded the air.

'Why the hell can't we light a fire?' Delacor whined. 'How are we ever supposed to dry our clothes?'

'Or cook any food, if we had any,' Joubert added, the rain dripping from the peak of his helmet.

'We cannot light campfires,' Lausard told the other dragoons. 'You know that. No one knows how close the Austrians are. Bonaparte does not wish to give away our strength.'

'What strength?' Roussard demanded. 'We are short of supplies; many of the men are wounded. God alone knows how many Austrians are out there.' He gestured off into the night.

'They are all sleeping warmly in comfortable billets inside Alessandria itself,' Giresse mused, wiping rain from his face.

'At least the dog-faces in Marengo have roofs over their

heads,' Delacor grunted, pulling his cloak even tighter around him. 'But here we sit like sheep in a field, with that stinking stream threatening to burst its banks and drown us.' He pointed towards the swiftly flowing Fontanove. The stream, swollen by the continual rain of the past few days, cut a path through the flat ground ahead of the village of Marengo. There were several infantry demibrigades camped close to it. Other units had occupied the village itself. Cannon had been placed between the gaps created by the infantry units, the gunners trying to sleep as best they could on the sodden ground.

'I'll wager Bonaparte and his generals will all be sleeping soundly tonight too,' Rocheteau offered. 'On fresh sheets, and on mattresses without fleas.'

'Bonaparte will not rest until he has beaten the Austrians,' Bonet said.

'Don't you mean until *we've* beaten the Austrians, schoolmaster?' Delacor hissed. 'Wherever the hell they are.'

Lausard chewed on a piece of stale bread and looked to the west. 'They're out there somewhere,' he mused. 'Waiting for us to attack them – or gathering themselves to attack us. That seems to be an eventuality no one has considered.'

'Word is that they are running,' Rocheteau said.

'They have no need to run,' Lausard told the corporal. 'They are equal to us in number. Superior in cavalry.'

'They have the best cavalry in Europe,' Bonet added.

'We will see,' Lausard murmured. 'I would take one of *us* over two of them any time. Their strength in arms is superior, not their ability as fighting troops. This army is the equal of anything sent against it. Bonaparte knows that and so do the Austrians. That is why they are keeping their positions secret. They do not want to force a battle unless they have to.'

'Do you think they will, Alain?' Rocheteau asked.

'Surprise may be the only thing in their favour. Should they care to use it. If they stop running and decide to fight, then it will be a bloody day.'

Using his cloak to shield the ammunition from the rain, Karim opened his cartouche and counted the contents.

'I have sixteen cartridges left,' he said quietly, pressing each of the small waxed packages gently between his thumb and forefinger to ensure the seal was still intact.

Some of the other men counted their supply.

'Twenty-two,' Rocheteau said.

'Twelve,' Sonnier murmured.

'We are supposed to fight these Austrians with no food in our bellies and no ammunition,' Delacor rasped.

'Yes, we are,' Lausard told him flatly. 'And we are expected to beat them. Just like we have done before.' He pulled his sword from its scabbard and began cleaning it with a piece of oily rag. As he gripped the hilt, he felt the stiffness from his wound more acutely, but the more he persevered the easier it felt.

'Well I don't know why we're sitting around here up to our arses in mud. Why doesn't Bonaparte let us destroy these damned Austrians and have done with it? Let us chase them as hounds would a fox until we have them at our mercy. Then let us ride them down.'

'Are you truly tired of sitting around, Delacor?' Lausard asked. 'Because if you are, go and relieve Tabor from sentry duty. You too, Moreau. Charvet has been at his post for more than two hours now.'

The other men chuckled as Delacor got to his feet irritably.

'Come on, your holiness,' he snapped at his companion. 'Let us go. Perhaps you can get your God to show us where the Austrians are hiding.' He cursed as he almost overbalanced, slipping in a deep puddle. 'We are more like infantry than cavalry. We spend more time on our feet than on our horses.'

'You have much in common with the infantry, Delacor,' Lausard told him. 'They are forever complaining too.'

More laughter greeted the remark, as Delacor and Moreau disappeared into the gloom.

Moments later, the bedraggled figures of Charvet and Tabor came struggling across the wet terrain. Lausard watched as Charvet seated himself then pulled a battered old pipe from his pocket. He had no tobacco but pushed it between his lips anyway.

'Someone is very busy,' he said, looking directly at Lausard. 'We heard much activity coming from Alessandria.'

'Perhaps the Austrians are fortifying the city against attack,' Rocheteau suggested.

Lausard nodded. He offered Tabor some of his bread and the big man gratefully accepted.

'Other sentries heard the noises too,' Charvet continued. 'What few of them have been posted. There are no more than a handful of men on duty tonight, Alain. Even the infantry officers have detailed only small numbers of troops to act as guards.'

'They must be certain of their position,' Bonet offered.

Lausard nodded gently. 'Or ignorant of it,' he murmured.

'We saw General Bonaparte.' Tabor looked across at Charvet as if for confirmation. 'He rode past us many times. I saluted him.'

'It's true,' the other trooper verified. 'Bonaparte and some of his staff are out and about tonight. I saw General Lannes and General Bessiéres too.'

'It *must* be important to tempt him out on a night like this,' Lausard muttered. 'What was he doing, inspecting our positions?'

Charvet shook his head. 'It didn't look like it,' he answered. 'We didn't see him stop to speak to any men as he normally does. He even asked us not to shout his name.'

'He looked worried,' Tabor added. 'As if he had something on his mind.'

'He has,' said Lausard.

A nudge from Rocheteau made the sergeant look round. He saw a group of horsemen making its way through the woods and vineyards that flanked the areas close to the dragoons' campsite. It took Lausard only a moment to realise that the horseman at the head of the small group was Bonaparte himself. As the riders came closer, the dragoons and, indeed, the other troops in the vicinity got to their feet to salute the general. But it was not the commanding officer who Lausard had fixed his gaze upon – it was the figure riding to his right, clad in the uniform of a hussar, his fur kolpack bobbing as he rode. The three long plaits of hair and the thick, bushy moustache made him immediately recognisable. Lausard wondered what Captain Feraud was doing in the company of the First Consul and so many other staff officers.

Bonaparte, unlike most of his officers, wore no cloak and Lausard could see that he was bedecked in the uniform of a grenadier. He waved occasionally to troops who called his name, but for the most part his passage through the troops was hasty and, it appeared, almost perfunctory. Lausard watched and saw that Bonaparte's eyes were not on the infantry who raised their headgear aloft on the end of their muskets as he passed. Neither were they directed towards the cavalry or artillerymen who joined in the salute. He appeared to be looking beyond his men, towards the river Bormida and the city of Alessandria beyond it. Although both, naturally, were hidden by the gloom of night.

Lausard watched Feraud for a moment, aware that the officer had seen him. The hussar passed within yards of the NCO, met his glance, then guided his horse on, away from Lausard's prying eyes. The horsemen wheeled their mounts, heading off to the north towards Marengo. As their commander left the area, the dragoons, like the infantry nearby, sat down again.

'I wonder why he didn't speak to us,' Tabor mused.

'No proclamations have been read either,' Carbonne said. 'Before a battle Bonaparte usually addresses us, doesn't he?'

'Perhaps there will be no battle,' Sonnier offered hopefully. 'If no one knows where the Austrians are, then we cannot fight them, can we?'

Lausard didn't answer. He sat on the wet ground, watching as the group of riders disappeared from view, his gaze fixed on Feraud.

'I see nothing,' said Napoleon Bonaparte, straining his eyes to the west in an effort to pick out any hint of an Austrian campfire. 'Perhaps Murat was right. It is as if our enemies have been spirited away.'

'If there is an army camped on the plains beyond the Bormida then they will not wish to show themselves,' Bessiéres suggested. 'Perhaps their men have received the same orders as ours and have been forbidden to light campfires.'

'There is no army there,' Bonaparte said defiantly. 'I fear we are chasing phantoms. Melas has run.' He looked across at Feraud. 'And you are sure that you saw nothing, Captain? No evidence to suggest that General Gardanne could have been mistaken?'

Feraud shook his head. 'No, sir,' he said, with an air of conviction. 'I followed your orders as conveyed to me by

Colonel Vernier. Neither I nor any of my unit saw evidence of an Austrian presence on this side of the Bormida.'

'The bridges had been destroyed?' Bonaparte persisted.

'To the best of my knowledge. I saw no passable bridges remaining intact across the river, sir.'

'Gardanne was correct with his first report then?' Bessiéres added.

Bonaparte didn't answer. He was still looking in the direction of the river. He turned his horse and began to ride slowly back across the front of the French positions. They snaked from the section of General Chambarlhac's corps holding the ground around and beyond the village of Peterbona back to the main bulk of the general's command, with its six cannon, and cavalry support from Murat and Kellerman of over one thousand horsemen. Moving northwards, the men commanded by Victor and Gardanne held the village of Marengo. Behind them, in reserve, were those troops under the command of General Lannes. The farthest reaches of the French position were guarded by Watrin's infantry, some of whom had occupied the village of Barbotta. Their right flank was protected by the men of the Consular Guard and by a further thousand more cavalry headed by Champeaux. The most north-easterly points were held by Monnier's corps who, if the need arose, were within striking distance of Castel Ceriolo.

Bonaparte had around twenty-four thousand troops at his disposal. Troops, he had convinced himself, he would not need on the following day, or even the day after. As he guided his horse over the open ground, glancing at soldiers who greeted him, his conviction that his enemy had fled was growing. It seemed that the Austrians' only objective was to avoid battle, and Bonaparte felt frustration and anger in equal measures as he rode.

'It is Sunday tomorrow, is it not?' he asked, his question directed at any who may care to furnish him with an answer. 'There may be a church nearby that some of you wish to visit. It seems that paying one's respect to a God will be the best and only way of passing the day.'

The group of riders around him laughed.

'We will strike camp at daybreak,' Bonaparte continued. 'Move on from these positions. If Melas means to run then we will chase him. If necessary, all the way to Genoa. In the meantime, gentlemen, I suggest we all get some sleep.'

He took one final look over his shoulder at the Bormida. As before, he saw nothing.

Twenty-Two

There could be no mistaking the roar that woke Lausard. The deafening eruption shook men from sleep like a giant hand upon their shoulders. The sergeant scrambled from beneath his blanket, keeping low, and looked to the west. Even as he did so he saw more tongues of flame burn through the early morning air. Squinting through eyes still blurred with sleep, he spotted the all-too-familiar brown uniforms of Austrian artillerymen. Seconds later, the three- and six-pounders they tended sent another torrent of shot hurtling towards the French lines.

The other dragoons were awake by now, some still dazed from the sudden onslaught. They fought to regain their wits, unsure from where the salvos were coming. Some gathered up their belongings, rolling up their blankets, jamming helmets on to their heads. Others didn't even bother with their possessions, grabbing for weapons, unsure as yet how close their enemy was.

The same scene was repeated throughout the length of the French line. Infantrymen, ripped from sleep by the opening cannonade, struggled to form battlelines, not even sure which side of the field the cannon fire was coming from. Some thought it was their own artillery until the shells began to land among them.

Lausard pulled Joubert and Carbonne to their feet and joined the others as they snatched up carbines and loaded. Why had there been no warning of this attack? he wondered. Why hadn't the French outposts alerted the remainder of the army to a danger so close? Thick smoke was already billowing upwards from the west as the Austrian cannon seemed to redouble its rate of fire.

Rocheteau, still somewhat dazed, pulled the telescope from his jacket. But before he could peer through it, Lausard had snatched it from him and trained it on the Austrian guns. Even through the rolling smoke Lausard could see movement. A mass of white-uniformed Austrian infantry was moving on to the plains beyond, slowly deploying into three columns. On either side of the columns, cavalry manoeuvred and more artillery was hauled into position to join that already pouring rounds into the surprised French.

Lausard could see that not only were the Austrians advancing across one main bridge that spanned the Bormida, but a pontoon bridge had also been erected and more of them swarmed over that. The main force appeared to be heading towards the village of Peterbona, just ahead of the French lines. Lausard could see more cannon being brought to bear upon buildings that were already aflame. In places, French infantry were fleeing from the inferno back towards their comrades. Austrian infantry was pouring musket fire into the Frenchmen who chose to defend the remains of the village, but the battle was shortlived and the last of the defenders either were killed or fled for their lives after some hand-to-hand fighting.

The cannon fire continued. The landscape was now covered

by drifting smoke, which made it virtually impossible to see. Lausard snapped shut the telescope and handed it back to Rocheteau. All around him his men stood, knelt or lay on the ground, unsure of what to do, still mesmerised by events. They were waiting for orders. Desperate for someone to instruct them on whether to mount up or to fight on foot. Advance or pull back. Lausard looked around and saw Lieutenant Royere hurrying towards him.

'Have you orders for us, Lieutenant?' he called out.

Before Royere could answer there was a sound like a scythe cutting through the air. Both men recognised it as roundshot and threw themselves down.

The six-pound ball struck several men behind them, bowling them over as if they were human skittles. It left a heap of bloodied bodies and, seconds later, several more of the deadly projectiles came hurtling in their direction. One struck the ground and buried itself harmlessly in the earth. The others ploughed on, killing more men and several horses. Soldiers went to the aid of their downed comrades but, for the most part, it was a futile exercise. Roundshot did not wound. They smashed men to pieces. The ground was already slick with the blood of man and beast.

'Mount up immediately!' Royere ordered, brushing mud from his face. 'We are to support the infantry of General Gardanne and General Chambarlhac around Marengo.'

The lieutenant had barely finished speaking when a howitzer shell exploded in mid-air, raining its lethal deluge of metal splinters on to the men below. Lausard saw one man stagger back clutching his face. Another was hit in the stomach by a steel splinter the size of a man's fist. He fell to the ground, trying to hold on to his intestines, which had burst through the savage rent in his belly. A steady stream of wounded was now being dragged or carried away from the positions to the front and right of him. Some of them dragoons.

The deafening cannonade continued.

Captain Deblou of the 2nd Chasseurs tugged hard on the reins of his horse, bringing the animal to a stop only yards from the mass of blue-uniformed guides that surrounded Napoleon Bonaparte. The First Consul looked up and saw the aide-de-camp hurrying towards him, noticing that the officer's uniform was spattered with a combination of mud and blood. The ADC's horse had been grazed by a bullet and the animal was badly lathered.

Deblou saluted and sucked in several deep breaths, the ride from the frontline having tired him almost as much as his horse. One of the guides stepped forward to hold the animal's reins as the ADC stood before Bonaparte.

'General Gardanne requests reinforcements, sir,' Deblou said breathlessly. 'Or he fears that his position will be overrun.'

Bonaparte smiled wanly. 'Overrun by what? This Austrian action against us is merely a probe.'

'It is not a probe, I assure you, sir. It is an attack in force,' Deblou insisted. 'The position is quite clear from where General Gardanne is.'

'Captain, you will tell General Gardanne to hold his position,' Bonaparte ordered flatly. 'Those are my only orders.'

'With respect, sir, you are five miles from the frontline. Surely you can hear the guns. They are Austrian guns. Our divisions have just five cannon to support them. They will not be able to stand unless they are reinforced.'

'What if Gardanne is right?' Eugene de Beauharnais questioned his stepfather. 'If this Austrian attack is as concentrated as we are told then it may be prudent to commit more men to our defence.'

'The Austrians are supported by over one hundred cannon, sir,' Deblou continued. 'They have formed into three distinct columns. The first has already driven back General Gardanne's outposts from beyond Peterbona. The second has been attacking the village of Marengo and our centre for the past two hours. A third column is moving towards Castel Ceriolo on our right. The only thing that has prevented General Gardanne's men from being destroyed so far is that the Austrians have taken so long to deploy from their bridgeheads.'

'They *had* no bridgeheads, so how can this be?' Bonaparte snapped. 'This show of aggression is nothing more than a ruse by Melas to shield his withdrawal towards Genoa. One hour ago I confirmed an order for General Lapoye's division to march north for Valenza. I have also instructed General Desaix to press on from Rivalta for Pozzolo Formigioso. What you are seeing, Captain, you and General Gardanne, is a screen with which the Austrians hope to fool us.'

Deblou sighed exasperatedly. 'General Gardanne is convinced that the Austrian force facing us is over thirty thousand strong, sir,' he insisted.

Bonaparte merely held his gaze.

'What if Gardanne is right?' Eugene pressed.

'He told me himself that he had seen no Austrian bridges over the Bormida, now he tries to tell me that Melas is not only attacking but doing so with his entire force,' Bonaparte countered, an air of incredulity colouring his tone.

'We are outnumbered two to one, sir,' Deblou insisted. 'The troops of Generals Murat and Lannes have moved up in support and yet still the Austrians have double our strength and their superiority in guns—'

Bonaparte raised a hand to silence the ADC. 'I will see for myself,' he said finally. 'Ride back to General Gardanne and tell him that I will assess this situation for myself. I will show him that he need have no concern about this attack.'

Deblou saluted, leaped into his saddle and wheeled his horse, galloping away quickly.

Bonaparte watched him disappear through some trees then glanced up at the clear blue sky. It was a marked contrast to the previous days of torrential rain. Yet still the atmosphere was heavy and the Corsican wondered if the mugginess threatened a storm.

'Gardanne's reaction is too extreme,' he said, standing to listen to the distant roar of the guns. 'There are sufficient troops under his command and those of Chambarlhac, Lannes and Murat to deal with anything the Austrians may offer.'

'Perhaps it might be sensible to recall either Lapoye or Desaix,' Eugene suggested. 'In the event that the Austrian attack should develop, we will need their men.'

Bonaparte shook his head. 'It is ten thirty now,' he said. 'By noon this action will be over and Melas will be halfway to Genoa. I tell you again, Eugene, this is merely a covering manoeuvre to mask the true nature of the Austrian strategy. There is no need for concern.'

Lausard cut downwards and sliced off a portion of an Austrian infantryman's face. Blood sprayed from the wound and spattered the sergeant, darkening his already sodden jacket and breeches. He struck to his left and right with devastating power, downing men with each stroke. All around him his companions fought with similar desperate savagery as, everywhere they looked, white-uniformed troops appeared. Smoke covered the battlefield like a dark shroud and Lausard could barely suck in breath through the sulphurous fumes. His eyes stung and his throat was parched. He had no idea how many rounds he'd fired from his carbine but there were few left in his cartouche. On foot and on horseback, the dragoons had fought without respite, and all the time the Austrian cannon poured shot into them and into the hapless infantry defending the village of Marengo and the outlying areas.

The French artillery tried its best to support its comrades but it was a futile task. Lausard saw several more horsemen crash to the ground, blasted to death by the close-range volleys of musket and canister fire that were ripping into the French from, it seemed, every angle. The ground was littered with corpses of both sides but, Lausard noticed, most were clad in blue.

Many of the infantry had been reduced to lying flat on the ground, hands clasped over their heads, in order to try and stay clear of the deadly artillery fire pouring forth from batteries all along the line. Lausard himself felt something strike his brass helmet and he actually saw the bullet drop to the ground. He shook his head and swung his sword at the man who had fired at him. The Austrians immediately before the dragoons were pulling back slightly, but when a respite seemed forthcoming, it was immediately shattered by more cannon fire or the approach of yet more infantry.

Captain Milliere drew men around him and led them back towards the high bank that bordered the stream of Fontanove. Lausard leaped from his saddle, pulled his carbine free and took up position behind a dead horse. The water of the stream was crimson and many bodies were already clogging it up and down the French line. The stench of smoke and black powder mingled with that of blood and excrement. And, continuously, the guns thundered. Many of the troops, Lausard among them, had difficulty hearing any orders shouted at them and more than one man had blood trickling from his ears, a testament to the ferocity of the cannonade.

Lausard could see some wounded men dragging themselves away from the action. He spotted one grenadier crawling along, his leg severed below the right knee, leaving a thick trail of blood behind him. Another man stumbled along in a daze clutching at the stump of his arm, which had been torn off just below the elbow. Blood jetted madly from it, spattering those nearby. Others were aiding fallen comrades, using the opportunity to escape the carnage. Lausard saw two infantrymen carrying a comrade between them, struggling to hold him upright, seemingly unconcerned that half of his head was missing. Their only thought seemed to be escape.

To the north of Marengo a cornfield had caught fire and the smoke and flames added to the pandemonium. Those who had fallen there, the wounded who were unable to move or men who were trapped, were being incinerated. The sickly sweet stench of burning flesh mingled with the other more familiar odours of the battlefield. And even over the relentless pounding of the cannon, Lausard could hear the shrieks of the poor wretches being burned alive.

Rocheteau, his face blackened by powder, his uniform splashed with blood, rolled over to join Lausard. Both men reloaded. They bit the ends from their cartridges, spat the ball down the barrel, pouring powder after it, and rammed the whole package down with the ramrod and fired. They repeated the procedure with robotic and flawless skill, every movement sapping more of their strength.

'I'm nearly out of ammunition,' Bonet gasped from close by.

'You and most of the army,' Giresse said, squeezing off another shot.

Lausard looked around at the dozens of bodies lying close to them. He motioned to Karim and Gaston to follow him and he scrambled to his feet. He ripped the cartouche from the crossbelt of the nearest corpse and flipped it open. There were half a dozen cartridges inside. He stuffed them into his pocket and moved on to the next body, collecting just three this time.

'Get as many as you can,' he roared at his two colleagues, who had realised what he was doing and were now duplicating his actions, ducking low as more gales of grapeshot swept the French positions. Geysers of dirt erupted from the ground every time one of the heavy balls struck.

They heard screams as a howitzer shell exploded overhead but Lausard could not see through the dense clouds of smoke who had been hit. He could barely see his hand in front of him as he moved swiftly from corpse to corpse gathering cartridges. To his growing horror, he found that more and more of the cartouches were already empty; Karim and Gaston were discovering the same; the young trumpeter in particular collecting fewer than a dozen of the desperately needed bullets. As he pulled at one body, trying to free the cossbelt holding the cartouche, the corpse turned over, flopping on to its back like a dead fish. The face had gone. A roundshot had caught the man squarely, staved in his features and punched a hole through the back of his skull, miraculously leaving his hair attached to a portion of jawbone and temple. Gaston ignored the sight and moved on.

Lausard was already back with the men, distributing the cartridges as best he could. Three to a man was the limit, and as he moved down the line, he had to duck constantly to avoid more shot and shell as it swept the French positions. Only the deep water of the stream was preventing the Austrian infantry and cavalry from mounting a sustained attack and, as more and more bodies littered the water, piling up in the red-stained flow, Lausard knew it was just a matter of time: the dead were forming a reeking bridge that would allow the enemy across. The onslaught was inevitable. Even as he fired off another round he heard a voice somewhere shouting and he turned to see an infantry officer gesturing to his men to fall back. At the same instant, Captain Milliere appeared from behind a reeking bank of smoke, rose in his stirrups and shouted to the dragoons to remount.

It was as Lausard got to his feet that he heard a deafening explosion just behind him. It blew him off his feet, dazing him momentarily, but he rolled over and glanced back to see that a howitzer shell had landed squarely on the bank of the Fontenove and blasted a deep crater in it. More than a dozen men lay round about, dead or wounded, and as he dragged himself breathlessly to his feet, through the drifting smoke, he saw the Austrian infantry begin to advance.

'To horse!' he roared, echoing the order of Milliere.

Many of the dragoons were cut down by bullets or artillery fire as they fled from the stream but Lausard saw most of his companions reach their mounts and clamber into the saddles. Moreau was limping slightly, blood running freely from a wound in his thigh. Tigana's face had been grazed by a fragment of shell that had dented his helmet. Roussard ran on with just the butt of his carbine in one bloodied hand. The remainder of the weapon had been destroyed. He discarded it and snatched up an infantry musket complete with bayonet. Equipment of all kind was scattered across the bloodied ground.

Lausard, barely able to suck in air, dragged himself into his saddle. His lungs felt as if they were filled with red hot coals and every breath he took was as if it had been drawn from within a furnace. The air was full of millions of tiny cinders, which floated around like minuscule black insects, filling the men's mouths and blinding them as surely as the thick smoke.

Somehow the dragoons formed up into a column, protecting the flank of the infantry as it withdrew from the oncoming Austrians. On the far side of the blue-jacketed foot soldiers, Lausard could see mounted chasseurs doing a similar job, close to the village of Marengo. Most of the dwellings were ablaze by now but the French troops within kept up a steady fire against their attackers, slipping out a few at a time.

'Why the hell don't we just get out of here?' Delacor roared, watching the oncoming Austrians.

'You stay close to me,' Lausard snarled at him, his face a mask of blood, powder and grime.

Sonnier raised his carbine to his shoulder and fired from the saddle, the shot bringing down the standard bearer of the enemy troops. The black, red and gold flag fell to the ground, only to be retrieved by another of the advancing horde.

'Draw swords,' Milliere roared, himself gasping for breath.

Those within earshot did as they were instructed. The remainder of the dragoons, unable to hear the bellowed order above the thunderous roar of cannon, simply mimicked their comrades. Lausard gripped his sword tightly and prepared to put spurs to his mount when the animal suddenly crashed down, pitching him from the saddle. He hit the ground with a bone-jarring thud and rolled over once, just avoiding the dying horse as it fell. A metal ball from the Austrian canister fire had caught the animal in the neck, and Lausard found himself sprayed with its blood as it writhed in its death agony. He looked around and snatched at the bridle of a riderless horse nearby, noticing as he did a single boot still stuck in one of the stirrups. He hauled himself up into the saddle, his head still spinning from the fall.

At first he thought that the blow to his head was causing

him to hallucinate. Blue-jacketed French infantry were moving forward to meet the oncoming Austrians. Men, their uniforms in tatters, some shoeless, some desperately wounded and some even without weapons, were forming a line to meet the enemy advance. Lausard grinned, his teeth gleaming whitely in contrast to the dirt and blood that covered his face. It seemed that nothing could break the resolve of his countrymen. They would retire a few dozen yards, reform, then return to the savage battle. Even as canister shot cut them down and volleys of Austrian musket fire poured into them they stood firm, ready with their fifteen-inch bayonets to fight for the ground already red with blood.

The dragoons moved into a linear formation, preparing to charge the Austrians, and Lausard, his ears still ringing, saw Captain Milliere roar at them to advance. Gaston raised the trumpet to his lips to signal the order but few heard it. The line moved forward, the ranks ragged. Lausard gripped his sword and roared his defiance at the oncoming Austrians as the dragoons went forward once more.

Napoleon Bonaparte squinted through his telescope and swept it back and forth from one end of the French line to the other. Much of it was shrouded in choking smoke, but he could see enough to know that he was confronted by a waking nightmare.

He held out a hand and took Bessiéres telescope, scanning the battlefield again through his companion's glass, as if by doing so he would be presented with a more acceptable scenario. As his ears filled with the incessant roar of Austrian guns, he looked from the left flank of the French position, where one of the Austrian columns was battering against the troops of Chambarlhac, pushing them steadily backward. Five thousand infantry and over one thousand cavalry were barely holding back the waves of enemy troops, crashing against them like the sea smashing into rocks. His gaze travelled to the centre of the line where hundreds of French bodies were already scattered behind the village of Peterbona, leading like some kind of macabre paper trail to the blazing inferno of Marengo. Watrin's division, stationed to the right of the village, was under heavy frontal attack by the largest of the Austrian columns. While on the far right of the French position, the Austrian corps, commanded by General Ott, were preparing to drive their way into the exposed French flank. There seemed to be no ebb and flow to the battle, just the unceasing advance of the Austrians, who seemed unfazed by the measured volleys of musket fire poured into them by the French. Sometimes the white-massed ranks engaged in savage hand-to-hand combat with the French – Bonaparte even saw several regiments formed into squares to protect themselves against the French cavalry – but he knew his horsemen were too few in number to be effective, and each discharge of Austrian canister brought with it more death and destruction.

Bonaparte, his face pale, handed the telescope back to Bessiéres. 'If the Austrians seize control of Castel Ceriolo they will be in a position to outflank our entire line,' he snapped, pointing to the far right of the French position. 'Perhaps even to press on towards the Po and cut our lines of communication. That area must be reinforced immediately. Order Monnier's division forward.'

Bonaparte spurred on his horse, through trees that had already been splintered by roundshot. Many of the wounded sheltered there, and as he drew nearer to the battleline, he could see bodies strewn everywhere. Men carrying wounded comrades were pouring away from the fighting, some using their colleague's misfortune as an excuse to save their own lives.

Eugene de Beauharnais rode up alongside his stepfather, his eyes never leaving the scene of battle before him as he asked, 'What do we do? They will destroy us. Our men cannot hold the line for much longer.'

'We must send gallopers after Desaix and Lapoye. We need more men. Those we have must be drawn together to form a more solid front but I must have reinforcements.' He grabbed an aide-de-camp by the arm. 'Find General Desaix,' he ordered, struggling to retain control of his breathing. 'You must find him. Tell him to return to me immediately with his men.' Bonaparte grabbed a piece of paper from Bessiéres and scribbled on it with a shaking hand, the quill almost cutting through the parchment. 'Take it!' he roared at the ADC, who could not help but see the scratchy message the First Consul had scrawled.

I had thought to attack Melas. He has attacked me first. For God's sake come back if you still can.

The roar of cannon continued.

Twenty-Three

Lausard thought he was choking. Thick smoke filled his lungs and cinders burned his throat every time he tried to breathe. It seemed, to him and to those who fought alongside him, that the world had been turned into an endless cloud of smoke and flame. In many respects it had. The world of the French soldiers had become one of fire and smoke, filled with the stench of cordite, black powder, blood and excrement. Of dead horses, sweat and vomit. The sky above was blue but all they saw was the reeking blanket of man-made fog. Life had been reduced to the two or three bloodied yards of ground around them.

Lausard stood beside his horse, the animal wounded in two places and losing blood. Indeed, many of the cavalry mounts had sustained injuries. Rocheteau's horse had lost part of its left ear to a bullet and most of its tail had been ripped away by a roundshot. Karim's horse was virtually lame due to a steel splinter that had shattered one of its front hoofs. It pawed at the ground with the injured appendage, tossing its head in pain every now and then. The neighing of injured animals, mingled with the groans of wounded men.

Lausard looked towards the Fontanove stream, or at least what he could see of it. Bodies were piled high on both sides. Austrian and French. In some places, corpses had been hauled together to form vile ramparts and every fresh volley of fire tore more holes in men already cut to pieces. Pieces of shattered bodies lay everywhere and it was difficult to walk a yard in any direction without stepping on ground slicked with blood. Discarded knapsacks, muskets, shoes, uniforms, headgear and cartouches littered the field.

Lausard saw that many of his companions were slumped forward in their saddles, overcome with exhaustion. Lieutenant Royere was wandering around a few yards away, a broken sword in his hand, blood running freely from a bayonet wound in his left arm. He finally took a new sword from a dead trooper, hefted it before him and nodded to himself.

Elsewhere, men were scampering amongst the dead collecting whatever ammunition they could find. With bullets, the Austrian attacks could be withheld, but without ammunition and against the cannon fire and incessant infantry attacks, the French were too badly outnumbered to hold their position for much longer.

Lausard looked towards Marengo, almost invisible beneath smoke, most of which poured from the blazing buildings. Infantrymen tugged at the crossbelts of dead companions as they too desperately searched for more cartridges.

'How long has it been since the last attack?' Lausard gasped, wiping one bloodied hand across his forehead.

Rocheteau looked at his pocket watch. At first he could only shrug, gazing at the watch as if mesmerised. 'An hour,' he said finally, coughing as the smoke filled his lungs again.

'What are they waiting for?' Carbonne asked, gently fingering the wound in his right shoulder. A bullet had caught him just below the collarbone and lodged there. Every time he poked his index finger into the wound he could feel the heavy lead ball about an inch below the surface.

Lausard didn't answer. He was trying to catch sight of the lumbering Austrian column through the rolling banks of smoke. He knew that it must be deploying for its next assault; it was the only logical step. There would be another attack, it was just a matter of when. The incessant cannon fire had eased somewhat during the last hour but now it began to intensify once more – a sure signal that an attack was about to be launched.

'Heads up, my fine troopers.'

The shout made Lausard turn and he saw General Francois Etienne Kellermann and three officers ride past, swords in hand.

'There will be more work for you today,' the cavalry general shouted.

A chorus of cheers greeted his remark. Even Lausard managed a smile. Kellermann had already led the dragoons forward against the advancing Austrians three times that morning, more men falling with each fresh charge, but each time he had reformed them and sent them hurtling back into the enemy troops. Each charge had relieved pressure on the hard pressed infantry but, looking around at the number of riderless horses, Lausard was beginning to wonder at what cost.

'Here they come again,' Giresse called out, wincing as he spoke. He was clutching a wound in his side, grateful that the ball had torn straight through the fleshy part of his abdomen and not damaged any internal organs on the way. He was bleeding but not badly and the wound was painful rather than dangerous. He pointed through a gap in the smoke.

Lausard saw the Austrian column moving forward. A great

unwielding monolith up to a hundred files wide and forty deep, it moved at over one hundred paces a minute towards the waiting French infantry, many of whom had laid out their remaining ammunition on the ground so they could see exactly how many cartridges they possessed. In some cases it was fewer than five. The dragoons had also reloaded, some down to their very last cartridge. Lausard himself had no ammunition left except that in his pistols. A number of the men had given their bullets to Sonnier, knowing that his skill with the carbine was more likely to bring down Austrian troops than their own. They sat and waited.

The Austrian column drew nearer, the second and third ranks firing, a manoeuvre peculiar to the Austrians who, rather than permit the front three ranks to open fire, saved the volley of the leading line for a crisis.

The French troops wavered under the latest onslaught and Lausard saw more men falling back, some wounded, some simply terrified by the massive force facing them.

From the far right of the French position there was movement. Lausard heard the strains of '*Le Marseillaise*' ringing out, mingling with cries of '*Vive Bonaparte*!' and he guessed that his countrymen, at least on one part of the field, were taking the initiative.

However, he had little time to think about it any further, as the cannonade was once again unleashed with all its savagery.

Many of the dragoons ducked low as more shot and shell began to fall among them. Shells exploded both in the air and on the ground, canister fire cut swathes through infantry and cavalry alike and, as ever, the lethal roundshot tore through men and horses as if they were made of straw.

Lausard saw Roussard, blood running down his face, clutching the mane of his horse, his eyes tightly closed.

Moreau was whispering a prayer to himself. Gaston, his face blackened by powder, gritted his teeth. Even Rocheteau was sucking in anxious, tainted breaths, the knot of muscles at the side of his jaw pulsing madly. He looked across at Lausard, who felt his own heart thudding hard against his ribs.

From somewhere close by, what little French artillery there was thundered back. Lausard watched as the gunners worked furiously at the four- and eight-pounders, returning the massed fire of their enemies as best they could. Each piece hurtled back over eight feet as it spat out its deadly load but the gunners hurriedly rolled it back into position, swabbed the barrel, pushed in fresh loads, rammed them down and used their portfires to light the fuses. Lausard saw bloody paths cut through the Austrians and the sight heartened him somewhat.

As the shattered French gunners continued to fire, the smoke covering the battlefield thickened. It was as if clouds had descended on to the earth itself, only these clouds were raining lead. It was a storm of fire that showed no signs of abating. Lausard gripped his reins more tightly and waited.

'Time is of the essence,' Bonaparte said, guiding his horse along the edge of a ditch, where dozens of French grenadiers sheltered from the canister shot that periodically came their way. 'The Austrians move slowly. They have not pressed their advantage. That might yet be our salvation. Ott has been forced to slow his advance to deal with Monnier's division.' He indicated towards the far right of the French line. 'The battle will turn on the struggle for Castel Ceriolo.'

'I fear the battle turning will depend on whether Desaix and his men arrive in time,' Bessiéres observed, his tone dark.

Bonaparte swept the lines with his telescope and saw

that the Austrians were exerting incredible pressure on and around Marengo.

'We may have secured our right but the Austrians seem intent on turning our left,' Bessiéres continued, his own glass also fixed on the fighting.

Both men could see hundreds of French troops streaming away from the village, some moving in an orderly manner, others simply running as fast as they could. The wounded were often left where they fell.

Bonaparte saw an ADC riding towards him. The officer's head was heavily bandaged and blood was soaking through the gauze. One sleeve of his jacket had been ripped away at the shoulder, exposing another wound beneath. Part of his shabraque had also been shredded by fire. The mane of his horse was badly singed.

'The village is lost, sir,' he blurted breathlessly. 'Marengo has fallen. General Watrin's division has been destroyed. The men of General Gardanne and General Victor have no choice but to retreat. The Austrians are forming into column of route.'

Bonaparte nodded. 'Let our men retire to San Guiliano,' he said, his voice almost lost beneath the sound of the guns. 'And no further.'

'But if we manage to pull back as far as there, who is to say that we will be able to stop the Austrians then?' Bessiéres demanded. 'Even if the gallopers reach Lapoye and Desaix, they could not hope to reach this battlefield before five. That is almost two hours. We will never hold them that long.'

'We have traded space for time,' Bonaparte insisted, looking around as he heard the sound of approaching hooves. He watched the man who rode towards him. As he saw the gold-trimmed blue uniform spattered with mud and the white feathers fluttering atop the bicorn, a slight smile creased the face of the First Consul.

General Desaix reined in his mount close to Bonaparte and sucked in a deep breath.

'Boudet's division is close behind me,' Desaix barked. 'Three thousand men supported by eight guns.'

Bonaparte made an expansive gesture. 'Well, what do you think of it?' he asked.

Desaix cast a quick but telling glance at the savage battle and shook his head. He pulled his watch from his pocket and looked at it.

'This battle is completely lost,' he said flatly. 'But there is time to win another.'

The roundshot brought down two hussars, carving a bloody path through the swiftly moving horsemen as they hurtled across the front of the deploying Austrian troops.

'We're all going to die, aren't we?' Gaston said, his voice raw in his throat. He hadn't tasted water for over two hours and he could barely swallow. All over the battlefield, men were in a similar condition. The combination of the hot air and foul black powder was almost driving them insane with thirst. All canteens were empty and some of the infantry had even resorted to supping handfuls of bloody water from the corpse-clogged Fontanove.

Lausard felt blood running down his face from a wound on his temple. A steel splinter had gouged a rent in his flesh. Another had sliced through the upper lid of his left eye and blood was clouding his vision. He wiped it away and looked at the young trumpeter.

'We are *not* going to die,' he said with a conviction few of his colleagues shared.

'Why should it bother *you*, Lausard?' Delacor snapped.

'This is what you've always wanted, isn't it? Death on the battlefield. It seems as if you're about to get your wish.'

The sergeant grabbed Gaston by the arm and held him for a moment, looking into his eyes. 'We are *not* going to die,' he repeated.

There was another aerial shell burst and several steel splinters struck the ground and the men nearby. Four or five dragoons went down, some dead before they hit the ground. Others with slight injuries struggled to their feet. Lausard saw one, dazed by a wound to the head, trying to urge his horse to its feet despite the fact that part of the animal's skull had been staved in by the red-hot lump of lead.

Captain Milliere rode close by, Lieutenant Royere behind him, his badly gashed left arm still bleeding freely. Despite the lulls in fighting, it had been virtually impossible for the wounded to get help and most were still unattended. Many had simply crawled away to die in the vineyards and woods that flanked the battlefield on both sides.

It was towards a deep defile in the direction of San Guiliano, bordered on one side by a wood and on the other by a densely planted vineyard, that Milliere was now signalling. Many troops were already reforming there. If there was to be a final stand, Lausard assumed that that was where it was to be made. The dragoons pulled back by squadrons, many dismounting to take cover in the woods despite the orders of their officers and NCOs. Lausard saw Sergeant Delpierre, his uniform drenched in blood, physically dragging men back to their mounts. Sergeant Legier and Corporal Charnier of the third squadron were also doing their best to prevent men from fleeing the field on foot. Terrified loose horses dashed in all directions, hampering the movements of other troops.

The area inside the wood was like a gigantic mortuary. Wounded men were crying out for water or brandy. Others lay cowering on the ground. But worst of all was the number of soldiers who had been killed while seeking refuge. The incredible ferocity of the Austrian cannon fire had torn through the woods, hacking off tree branches and in places felling whole trees. Dozens of wounded men had been crushed to death beneath the timbers. A drummer boy, no more than twelve, was sitting on one of the pulverised stumps weeping, holding his drumsticks in his hand as if they were weapons. Close by, up to six men had been crushed by a fallen tree.

'Remain in the saddle,' Milliere roared, struggling to make himself heard. His own face was black with smoke and grime, rivulets of sweat having carved paths through the muck. He had lost one stirrup, the leather shot through; the other one had been dented by a musket ball. Both of his spurs and the heel of one boot had also been torn away during the course of the battle.

Lausard looked towards the remains of Marengo and saw hundreds of French troops still streaming away from the carnage. Every now and then a burst of cannon fire would bring them down in bloody heaps as the Austrian gunners fired into their backs.

'It *is* over, isn't it, Alain?' Rocheteau gasped, without looking at the sergeant. 'The battle is lost.'

'Do you want to die here?' Lausard snapped, looking at his companion. 'Or you, Karim? You, Sonnier? Carbonne? Charvet? Any of you?'

Those who met his gaze shook their heads.

'Then fight on with me,' Lausard gasped, ducking as a roundshot carved its way through the wood, tearing off branches and splintering a tree trunk close by.

'Here is the reserve!'

The triumphant shout came from the area in front of the

wooded ground and all heads turned towards the ADC who galloped across the front of the line, bellowing at the top of his voice.

'You will be reinforced within half an hour!' the ADC continued, waving his bicorn in the air.

'My God,' said Bonet, grabbing Lausard's arm and pointing to several more figures riding across the face of the now-cheering French troops. 'It's Bonaparte!'

'Soldiers,' Bonaparte shouted. 'You have retreated far enough. You know that it is my habit to bivouac on the field of battle. Steady now, here is my reserve.'

Cheers were now ringing out along the entire length of the French line and Lausard could hear shouts of '*Vive Bonaparte*!' For his own part, the sergeant looked ahead and contemplated the massive advancing Austrian column. He had no idea how many men it contained but it moved with inexorable purpose. As it drew nearer, its artillery was forced to cease fire for fear of hitting its own men, and the respite from shot and shell was a welcome one for the French. For the first time that day, the air was free of that terrible sound. However, it was replaced by the tramping of thousands of feet as the Austrian column drew nearer. With it came horse artillery and Lausard knew that the damage would be wrought again should the three-pounders open up.

The enormous eruption of fire that shook the dragoons in their saddles, however, came from French guns.

Massed into one lethal battery, eighteen cannon opened fire on the flank of the slow-moving Austrian column. Lausard could see General Marmont riding back and forth behind the guns, directing their fire and exhorting his gunners to even greater effort. A furious fusillade of canister and roundshot, many of the guns double-shotted, ripped into the white coated mass. Whole ranks disappeared as the lethal loads scythed through them and bodies began to pile up, their white uniforms crimson. The men behind stumbled over the corpses of their companions, trying to keep order in the column as officers attempted to make their orders heard above the roar of the guns and the screams of dying men. And yet still the column advanced.

Lausard wiped sweat from his brow and saw French infantry advancing in a counterattack. The men of Desaix's reserve moved forward in mixed order and Lausard recognised the infantry regiments as their standards waved in the breeze. Three battalions of the 9th Line infantry; two battalions of the 30th slightly behind them; then came the 59th. Horse artillery batteries were also moving forward. Lausard realised that the depth of the defile and the clouds of smoke swirling across the battlefield were providing much needed cover for the advancing French infantry, who were drawing closer to the oncoming Austrians. Somewhere Lausard heard music and he was surprised to see several Austrian bandsmen marching ahead of the main column.

'They think they have already won the battle,' he rasped through gritted teeth, watching as the column came on.

'How many do you think there are?' Bonet wondered aloud.

'Five or six thousand,' Lausard replied, his eyes riveted to the mass of enemy troops drawing ever nearer. They remained oblivious to the presence of Desaix's men, still hidden by the slightly undulating ground and the reeking smoke from the cannons, who were moving ever closer to their flank. French gunners, some having discarded their shirts in the incredible heat, rammed shot and shell home then stepped back as their pieces spewed forth their deadly load. Without waiting to see what damage they had reaped, the gunners reloaded and repeated the procedure with a speed and determination that was barely believable. Blinded by the muzzle flashes, deafened by the thunderous roar from their guns, they worked like demons to keep up the salvos that were still cutting great swathes through the Austrian column. However, the advancing French infantry was moving into the path of its own guns and Lausard realised that the French cannon would have to cease fire. The exhausted gunners reloaded, prepared to open fire again when their chance came. For what seemed like an eternity, a relative hush settled over the battlefield, then, rising in his stirrups, General Desaix pointed his sword at the Austrians and bellowed at his men to charge.

The volley of musket fire from the Austrians was devastating, an incredible discharge that brought down countless French infantry. Desaix himself, hit in the head and chest, crashed to the ground in an untidy heap. His horse galloped away, itself bleeding from several wounds.

Everything seemed to freeze. The French troops wavered, shocked by the ferocity of the volley and by the death of their commander. The Austrians also hesitated, knowing they had no time to reload should the French now attack.

'With me,' roared General Kellermann, and Lausard pulled his sword from its scabbard and spurred his horse forward along with the rest of the dragoons. It seemed as if every remaining French cavalryman was hurtling towards the massive Austrian column. 'They are unarmed!' Kellermann shouted, his powerful voice echoing even above the thundering of hundreds of hooves. 'They have nothing but empty muskets.' Lausard looked to his right and saw four of the French cannon open fire with canister, vomiting the heavy lead balls into the tightly packed ranks.

There was an explosion of incredible ferocity and power, one that seemed to shake the very air itself. The concussion blast forced men to cling more tightly to their mounts for fear of being unhorsed and, somewhere in the centre of the Austrian column, came a blinding eruption of red and white flame. It burst upwards and outwards, forming a huge choking cloud of black smoke above the column.

'We've hit an ammunition wagon,' Lausard shouted, watching as the Austrian column seemed to shudder. The entire formation wavered. It was then that the dragoons ploughed into it.

They fought like men possessed, striking to right and left, carving paths through the stunned infantrymen, who seemed more concerned with running than fighting. Despite being hugely outnumbered, the savagery of the cavalry's attack was overwhelming. Lausard hacked down four men, his blade coated with blood. Even those who tried to surrender were cut down or ridden over as the dragoons tore their way deeper and deeper into the mass of white. A mounted infantry officer swung his sword at Lausard but the sergeant ducked and brought his sword upwards, driving the blade through the chin of his adversary. Lausard ripped the sword free and struck madly again in all directions.

Holding the reins in his teeth, Delacor was using his sword in one hand and his axe in the other, his arms pinwheeling as he cut down men at will. Karim sliced the head from one corporal then laid open the skull of a fleeing man. Carbonne rode down two Austrians, driving his sword into the back of another. Even Gaston, wielding his blade expertly, caught a man across the throat, ignoring the gouts of blood that spattered his already crimson jacket. The horses were biting and snapping at the Austrians too, seemingly infected with the same savage madness as their riders. The French dragoons forced their way deeper into the reeling column and Lausard raised his head long enough to see that the formation was breaking up.

'They're running!' he yelled, bringing his sword down again with devastating force, carving the shako of an Austrian cleanly in two and splitting his skull.

On the other flank, the French infantry ran forward and drove bayonets into any Austrians they could find. The crush became intolerable. Men were unable to fight back and were butchered where they stood.

More and more gaps began to appear in the Austrians' dense formation until, at last, it began to break. There was no order to its withdrawal; men threw away their weapons and equipment in their haste to escape the slaughter.

Barely able to raise their arms from exhaustion, the dragoons rode after the fleeing men, now only too happy to take prisoners. White-coated men flung their arms into the air and begged for their lives as the horsemen bore down on them.

Gun crews abandoned their cannon.

Lausard snatched a standard from the shaking hands of a terrified man and brandished it above his head before tossing it aside, to be ridden over by the horsemen following.

Lausard saw Austrian cavalry ahead. They had come forward in support of the column but now, as they saw the ferocious attack reach its climax, they too turned and fled. Lausard saw at least two officers pull pistols from their saddles and shoot their own horses, fleeing on foot to the nearest body of infantry.

All over the battlefield, Austrian troops were running, many not even knowing why. But panic spread quickly and the exodus increased momentum.

Rocheteau rode up alongside Lausard and watched as the Austrian dragoons fled, hurling away their swords, portmanteaus and helmets in the process, wanting nothing to hamper their flight from the field where victory had seemed so close little more than twenty minutes earlier. All that remained was defeat and death, and the entire army fled in the direction of Alessandria. The French infantry pursued them, driving bayonets into those who resisted, taking prisoner those who threw up their arms in surrender.

'Bonaparte has his victory,' Lausard gasped breathlessly.

Rocheteau looked around at the battlefield piled high with bodies from both sides. The cries of dying men and horses filled the stinking air. The corporal nodded and raised a hand to his face. Lausard could see tears in the other man's eyes.

'Am I weak, Alain?' Rocheteau pleaded, his voice cracking, tears now rolling down his cheeks. 'Do you think me a coward?' He sniffed back more tears.

The sergeant gripped his comrades forearm tightly and shook his head. 'Be grateful you still have feelings enough to experience sorrow at what has happened here today. Many will shed tears because of this day.'

Rocheteau wiped a bloodied hand across his face and nodded, regaining some of his composure.

Lausard could still hear cannon fire and saw that several of the French guns were still firing at the fleeing enemy. But, on a slight rise away to his right, he saw a battery of Austrian artillery attempting to cover the flight of their countrymen. Several roundshot struck the ground, one ricochetting into some infantrymen, who were struck down. High above, a shell burst in the air and splinters of hot steel rained down over the French.

'Will these bastards never give up?' Delacor roared, waving his sword at the battery.

A roundshot took out his horse, catching it in the side and almost cutting it in two. Delacor was sent flying from the saddle, drenched in the blood of his mount.

Giresse rode up, guiding a spare horse, a black, well-groomed Austrian mount, which Delacor accepted with a smile.

They heard the high-pitched whistle as the shell came hurtling out of the sky.

Rocheteau and Giresse instinctively ducked down low over the necks of their horses. Delacor tried to keep control of his new mount.

Lausard saw the shell as it hit the ground and lay spinning. He could actually see every inch of it, the crackling fuse burning down and the spinning ball. It was as if time had slowed down; he felt as if he had time to dismount, run across to the shell and snuff out the fuse. Then it exploded with a deafening bang.

The blast took all four of them.

Twenty-Four

The field hospital that had been set up in the Château of Marengo was little more than a charnel house. Bodies of wounded men lay on the floors of every room and a large proportion had been unlucky enough to be laid out in the large courtyard. Medical orderlies moved among these wretched individuals dispensing help where they could, but for the most part a wounded man knew his own fate. If the damage was to a limb, then, more often than not, it would be amputated. If a wound had been inflicted by a bullet or piece of shrapnel then the projectile would be either probed for or simply left to work itself free. Sometimes it did, sometimes it did not. Lausard knew of men who still carried lead balls inside them from wounds they'd received four years before. For many of those, there was the possibility that lead poisoning might kill them even if the original wound hadn't. Infection and fever were to be feared as much as roundshot and bullets. Brandy was used both as anaesthetic and antiseptic. When it was available.

Lausard rolled over on his straw mattress and felt pain gnawing at his side. He looked down to see that his torso had been heavily bandaged, blood soaking through the gauze. He wore only his breeches and his boots. He had no idea where his jacket was.

Beside him, Rocheteau was still unconscious, his face swathed in bandages. Every now and then his fingers flexed, but other than that he showed no signs of movement.

Delacor was propped up against a wall, looking down at his left leg. A portion of metal had carved through the calf just below the knee, just missing the patella but cracking his tibia in two places. Most of the metal had passed through but there was still some lodged in the wound.

Giresse had fared a little better. The exploding shell had blasted him from his horse and the animal had taken the brunt of the detonation. He had sustained a deep wound to his right shoulder and chest but the metal had passed through cleanly. He had lost a great deal of blood though and Lausard thought how pale his skin looked as he lay on the filthy floor.

The room was filled with wounded men, men still stained with the blood of their wounds, their faces still blackened by the smoke of the day's battle. The air reeked of blood, urine, faeces, sweat and damp straw. Orderlies in dark blue frockcoats moved among the men with buckets of water, offering the wounded a drink from a ladle. Those who could drank the pitiful amount of fluid but many were unable to and had to contend with the misery of their raging thirst as well as the pain of their wounds.

In the courtyard, Lausard had spotted two makeshift operating tables, both constructed from doors secured to barrels. One was being used specifically for amputations. A pile of severed limbs fully three feet high stood close by. As each shattered arm or leg was amputated, it was tossed on to the pile with the others. Surgeons, stripped down to their shirts, toiled and sweated over each new man placed on the table and there was a never-ending cacophony of screams as limbs were hacked off. Even the assistants who held down the wounded were sweating; it wasn't unusual for them to lose fingers if the doctor performing the amuputation was overzealous with the knife or saw. The other table was for bullet wounds, sword cuts and other injuries.

Out on the battlefield, details of infantry collected dead men and horses, bundled them into piles and burned them to prevent the spread of disease. A number of burn victims had been recovered from the wheat fields to the north of Marengo but there was little anyone could do for them other than lie them on the ground and cover their scorched bodies with damp cloth while they died slowly and in excrutiating agony.

Austrian troops were among the wounded in the field hospital and Lausard glanced across at an infantryman who was sitting with his knees drawn up before him, slowly rocking himself back and forth, his sightless eyes staring ahead. A portion of his skull had been hacked away by a sword, exposing part of his brain. Lausard continued to watch as the man swayed relentlessly, his mouth occasionally opening and closing soundlessly. Beside him was a French grenadier who had been hit in the chest by a musket ball. A purple foam spilled over his lips every time he coughed. He was clutching the hand of a companion, who sat beside him, part of his bottom jaw missing.

An artilleryman, his feet crushed almost beyond recognition by the steel-braced wheels of a cannon, lay on his stomach close to Lausard, pulling at the strands of straw protruding from the mattress next to him. He also had a bayonet wound in his back, which had yet to be dressed. Blood was running freely from it.

Lausard moved slightly and felt the pain of his own wound. He grunted but the sound was eclipsed by the chorus of suffering that echoed around the château and its courtyard.

One of the orderlies distributing water was heading in their direction. Lausard took the ladle from him and passed it to Giresse, who drank deeply before handing it on to Delacor, who supped a ladleful then demanded more.

'Have you heard the news of our great victory?' the orderly said delightedly. 'Over six thousand Austrians dead, eight thousand captured as well as fifteen colours taken and over forty cannon. It is indeed a great day for France.'

'And how many Frenchmen have died to *make* this day great?' Lausard's tone was menacing. 'Five thousand? More?'

'Word is that we have suffered no more than four thousand killed. It is a glorious victory. I hear that the Austrians have already asked for peace.'

Lausard snatched the ladle from him and drank.

'And where were *you* when the fighting was going on?' Delacor demanded.

'I was doing my duty as you were,' the orderly countered, trying to retrieve the ladle from Lausard. But the sergeant refilled it and drank again, much to the consternation of the orderly who shot him an angry glance. 'One ladle per man,' he snapped.

'We have earned that,' Lausard told him. 'And much more. Every man in this hospital has.'

The orderly glanced quickly at the wounds each of the men sported. He looked more closely at Delacor's. 'The surgeon will be here to inspect your wounds soon,' he said. 'It looks as if you'll lose that leg.'

Delacor aimed a kick at him with his other boot. 'Get out of here, you stinking vulture,' he snarled then turned to look at Lausard. 'Don't let them take it, Alain. I could not bear that. I do not wish to become some hobbling cripple.' There was genuine fear in his voice. 'I have faced all the dangers this army can find for me and I have bested them, but I cannot bear the thought of losing my leg. I would rather die.'

'See what the surgeon says,' Lausard told him. 'There may be another way of treating the wound. It might not be as bad as it looks.'

'They will take my leg. Those butchers know no other way.'

'It might save your life.' Giresse's voice was low. 'Men have fought on with only one leg. Look at General Caffarelli.'

'I told you, I do not wish to hobble around like that for the rest of my life.' Delacor sucked in a deep breath. 'If I believed in a God I would offer a prayer to him now.'

Lausard leaned over and ducked his head close to Rocheteau. The corporal did not move.

'Rocheteau, can you hear me?' Lausard said softly. He slipped his hand into that of his companion and squeezed. 'Listen to me. Hear the words I speak. I know you are in pain, I saw the wounds to your face. But if you can understand me then let me know.'

Rocheteau didn't move but Lausard felt the pressure on his hand growing as it was gripped tightly for a moment then released.

As the men lay in the field hospital, they were aware of a constant stream of wounded being brought in. Men from both sides. Men from all arms of the service: officers, enlisted men, conscripts and veterans. Battles treated all men with equal disdain and violence. War, Lausard mused, bestowed an equality upon men that all manner of revolutions could never hope to do. Death cared nothing for rank, age or social standing. Bullets, roundshot and swords were not discerning.

As the sergeant watched, two orderlies carried a hussar into the room and laid him down in a corner. The man was babbling incoherently, a combination of pain and fever. His face was the colour of sour cream and Lausard could see that he was bleeding heavily from wounds in his legs and stomach. Apart from his headgear, he still wore his full uniform, even his dark blue pelisse, one arm of which had been ripped from the jacket by a roundshot and the rest of the distinctive outfit was blackened by smoke and discoloured by blood, much of it his own. Lausard could make out from the red lace that adorned the man's dolman and pelisse and the blue-grey breeches that he belonged to the third regiment. It was only when the orderlies finally moved away from the man that Lausard heard some of the words he spoke.

'We are betrayed,' the hussar rasped, the words disappearing beneath a cough. 'Let us find the spy.'

The word seemed to hang in the air.

'He is delirious,' one of the orderlies said. 'A fever has gripped his mind that is as serious as his wounds. He will not see the dawn.'

'We are betrayed,' the hussar said again, his voice slowly fading.

His rantings slowly degenerated into low mutterings that could be heard only by those closest to him and they were too concerned with their own pain to care for his fevered outpourings. By nightfall, he was silent.

The night brought no respite from the chorus of mournful wails that filled the field hospital. Men still desperately in need of treatment lay crammed together in the foul surroundings, some slipping into the welcoming arms of death without ever being examined by a member of the medical staff.

Lausard had drifted into a troubled sleep around midnight but he had woken again less than thirty minutes later, partly due to the pain of his wound but also because of the continuous shrieks of agony from those around him. Candles had been placed at either end of the room and they provided a sickly orange light, casting deep shadows over the wounded men. Lausard glanced at his companions. Giresse was snoring quietly. Delacor was still propped against the wall, his head resting on his chest as he slept. Rocheteau had murmured a few words during the evening but had drifted back into unconsciousness. Lausard leaned close to the corporal again, checking for the sound of his breathing. More than once he'd dug his thumb into Rocheteau's wrist, searching for a pulse.

Outside, illuminated by burning torches, the surgeons continued their grisly work, but even they were close to exhaustion and those men not already attended to would have to wait until the next morning. Delacor among them.

Lausard looked over at the wounded hussar but could hear no sound. Moving slowly, wincing at the pain of his wound, he eased himself up, shooting out a hand to steady himself against the wall. He swayed on unsteady legs for a moment, his head spinning slightly, the pain making him suck in a deep breath. The moment passed and he wandered cautiously in the direction of the hussar, careful not to step on any of the outstretched limbs of other men lying on the floor. An infantryman with a sword cut across his face and neck lifted a hand in Lausard's direction and croaked something, imitating the action of drinking. The sergeant had no liquid to offer him and continued past. In the dull light of the candles he could see many open, pain-filled eyes watching him. Men unable to sleep because of their agony followed his every move as he finally knelt beside the blood-spattered hussar.

He leaned close to the man and heard guttural breathing, followed by a liquid rasp.

'He is as good as dead,' a voice close by croaked and Lausard glanced around to see a man in just a pair of long-johns and a torn, bloodied shirt propped against the wall, gazing at him. It was impossible to tell from the lack of uniform which unit the man was from. 'His mind has gone.'

'Do you know him?' Lausard asked, looking back at the dying hussar, who was lying on his side, his knees drawn up in a foetal position.

'His name is Vernet,' the man said quietly, wincing with every word. 'He was in my unit.'

'Third hussars.' It sounded more like a statement than a question. 'I recognise the uniform. What is *your* name?'

'Francois Gassendi. I am Breton. What is your interest in this man?'

'When he was brought in, he was shouting about betrayal, about catching spies and traitors.'

'I told you, his mind has gone. He will be dead before morning. What are the ravings of a dying man to do with you?' He coughed, bright red blood spilling over his lips and down his chin.

'Dying men usually call for their mothers not for justice. Do you have any idea what he was talking about?'

Gassendi bowed his head slightly and tried to draw in a breath but the effort made him start. He grunted in pain. Lausard put a comforting hand on his shoulder.

'Six or seven days ago my unit was detailed to follow the Austrians,' the Breton said, wiping sweat from his upper lip, 'to reconnoitre and send back information about their strengths and dispositions. We were ambushed in some woods close to Montebello. Every man was killed or captured. Vernet and I were taken prisoner but we escaped and returned to fight again. Vernet was convinced that we were sent into a trap. He suspected our captain of being a spy.'

'Captain Feraud,' Lausard murmured.

Gassendi nodded.

'Why did your companion suspect Feraud?' Lausard pressed.

'He joined our regiment at Lausanne, before we crossed the Alps. Our former commander, Captain Agossian, was transferred just before we left. No one knew why. He was replaced by Captain Feraud.'

'But that still does not explain why Vernet thought him to be a spy.'

'The night before the battle, Captain Feraud was sent to report on the Austrian positions behind or before the Bormida river, to report directly to the First Consul on whether or not the Austrians had built bridges. Vernet accompanied him. He saw two pontoon bridges but Feraud said he was mistaken. He threatened Vernet with a firing squad if he reported what he had seen.'

'Could Vernet have been mistaken?'

'It's possible but given the ambush in the woods, the fact that Feraud was the only one to survive, that he did not report the bridges . . . plus there was talk among some of the men that the Austrian officer General Zach was paying a double agent for information . . .' The sentence trailed off as he coughed, gasping for breath.

'Do *you* think Feraud is a spy?' Lausard asked.

'If he is, I fear I will not live to avenge those whose deaths he has caused.' He pulled his torn shirt to one side to reveal a gaping wound in his chest. Every time he breathed, Lausard heard a liquid gurgle. It sounded like a set of punctured bellows and Lausard realised it was the air rushing in and out of the wound in Gassendi's lung.

'Did you see Feraud during the battle?' Lausard persisted.

Gassendi shook his head. 'Some men in my unit told me he had been captured during the fighting around Marengo.'

The sergeant made to straighten up but Gassendi gripped his hand. 'Will you sit with me, please?' he asked, blood dribbling over his lips. 'I don't want to be alone.'

Lausard understood. He felt his hand being squeezed with incredible pressure, particularly given the weakened state of the hussar.

He heard the breath hissing slowly out of Gassendi's lung wound. The pressure in the grip eased gradually. Gassendi looked directly into his eyes.

'It was a great day today, was it not?' he murmured. 'A great day for France, for Bonaparte and for the Republic.'

Lausard nodded.

'A great victory,' Gassendi continued, his grip loosening by the second. His eyes brimmed with tears. 'I want to go back to my wife and family,' the dying man whispered, a single tear trickling down his cheek. He slumped forward slightly, his tortured breathing now silent. Lausard gently eased his hand free of Gassendi's and stepped away from the dead hussar.

All around, the other wounded men continued to cry out in their pain.

Lausard had no idea how many men had died during the night. As he looked around the room full of suffering troops he couldn't help but think of Gassendi and his slow, painful death. He feared that many more had met the same fate during the hours of darkness. Now, as the sunlight poked through the windows of the field hospital, the cries of the wounded seemed to increase in volume. Many had still not been attended to since they had been brought in, and throughout the night Lausard had heard movement in the courtyard, which indicated the arrival of yet more injured.

Orderlies entered the room, accompanied by two surgeons, both dressed in dark blue jackets and bicorns. Each took one side of the room and passed along it slowly, inspecting all of the wounded in turn, deciding who was to be operated upon. At the same time, the orderlies removed the corpses of those who had died during the night. Lausard watched them carry out the body of Gassendi.

Lausard's wound was still very painful but he ignored the discomfort, intent on leaning across to Rocheteau. He squeezed the corporal's hand and was relieved to feel the pressure returned.

'Can you hear me, you old pirate?' Lausard whispered.

'I hear you, Alain,' Rocheteau croaked, his voice muffled by the bandages wrapped so tightly around his head.

'We thought you were a dead man.'

'No one gets rid of me *that* easily. You should know by now,' Rocheteau retorted. He attempted to sit up but Lausard urged him to remain where he was on the cold floor.

The surgeon was drawing closer; Delacor looked at the uniformed man then down at his injured leg. Part of the metal fragment was protruding from the wound just below his knee. It glinted against the crimson background of blood.

'If that butcher thinks he is taking my leg then he is very much mistaken,' Delacor snarled as the surgeon drew closer.

Lausard could see that the surgeon was carrying a small black box and as the man paused beside the soldier next to Lausard and his companions, he saw that the contents of the box seemed to move of its own accord, slithering with liquid movements; it took him only a moment to realise that the box contained leeches. The surgeon called over an orderly and said something to him, handing him the leeches and indicating the wounded artilleryman, who looked on in horror.

'A portion of your uniform has been carried into your wound,' the surgeon explained to the man. 'If it becomes infected, it could lead to fever of the blood. These leeches will prevent that.'

The artilleryman looked aghast at the prospect of having the leeches applied to his skin, but he knew he had no choice.

The surgeon moved on to Giresse, who was still pale from loss of blood.

'You need to drink some broth,' the surgeon instructed. 'Replace the liquids you have lost. One of the orderlies will mix some gunpowder and horses' blood for you. It will help you regain your strength.'

He looked at Lausard and began unfastening the bandage around his stomach. The patch of gauze over the wound was soaked in crimson, but despite the raw look of the injury, the surgeon nodded.

'The wound was a clean one, you are lucky,' he said. 'You should be fit to return to service in two days.' He called an orderly over to rebandage the wound.

He passed on to Delacor, who swallowed hard as the surgeon inspected his leg.

'I will remove the leg later this morning,' he stated flatly.

'No you won't,' Delacor told him. 'I will not allow you to turn me into a cripple.'

'Don't be ridiculous. Your leg is broken and there are metal fragments inside the wound. If it is not amputated you will die.'

'Remove the fragments.'

'That is impossible. I haven't the time. You are not the only injured man I have to attend to.'

'If you take my leg, I will take your head, you butchering bastard,' Delacor hissed.

The surgeon met Delacor's stare. 'How dare you speak to me like that! I am an officer, I—'

Delacor cut him short. 'I don't care if you are the First Consul himself. If you try to remove my leg, I will kill you.'

'Probe the wound,' Lausard interjected.

The surgeon looked at him in astonishment. 'I haven't the time,' he said, waving away the suggestion.

'Make time,' Lausard told him.

As the surgeon prepared to straighten up, he felt something cold pressing into his back. He looked round to see that Rocheteau had propped himself up on an elbow and was holding a knife to the base of his spine. The orderly who had been bandaging Lausard's wound looked at the knife then at the surgeon. He reached into his tunic pocket and handed the surgeon a metal probe.

'I could have you all shot for this,' the surgeon snapped, snatching the instrument from the orderly. He moved it gently around the extremities of the wound in Delacor's leg then guided it carefully into the hole.

The dragoon gritted his teeth as the surgeon foraged within the deep gash, the probe connecting almost immediately with metal. Discarding the instrument, the surgeon used his fingers to delve deeper into the hole. He could feel bone as he fastened the tips of his index and middle fingers on to the splinter and pulled, ignoring the grunts of pain from Delacor. The metal came free and the surgeon brandished it before him. It was over two inches long and jagged on one side.

'There could well be other fragments,' he said, dropping

the piece of shell to the floor. 'There is still a danger of the wound becoming infected.'

'I'll take that chance,' Delacor declared, perspiration beading on his forehead and cheeks. He turned to the orderly. 'Bandage it.'

The man did as he was instructed.

'Thank you for your time, doctor,' Lausard said quietly, holding the surgeon's stare. 'We all thank you for your expertise.' He watched as the medical man dropped the bloodied probe into his pocket and moved to the next wounded soldier.

Lausard managed a smile.

As Alain Lausard made his way slowly across the courtyard of the Château of Marengo, he sucked in deep lungfuls of fresh air, savouring each one as if it were fine wine. It was the first time he had left the field hospital since being carried in two days earlier.

The sun was shining brightly in the cloudless June sky and Lausard looked up to see birds arrowing across the firmament. They swooped and dived, as glad, it seemed, to be beneath the warming rays of the sun as he was. Beyond the château he could see the battlefield where so many had died just forty-eight hours earlier. Crows were circling the shattered landscape and he imagined that, come nightfall, rats and foxes and all manner of predatory creatures would venture forth to eat their fill, feasting on the thousands of corpses that remained unburied. Most had been burned but elsewhere the burial details had not finished their vile task and were still shovelling the bodies of men and horses into huge communal graves. They worked with scarves tied around their faces to protect them from the foul odours and disease.

However, for now, the only air that Lausard breathed was clear and clean. A wonderful contrast to the rank, fetid stench that filled the field hospital.

The bulk of the army, he had learned, had advanced more than forty leagues. The Austrians had withdrawn behind the Mincio river, seeking refuge from their foe. Despite the crushing victory at Marengo, they had not been destroyed. The war was still on. Rumours circulated within the confines of the hospital; some said that the Austrians had accepted truces but had not surrendered, that even now, the Austrian Emperor, under the prompting of the English Prime Minister, Pitt, was resisting the lure of peace. Lausard wondered how much longer the war would continue.

He walked on to the gates of the château and looked out towards the road that led towards Alessandria. Blue jacketed troops moved along it in an untidy column, away from the city. Infantrymen, artillery gunners and cavalrymen, most of whom, Lausard noted, were on foot. This dishevelled band strode wearily along the dusty road and Lausard could only watch them and wonder: why were his fellow countrymen marching back towards Marengo?

'Melas released our prisoners today,' said a voice behind him.

Lausard turned to see one of the orderlies standing watching the forlorn procession as it trooped by.

'They don't look very happy for victorious men, do they?' the orderly continued.

'How many of them are there?'

'About twelve hundred.'

Lausard scanned the ranks, all arms intermingled. He searched faces as best he could but most were too far away for him to pick them out. But he saw uniforms. The blue of the infantry and artillery, many of them in tatters. He even saw some green-jacketed dragoons and a handful of hussars. His eyes narrowed as he saw the grey-blue of a couple of troopers from one particular regiment: the third hussars. One had his head bandaged, the other was limping badly.

'More work for us,' said the orderly, running appraising eyes over the men.

'What about those who are not wounded?'

'They will rejoin their units within a day. What about you? When do you leave us?'

'As soon as I can.'

'The war is still on. Perhaps you would be better off here.'

'My place is with the living. With the rest of my men. If there is more fighting to be done then I want to be a part of it.'

'Your patriotism is to be admired, Sergeant. General Bonaparte would be proud of you.'

'My desire to fight has nothing to do with patriotism. Nor do I seek the approval of Bonaparte. I have my own reasons. Reasons I would never expect you to understand.' He stood watching the column of returning prisoners for a moment longer then turned and headed back across the courtyard.

When the time came, Lausard found that he could not button his tunic completely because of the bandages still wound so thickly and tightly around his torso. Giresse, Rocheteau and Delacor watched as he strapped on his sword, the three-foot-long blade, encased in its scabbard, bumping against his boot. He fitted his helmet gently on to his head, feeling the dent in the side of it with his index finger. Then he bent, wincing with the pain, and attached his spurs, finally straightening up.

'So, the time has come for you to abandon us,' Rocheteau said, grinning.

'You will join me soon. All of you.'

'In which direction will you ride?' Giresse asked.

'West. The army has just two days start on me. It will not take me long to catch them up. By noon tomorrow I will be drinking Rostov's foul broth. Listening to Sonnier telling me how lucky we all are to be alive and hearing Moreau reciting prayers to his God.' Lausard smiled.

The three men lined up and each shook hands with their sergeant.

'Take care of yourself, Alain,' Rocheteau said quietly.

'And you, my friend,' Lausard intoned, gripping his colleague's hand in both of his.

'Are you *so* anxious to get yourself killed that you cannot wait for us to join you?' Delacor wanted to know. 'We could have all left here together.'

'You must remain until that leg is properly healed, Delacor. Besides, there is something I must do that cannot wait.'

'What is so important that you leave us here to rot?' Rocheteau asked.

'Call it an unpaid debt.'

'Say hello to the others for us.' Giresse grinned. 'Ask them if they have seen any pretty women on their travels.'

'And make sure that fat bastard Joubert doesn't eat all of your rations,' chuckled Delacor.

'*Vive Bonaparte!*' Rocheteau called as Lausard walked towards the door, pausing momentarily, silhouetted there.

He raised one hand in salute, then he was gone.

Twenty-Five

As he rode, Lausard occasionally felt intense pain in his side, but the spasms usually passed quickly and he was forced to stop and dismount only once.

He had ridden north-west for almost fifteen miles, passing through towns and villages which the victorious French had already visited, sometimes welcomed by the locals, sometimes resented. Whatever they wanted, the soldiers took, often stripping the towns clean of food and drink. Injured troops had been left behind in some of these towns, men suffering from minor ailments – twisted ankles from traversing difficult terrain or fevers that required rest for a day or two – which could not be cured on the march. Everywhere Lausard found his fellow countrymen, he asked them the same question. On every occasion he received more heartening news. The main army was only a matter of miles ahead.

He crossed the Po just south of Valenza, slowing his mount as he reached the far side of the river. He felt pain from his wound and eased the horse into a trot. He guided it along the bank for about a mile, gazing at the river that had been such a significant part of his life during the Italian campaigns. He thought of the battles involved crossing it four years ago; its importance then could not be overestimated.

Lausard felt the pain building once again and he swung himself from the saddle, walking to the bank of the swiftly flowing river. He sucked in several deep breaths and watched the sun dancing on the surface of the water. As he knelt to fill his canteen, he saw his own reflection. Beside him, his horse drank deeply. The animal was lathered from having ridden hard for over a day and, like its rider, was enjoying this moment of tranquillity.

Lausard undid his tunic and eased the bandages down slightly, inspecting his wound. It was still raw, the edges beginning to scab over slightly. He realized how lucky he'd been. Two inches to the left and he would have been killed by the lethally sharp metal splinter. Instead, it had passed through the fleshy part of his side above his pelvic bone. He thought about cleaning it with river water but decided against it. At this time of the year, mosquitoes were flourishing on and around the rivers of Italy, the swampy areas like magnets to the disease-spreading insects. He rebandaged the wound, took a few more deep breaths and climbed into the saddle once again, urging his horse on.

It was another two hours before he saw the first troops on the road ahead of him.

The sky was already the colour of blood as the sun sank slowly, weeping its bright red hues across the purple and blue heavens. Clouds were moving in, shunted by the strong breeze. Lausard reined in his horse and sat atop the crest of a low ridge, looking down on to the road that stretched before him. It snaked through a shallow valley and he watched the men trudging along it. There were about a hundred infantry, mostly grenadiers, immediately recognisable by their large bearskins. They marched on either side of a disorganised mass of Austrian prisoners, who shuffled along with their heads down. Some carried slight wounds, some were being supported by comrades. Two wagons carried the more severely injured, men who had suffered leg wounds and could not march.

To the rear of the untidy column and on either side of it, some fanning out into the woods and vineyards that flanked the road, were French light cavalry. Lausard counted some fifty troopers. All hussars. All dressed in grey-blue dolman jackets, pelisses and hungarian breeches, their uniforms trimmed with red lace. The unmistakable uniform of the third regiment of hussars.

He glanced up again and saw that the evening sky was darkening. Birds returning to their nests were black arrowheads against the sunset.

Lausard snapped the reins and sent his mount down the gentle slope towards the slowly moving column. Clouds of dust surrounded it as it moved.

Several of the hussars towards the rear of the column saw him approach. One of them, a tall man with a gold earring and a scar on his left cheek, nodded a greeting.

'You're a long way from your friends,' the hussar said. 'The dragoons are with the advance guard about ten miles ahead. What's wrong, did you get lost?' He and his companion laughed.

'I am looking for someone,' Lausard told the troopers. 'One of your officers as a matter of fact. Captain Feraud. Do you know where I can find him?'

'That bastard,' snapped the other hussar. 'He's up at the head of the column.'

'Why do you call him a bastard?' Lausard asked.

'He volunteered us for this task,' the hussar grunted. 'The remainder of our regiment scout ahead of the army. They have their pick of the supplies they find, while we are back here playing nursemaid to these Austrians.'

'Why do *you* want to see Captain Feraud?' the hussar with the scar asked.

'I have a message for him,' Lausard murmured, tugging on his reins and sending his horse forward. He cantered past the ragged column, sanguine Austrian faces sometimes turning in his direction. He rode on, glancing at the hussars who swarmed the flanks of the column like bees around fresh flowers. His eyes were constantly alert for the face of the man he sought, but to his dismay he could not see him. Thoughts tumbled through his mind. What would he do when he finally came face to face with the man he suspected of being a traitor? A spy. The word stuck in his mind. What could compel a man to betray his own side? To cause the deaths of those he fought with? There was a bizarre irony to the situation, which Lausard was not slow to appreciate. Surely the fate of his family five years earlier had been little more than an act of betrayal. Had they not been condemned to the guillotine by their own countrymen? Taken to the place of their deaths by those who shared their language. Executed by people who loved their country as much but hated its extremes of wealth and privilege.

Lausard spurred his mount to the head of the column, still scanning the area around him for any sign of those familiar long plaits, that thick, curling moustache, the brown fur kolpack which distinguished officers from troopers. Perhaps Feraud had ridden off somewhere. Disappeared into the oncoming gloom, to seek out those he supposedly served. Then again, what if Gassendi had been wrong? There was only one way to discover the truth. He had to confront this officer. But first, he had to find him.

There was a vineyard off to the right, at the top of a gentle rise. Lausard could see that a swiftly flowing stream cut through it. He guided his horse up towards the crest, the animal splashing through the water. The sergeant looked down and thought back to the blood-stained flow of the Fontanove at Marengo, to the men and horses that had crashed into it during the battle. For fleeting seconds he thought this stream too flowed crimson, then he realised it was the rays of the dying sun colouring it.

A grey horse was tethered to one of the trees of the vineyard, the dark blue shabraque and white sheepskin slung across its back slightly discoloured with dust and dried blood. The grey tossed its head as Lausard drew nearer, then returned to chewing contentedly on the grass. It obviously had a rider. Someone had tied it to this tree. He could also tell that the animal belonged to an officer because of the gold lace on the saddle cloth.

Lausard dismounted and wandered across to the animal, patting its neck, glancing into the gloom of the vineyard for any signs of the rider. He saw nothing. He hurriedly unfastened the straps that held the rider's valise in place and opened it. The gold coins fell out immediately. Lausard stooped to pick them up. They carried an eagle on one side, the head of the Emperor on the other; the gold was Austrian. There were several pieces of paper in there too and he hurriedly unfolded them, scanning them, recognising that they were written in German. The signature on each was the same.

Zach.

The Austrian general's sweeping scrawl was easily readable.

Lausard heard movement behind him then the metallic hiss of steel as a sabre was pulled from its scabbard.

'I have caught a thief,' said a familiar voice.

Lausard felt the cold tip of the blade against the back of his neck. 'And *I* have found a spy.'

Behind him, Captain Feraud held the sabre at arm's length, ensuring that the needle-sharp point never broke contact with Lausard's flesh.

'What are you talking about?' the officer demanded. 'You try to steal my belongings and then you accuse me of being a spy. I should kill you on the spot.'

'Then do it, Captain. For if you do not, then I will surely kill you.'

'Where did you attain such a fanciful notion, Sergeant Lausard?'

'My own suspicions. Then I spoke to some of your men, and now I discover Austrian gold and communications from the enemy high command in your saddle.'

'A handful of Austrian gold and some letters does not prove I am a spy, Lausard. How many men in the French army are now carrying Austrian gold? Gold they picked up from the bodies of their enemies. The spoils of war.'

'And the letters? What is your explanation for those, Captain? Since when did men steal letters from the dead? They are communications from General Zach to you. They are proof of your betrayal. Have you any idea how many men have died because of your treachery?'

'And how many died because of Bonaparte's treachery?' snarled Feraud. 'He embodies the spirit of the revolution that destroyed my family, that forced them to flee from a country they had prospered in. A country where a mob of peasants decided that privilege was bad, where some filthy, unwashed scum appointed themselves judge, jury and executioner for all those who were better bred and more fortunate than themselves.' He pulled the sabre away, allowing Lausard to turn and face him. The sergeant could see fury in the officer's eyes.

'Eight years ago, my entire family was forced to flee from our estate outside Paris. Why? Because we had money, we had position and we had power. We had nobility. Something that men like Bonaparte and those who serve him could never hope to understand. We fled to Austria. We made a home there but it was not our *real* home. We were strangers there. Distrusted and disliked. I joined the Austrian army, so did my brother. I wanted to fight *against* Bonaparte and all he stood for. But then I realised I could be a part of his army and cause more damage to it.'

Lausard listened intently. Some of the words that Feraud spoke he could have echoed himself.

'Yes, Sergeant, I am a spy, if that is what you choose to call it,' Feraud continued. 'But I know you will never understand. You are just one more piece of rubbish that Bonaparte sweeps along with him in his quest for power. You can never hope to realise what I lost because of him.'

Lausard managed a smile. 'You would be surprised, Captain,' he said softly. 'Do not think yourself the only one to have suffered during the revolution. At least your family are still alive. Like you, I have reason to hate, but I would not allow my hate to consume me as you have. I would not let it cause the deaths of my fellow countrymen. Perhaps that is the difference between us.'

Feraud looked puzzled. He took a step back and lowered his sabre slightly.

'How can you know what *I* know?' he asked. 'Feel what I feel? You are gutter trash and nothing more.'

'Believe what you will, Captain. It is not important what you think of me. *I* know the truth. I came from a world of privilege, as you did. And that was taken from me by the men I now fight for. How do you want me to prove my breeding? By telling you the names of my teachers at the Carabinier school at Chinon, where I learned to ride, to shoot and to use a sword? Would the gutter trash you speak of even *know* of such a place? No. You stand looking at a man like yourself, Captain. A man who lost everything, even self-respect. Be grateful you still have that.'

'But if you are of noble birth, why do you not understand what I am doing?'

'Nobility does not come with birth, it comes with actions, and I have seen more nobility among some of the men I have fought with than among any of the upper classes I was once a part of.'

'What became of your family?'

Lausard never once allowed his gaze to drop. He fixed the officer in an unblinking stare as he spoke.

'They were murdered by the Paris mob,' he began, the knot of muscles at the side of his jaw pulsing angrily. 'I stood and watched as my father and mother, my sisters and my brother were all guillotined. I let them die, hiding like some filthy coward, protected by my charade. I had lived among the very people who had murdered them. I had stolen as they had. Any nobility I had I lost that day. There isn't an hour that passes when I don't think of them and despise myself even more. I should have died with them that day. Ever since I have been searching for the self-respect I lost then, knowing the only way to regain it is by fighting and possibly dying on some battlefield somewhere. Only by doing so will I find honour again.'

'Join me,' Feraud said softly. 'Work with me *against* Bonaparte and this rabble of an army of his. He will not survive forever against the rest of Europe. France will fall and when it does the rightful order will be restored. Men like you and me.'

'Is that what you wish? The fall of France?'

'If that is what it takes for my family to regain what it had before, then yes.'

'Those days are gone, Captain. We will not see their like again. I am a soldier. *This* is my world now. This world and the men in it. There is nothing beyond my squadron. Inhabited by those you despise. More gutter trash. How many of them have died for this gold, Captain?' Lausard tossed the Austrian coins into the air. 'Good men died because of this. Because of you. I cannot allow you to continue this deceit. And I have no wish to see France fall. Coward I may have been, but I am no traitor.'

The movement was performed with such speed and expertise that even if Feraud had realised what was happening he would have been powerless to prevent it. In one swift movement, Lausard pulled his sword from its scabbard and lunged forward, driving the point into the officer's stomach. He wrenched it free and struck again, the second blow piercing Feraud's chest close to the heart. Gouts of blood burst from the wounds and the officer fell backwards, his sabre falling from his hand.

Lausard stood over him, watching the slow rise and fall of his chest and the ribbon of blood at the side of his mouth.

Feraud coughed, more bright blood spraying into the air.

'You would kill a man like yourself?' he gurgled, clutching at his stomach wound. 'Someone who would see an end to this war?'

Lausard pressed the point of his sword to the officer's throat.

'Perhaps I don't want it to end,' he murmured. 'Not this, or any other war.'

'Why not?'

'Because I am afraid of what I would be without it,' Lausard admitted flatly.

He drove the sword down, through Feraud's throat and into the ground beneath. He put all his weight on the long blade for a moment then pulled it free. He looked down at the body of the officer, the eyes now sightless. Then, using a corner of Feraud's shabraque, he wiped the blood from the steel and sheathed it once more. He dug the toe of his boot under the corpse and flipped it over, watching as it rolled down the bank into the stream, blood flowing into the water around it.

Lausard ripped the portmanteau from the back of Feraud's saddle and tossed the contents into the air. Pieces of gold were scattered over the ground. As the sergeant walked back to his horse he trod some of the coins into the ground.

He swung himself into the saddle, sucking in a deep breath as he felt pain from his wound, but it subsided gradually.

The column was still moving slowly in the valley below. Lausard urged his horse to greater speed. It was only a matter of hours before he rejoined his regiment and the realisation brought a smile to his face.

BONAPARTE'S SONS

Richard Howard

With the Bourbon monarchy a distant memory, confusion reigns in the French republic in 1795 . . .

Crushing the resistance of the Paris mob at the guillotine, but facing annihilation on three European fronts, the ruling Directory resorts to enlisting condemned prisoners into the army. Alongside the murderers, rapists and thieves emerge men like Alvin Lausard, a military-educated aristocrat forced to live as a peasant during the hysteria of The Terror. Cheating execution for salvation on the battlefield, Lausard turns hardened criminals into a ruthless cavalry unit, spearheading – with stunning victories over the Austrian army – Napoleon Bonaparte's relentless drive through Piedmont and Northern Italy.

Yet tensions between the ranks remain, and when the regiment falls under the command of the despotic Cezar, a mission behind enemy lines threatens to push the mutinous atmosphere to the very brink of anarchy . . .